Spit and Polish

Dorothyanne Brown

Go with the "Flo"
[signature]

Published by arrangement with Somewhat Grumpy Press Inc.
Halifax, Nova Scotia, Canada.
www.SomewhatGrumpyPress.com
The Somewhat Grumpy Press name and Pallas' cat logo are registered trademarks.

ISBN 978-1-7387998-9-3 (paperback)

ISBN 978-1-7380743-0-3 (eBook)

First Printing, November 2023 v5

Contents

Nightingale Pledge, 1935

I solemnly pledge myself before God and in the presence of this assembly, to pass my life in purity and to practise my profession faithfully. I will abstain from whatever is deleterious and mischievous, and will not take or knowingly administer any harmful drug. I will do all in my power to maintain and elevate the standard of my profession, and will hold in confidence all personal matters committed to my keeping, and all family affairs coming to my knowledge in the practice of my calling. With loyalty will I endeavour to aid the physician in his work, and as a 'missioner of health' I will dedicate myself to devoted service to human welfare.

Chapter One

September

Nothing but observation and experience will teach us the way to maintain or to bring back the state of health. It is often thought that medicine is the curative process. It is no such thing; Medicine is the surgery of functions, as surgery proper is that of limbs and organs. Neither can do anything but remove obstructions; neither can cure; nature alone cures.... And what nursing has to do in either case, is to put the patient in the best condition for nature to act up on him.

Nightingale, Notes on Nursing, p. 142

Ruth dragged her feet up the stairs of the nursing residence, almost tripping on the risers. She was so tired. A long day of classes and reception duty hit her. At least she didn't have to ring the front doorbell—the thought of having to wake one of the housemothers terrified her. The students called them "dragons" for a reason.

Tiptoeing down the hallway, Ruth opened her door and started to undress and put away her uniform. She carefully took off her apron and cuffs, placing the cuffs on the windowsill and hanging her apron over the radiator. She had a spot on the chest of her uniform, darn it. At least the blue and white striped material seemed to wash easily. She'd have to sponge that out before class tomorrow. She was too tired to think about it now. She cringed as her warped wardrobe door shrieked. Everything else lay silent, all of her fellow students asleep or on their night shifts.

It appeared both eerie and lovely at night. Her window overlooked Lake Ontario, and the water glistened, flat as glass. She laid her black stockings carefully over the chair beside her bed and gazed out at the September moonlight.

Suddenly, her door banged open, and a terrifying shape filled it.

"What in the name of all that's good and holy are you doing?" The apparition, a grey-haired medusa in a long flannel nightgown, waved its arms at her. "Can't you be quieter? Some of us want to sleep!" It turned and stumbled along the hall, thumping its feet in its hard-soled slippers.

Ruth fell back on her bed, heart racing.

Her friend Betty peeked her head around the corner. She grinned. "I see you've met the new matron."

Ruth pulled Betty into the room and pulled her door almost closed. "Who WAS that?"

"Shhh. She'll hear you. That's our new supervisor," Betty whispered. "Her name is Mrs. Graham, but she wants us to call her Matron. Some British thing. She trained there."

Ruth rolled her eyes. "She scared me half to death! I'm trying to be so quiet!"

"I didn't hear a thing until she stomped in. She's afraid of prowlers or something. Ann got lambasted before you got in. She seems to have it in for first years."

"Oh great," moaned Ruth. "Just what I need is someone to yell at me unexpectedly. I thought I left that back at home with my father."

Betty nodded, put her hand on Ruth's. "It won't be that bad, surely. After all, she can't be everywhere, can she?"

"I hope not. That hair!" Ruth permitted herself another quiet laugh. "She looked like she'd been electrified!"

Betty gave Ruth another comforting hand pat and tiptoed out of the room. At the door she whispered, "We'll do a run to Vandervoot's for some grease for those hinges tomorrow. Sleep well!"

"As if I could!"

Betty closed the door almost completely silently, leaving Ruth alone with her thoughts. They weren't happy ones. She had hoped nursing school would be very different.

She'd been so excited when she realized she could escape Cloyne. Her father had other plans for her, mostly involving missionary work in the very near area. Ruth wanted to get out, and she didn't care how. Cloyne was a tiny resort town set in the middle of the woods in Ontario, north of Kingston. It filled with screaming children in the summer months and became dead quiet in the winter, when the lodges shut down. Nice trees, but they weren't much fun.

Reverend Maclean wouldn't discuss her going anywhere. The world wasn't safe for young women, he said, and besides, Ruth needed adult supervision. In vain Ruth argued that her brother already served in the Royal Canadian Army, training to fight with the British and without adult supervision. "He's a man," her father shouted. "That is different."

When she tried to add that lots of women had joined the Women's Royal Naval Service to help with the war effort, her father's face turned from red to persimmon.

"Your responsibility is to stay here and help your mother," he'd thundered at her. "And you are needed for the church. Why can't you see that?"

Ruth had gazed at Joan, her mother, saw only endless, thankless work. Joan, having birthed six children and raised five, was the ultimate home manager. She could cook like an expert, budgeted for them all on a minister's salary, sewed all their clothes, and knitted everyone socks and hats and mittens. She never stopped work. Even during this heated discussion, she darned socks.

"I'm no good at any of this!" Ruth gestured at the cluttered but welcoming house.

Joan nodded. "She isn't, Reverend. She can't crochet to save her life, and you've tasted some of her cooking. Let her go learn something she might be able to do. She can always come back after she's done, help then."

Over my dead body, thought Ruth. The comment from her mother hurt, but she caught her eye and Joan made the tiniest of smiles, letting her know she was leading up to something. Ruth felt a tingle of excitement.

"Besides," Joan said. "Meg is better at everything here. She'll help me." They felt a slight bang on one wall in their small house. Meg must have overheard. Joan continued, "You've always sung the praises of Florence Nightingale, haven't you? Maybe Ruth could train as a nurse."

"Florence Nightingale, a Unitarian! But you're right, other than that, she led an exemplary life..."

Ruth moaned. "As a celibate saint," she muttered. She wasn't sure that was her goal in life. Did Florence have any fun?

"And did you know? As a nursing student, they will clothe her—and feed her."

Her father straightened up. "They will?"

And that settled it. Ruth would go to nursing school in Kingston and live at the nursing residence, a lovely home where they had supervisors to watch over the girls, a curfew, exacting expectations of room cleanliness, and more. And she was to keep Florence as her guidepost. That and God.

It was thrilling to escape the enclosed atmosphere of Cloyne. The Macleans had been posted there a few years before from Napanee. Since they moved, the family had made slow progress with the town members. They suspected people came to church largely because of the delicious cakes Joan prepared for the Sunday services. It became obvious when they held a social after the service. Attendance trebled. Ruth wanted no part of this world.

When she first arrived in Kingston and started making friends with the other girls in training, it all sounded glorious. She glowed as she first put on her uniform, the blue and white marking her as a student. In a few months, she'd earn a bib, and then a cap. So exciting. Soon she'd be a respected professional, guiding her own life.

Of course, it was too good to be true. Nursing training in the first year seemed to consist of bedpan emptying and running errands for the doctors and just about everyone else. The students floated all over the hospital depending on the location of any mess. No one said thank you, and the room inspections were terrifying. The supervisors had a thing about hospital corners bordering on the pathological and Ruth had already lost track of the times she'd had her sheets pulled out to be redone. They also inspected the residence rooms, and if a spot of dust lingered anywhere, they'd have to clean the entire room from stem to stern again. Ruth wondered if her brother Billy had such demanding standards in the Navy.

And then there was all the standing! Standing up whenever a doctor passed, standing aside when senior students wanted to go into a room, standing to serve and saying nothing. Ruth, used to speaking her mind despite her father's blustering, soon found out that at the nursing school, this wasn't at all allowed.

She also hated fighting with her hair. She'd had it cut to match the requirements for it to be off her collar, but her red-brown curls refused to behave. She spent hours and buckets of hair spray trying to get them to look at least slightly professional. Her head made crinkly sounds on her pillow, and the spray, hardened, cracked into powder that left piles of dust everywhere. More cleaning.

Ruth felt tears prick her eyelids. She shook her head. It's got to get better, she told herself. I just need to prove myself. It will get better. I know it will. She pulled the quilt her mother had given her into a hug. "Mother, help me?" she begged. She wished for her strength.

She laid the quilt carefully over her bed and settled onto her knees for her goodnight prayer. Reaching under her pillow, she pulled out her blue book of prayers for nurses, a gift from her aunt. Turning to the page on prayers for the patients, she began.

Chapter Two

Doubts

A true nurse will always make her patient's bed carefully herself. Consider the importance of sleep to the sick, the necessity of a well-made bed to give them sleep. But a careless nurse doubles the blankets over the patient's chest instead of leaving the lightest weight there—she puts a thick blanket under him—she does not turn his mattress every way every day; and the patient would rather than not that his bed were made by anybody else.

Nightingale, Notes on Nursing, p. 89

S he had another occasion to doubt her choice to be a nurse the next morning. At 6 AM there came a loud bell ringing down the hall, accompanied by Mrs. Graham's yelling "Rise and shine, nurses! Time and tide wait for no nurse!"

As the matron walked down the hallway, she flung the doors open with a bang. Today, Ruth was glad to see, she looked slightly less threatening. She wore blue serge from head to toe, Medusa hair pulled back into a tight bun, nursing cap crushed on. A shiny nursing watch adorned her left breast, a cross hung from her neck. "Time for prayers, girls! Meeting room in fifteen minutes and you all better be spit spot."

Ruth stepped onto the freezing floor and splashed water on her face from the sink in her room. Even this early in September, the night winds from Lake Ontario made the residence rooms chilly. She did a quick once-over, trying to dress swiftly before she started shivering. Teeth brushed, check. Hair pulled back, sprayed to within an inch of its life. No hairpins allowed. She lifted out her nursing uniform and patted at the stain with a facecloth. It would look wet, but she hoped no one would notice. She only had two uniforms, and she struggled with keeping them up to snuff. The laundry took forever to send them back, so she tried to keep her uniforms lasting more than a couple of days with the plan of getting them laundered on her days off.

She tried to shake a little freshness into it. No time to iron now. She kicked herself for not ironing it when she'd come in. She tugged it over her head, added her black tights and shoes. Gazing in the tiny mirror over her sink, she thought she was acceptable.

She thought.

Mrs. Graham had other ideas. By the time Ruth arrived, most of the other students stood in the meeting room, presented for inspection and failing miserably. Ruth, shaking, took her place in the line.

"What have you done to your cuffs?" Mrs. Graham pointed to one girl. "Take them off at once. After prayers, take them and wash and starch them again. You have others for today?"

The nursing student under inspection nodded, head lowered. After Mrs. Graham walked on, she whispered to her neighbour. "Can I borrow a pair? Mine are still at the laundry."

She walked down the line, finding fault with everyone's appearance. By the time she got to Ruth, she seemed worn out. She waved her hand up and down in the air in front of her and sighed like a steam locomotive. "Start over."

Ruth turned to go.

"Not now! Prayers first, then fix yourself." Ruth nodded, wretched.

Mrs. Graham turned to the class. "Now, girls, on your knees."

Stunned, the girls obeyed. Mrs. Graham led them in a lengthy set of prayers, some of which were familiar. They were Catholic prayers, though, so many of the students limped through the words.

Mrs. Graham sighed again. "I will have catechism books placed in each of your rooms. Please bring them to morning prayers every day. Dismissed."

Ruth ran back to her room, pulled out her second uniform and put it on hurriedly, adjusting her hair back into the shell she'd created with the hairspray. Time for breakfast.

Betty met Ruth at the cafeteria. They sat, shocked into silence.

"That matron is scary. My dad would flip his lid if he heard we were praying Papist prayers," Ruth said, biting through a piece of toast with unusual vigour.

"Better not say that too loudly," said Betty. "Prayers are prayers, or so my minister says. Though he adds, 'As long as they aren't Catholic ones'."

Ruth snorted. "Why isn't Mrs. Graham teaching over at the Dieu school? She'd be more comfortable there, surely, with the other Catholics?"

Betty leaned over her cup of hot chocolate, peered around. "Shhh. Someone might hear you. I heard she wanted to work with the soldiers—her husband was military. More of them come here."

The students crowded around after breakfast and the upper years vanished to the wards for their early shifts. The others studied the basics of nursing in the basement classroom. Today they would be again practising making beds, changing sheets, giving bedpans. They'd done it all before, but Mrs. Graham felt they weren't up to snuff, so it was back to the training. It was hard not to burst into unapproved laughter, especially when they had to work with Mrs. Chase, the training dummy. They practiced making the bed empty, both a closed bed and an open one, folding back the blankets in the approved way. After that, they had to make a bed with Mrs. Chase inside it, flipping her side to side. Finally, one student lay on a bed, and they practiced changing the sheets with a floppy person in them. It was always much harder with a real person than the stiff and non-ticklish Mrs. Chase.

Ruth tried to master the layering of rubber sheets and flannel ones, but her sheets always hung crooked or lumped underneath. At the bottom of each bed, they had to fold a pleat to allow for room for the patient's feet and getting that just right was a torment. Betty came over to help, and with two it was easier, but so frustrating when the teacher untucked their bed yet another time. And, after wrestling with the sheets, they even had to arrange the casters on the beds to be parallel!

Washing the bedpans was another endless task. The instructors insisted they be left shining, and in Kingston's hard water, telltale spots lingered. They polished each one with alcohol and practiced walking with pans full and covered with a towel so they wouldn't spill them. The thin fracture pans were the worst—they tipped with the slightest jiggle. By the end of the class, every student was damp and stinking of alcohol from all the polishing. Poor Mrs. Chase got hoisted up and down so many times that if she were an actual patient, she'd have a spinal injury.

After hours of practice, Mrs. Graham took the students up to the wards. Groups worked through each ward, making beds in pairs under her sharp eye. The patients on the ward, soldiers back from the front, gave them advice to help them get the sheets tight and smooth. That was fun for everyone. Even Mrs. Graham laughed a couple of times.

The next day, the class endlessly took temperatures. Oral temperatures, axillary temperatures, and....

"Girls," the instructor said, "Sometimes the parts of the patient we take a temperature from are not available. For example, with mouth surgery, or...."

She faltered, but Jane called out, "If they have a head injury?"

"Exactly. So we take the temperature rectally in that case. Now, why else would we want to take a temperature rectally instead of orally, assuming all parts were," she cleared her throat, "in working order?" General laughter and giggles.

"Would that be if they were a naughty patient?"

"No. Don't be foolish, girls. This is serious. If Mrs. Graham hears you!"

Ruth and Betty looked at each other. Even the profs feared Mrs. Graham. This was interesting news.

"We won't be practicing taking rectal temperatures on each other. Look for opportunities on the ward. Now, let's discuss how we care for our equipment."

Ruth couldn't believe the administration it took to keep track of a few thermometers. Oral thermometers were, of course, kept separate from rectal ones, but the risk of mixing them up made a lot of careful management necessary. Oral thermometers were blue. Rectal ones, red. The axillary ones that were placed under the arm were stored with the oral thermometers. All of them had different 'normal' temperatures that had to be learned. And then they had to prepare the solution for cleaning the thermometers every day. The wet thermometers were slippery, and several slipped to the floor in practice. The teachers firmly reminded each nurse that the cost of replacing a thermometer was theirs to pay.

They learned how to clean the sphygmomanometers and the stethoscopes with alcohol and ether, and how to arrange gloves for sterilizing in the autoclave. Later they'd learn how to run the autoclave itself, but for now they worked on packaging the gloves and practiced trying to put the gloves on without contaminating them. It was harder than it looked. They had to open the wrapping with great caution and slip one hand into the turned-down glove and slide the gloved fingers under the cuff of the second and try to get that one over their hand without contaminating the outside. It took several tries and Ruth could feel her patience wearing thin, but at last they got it.

It took another morning to learn how to boil the needles. Ruth felt terribly clumsy as she dropped one bit or another, but the other students lost things, too. Eventually, the instructors got fed up and let them go to try again another day.

"My hands are so tired from the bed making and scrubbing. The tiny things keep slipping away."

Betty nodded. "Finger pushups this evening, for sure."

Ruth thought to the ward time ahead. It, too, would consist primarily of cleaning. When would she be doing real nursing? She wanted to work with patients, not bedpans.

Chapter Three

Struggling along

In the Dem Room 1947

In a bed beneath a window
Lies a female lightly clad
'Tis "Mrs Chase", that awful creature
Who sends all the nurses mad.
She is still and she is ponderous
And she sits up with a jerk
But she has no table manners,
Gives the nurses extra work.
And they feed her, and they scrub her
Every demonstration day,
Poor Old Chase, 'tis a wonder
That she's not washed away!

Crothers, p. 70

On the days they didn't practice nursing skills, the mornings were filled with teaching about medicine and surgery, anatomy, and body functions. By the end of the lectures, Ruth and Betty were confused and dizzy with all the unfamiliar words.

"I hate these class sessions," complained Betty. "I like it better when we are doing things. I can't get the information to stick, otherwise."

"I know. I'm going to hit the books tonight for sure."

"You're a saint. I'm heading out, I think. Some girls are going to the camp. Why don't you come with us? It's so much fun!"

"Can't. I have to get this stuff down. My father is checking on me all the time. I don't dare fail. He'll have me back in Cloyne in the blink of an eye." She grimaced. "At least we get fed to change sheets here! At home, I have to help cook and then fight for enough to eat. There's just too many of us."

Betty shrugged. "I suppose you could always marry that boy who keeps writing to you. He'd look after you, surely?"

"Ugh." Ruth shook her head. "He wants to have a big family. I'd be right back into it, cooking, cleaning, wiping noses."

"And back to having to fight for food, no doubt. Thank heavens the boys at the base get money. And they treat us! They're a laugh, though. I wish you'd come with us."

"Thanks, but I'm having so much trouble doing the ward work. I'm so clumsy and slow. I know they'll fail me if I don't get the studying part right. Now Betty, remember what my father told me about boys and peanuts!"

"I remember! Boys bring you bags of peanuts, all innocently, and they'll want something in return, right? Well, I like peanuts. And what if I don't mind giving them something in return, eh?"

"Scandalous!" Ruth laughed.

The day's classes ended at noon. Students were given an hour's break for lunch and to write to their parents, and then it was time to prepare for the afternoon shift. Their more senior classmates overlapped at lunch, sharing tales of their mornings at the hospital.

"Watch out for 305. He's a lech. He kept grabbing my legs when I was making his bed."

"And 316 wants pain medications every three minutes and would NOT understand I couldn't get him any yet. I hate not being able to do things for the patients. When do we get to give meds, anyway?"

The talk over lunch was loud and cheerful, everyone talking at once and laughing.

"Did you see Emmy spill that urinal? It sprayed EVERYWHERE! The head nurse was furious."

"Thanks for bringing it up," said Emmy. "Some of you may not have heard about that."

Everyone cheered. This was more like it, Ruth thought. Not that she would write anything like this to her family. Her father would make her come home if he read she was laughing about spilling male excretions.

After lunch, Ruth walked to the library to write the mandatory weekly letter home. The library had a view over the lake and a series of gently curved bookcases that Ruth was eager to explore. She hoped the atmosphere would encourage her. She wasn't sure how to phrase her adventures, so she was brief.

"Dear father and mother, I trust and pray all is well with you and the children. This week we learned about taking temperatures and blood pressures and how to make a comfortable bed. There's a science in it. Our teacher tested all our beds like a military sergeant—even bouncing coins off them! I am working the afternoon shift for the next week. I like it. It means I get to see the patients off to sleep. It's just like settling the children at night. You'll be glad to hear, father, the new matron in the residence is very strict and makes us say prayers every morning. I carry my blue book with me always and I try to read a bit of Florence Nightingale's book as well, every night. I'm making some friends here and they all seem like splendid girls, very serious and focused on learning. Thank you for letting me come here. I know I am learning useful things every day. My love always, Ruth."

She followed it with a much more gossipy letter to her sister Meg. She told her about the urinal, the prayers, the upcoming dances, all things she wouldn't ever tell her parents. Meg was good, sending back letters with all the gossip from home, offering support and laughter in return. Ruth missed her every day.

She posted the letters in the drop off box, finishing at the same time as a bunch of the other girls.

"You coming out tonight?" one of the second years asked her.

"No, sorry. It's my turn on the telephone." The students had to rotate through switchboard activities, answering the one phone at the residence. The receptionist screened the callers and brought a note to the student. No one could receive calls after nine at night. Ever. Even in the case of death.

The girls leaned closer and whispered, "Why not come out after? Everyone else does. The supervisors won't know. All the Air Force guys are in town training. They're great fun!" All the girls wanted one of the flyboys. They could always be counted on to buy dinner, and some of them even had cars.

"Oh, I wouldn't dare. Mrs. Graham caught me coming in the other night after work and scared me so much my hair curled. I can't imagine how I'd react if she caught me after being out with the men."

The girl laughed. "Your hair IS pretty curly already. Well, your loss. I think your friend Betty is coming with us. Maybe you could let us back in?"

Ruth looked at her, head tilted.

"When you get a moment, go open the coal chute. We can do the rest."

Ruth just nodded. She didn't want to be in the conversation anymore. Mrs. Graham was bearing down on them like the Titanic. She noted about the coal chute and made sure to remember to open it before she went to bed. Wiping her hands on her skirt, she realized she'd transferred some coal to it. Sighing, she hustled upstairs to rinse out the uniform again. She only hoped it would dry by morning.

Chapter Four

Patricia

"What is a student nurse?", by Laurel Leaf, RN 1967

Student nurses are found everywhere, underneath, on top of, running around, jumping over, or slithering past patients' beds. Doctors overlook them, mothers worry about them, and patients love them.

A student nurse is courage under a cap, a smile in snowy white, strength in starched skirts, energy that is endless, the best of young womanhood, a modern Florence Nightingale. Just when she is gaining poise and prestige, she drops a glass, breaks a syringe, or steps on a doctor's foot....

A student nurse is a wonderful creature; you can criticize her, but you can't make her quit. Might as well admit it, whether you are a head nurse, doctor, alumna, or patient, she is your personal representative of the hospital, your living symbol of faith and sympathetic care.

With Tender Loving Care, p. 88

Time flew, and the autumn breezes began to wind their ways around the hospital. The students felt a bit more confident, learning how to do bed baths and reapply dressings. Ruth was partnered with a senior nurse on the ward, Patricia Brannigan, as a mentor through the rest of her basic training. Just starting out, Ruth really knew she needed help. And Miss Brannigan looked so professional—her uniform spotless, her lace cap and hair perfect, her stockings and shoes all in perfect order. Even her voice sounded perfect for nursing: low, melodious, with no accent. Ruth looked at her and thought that she'd be a perfect model to form herself after.

But Patricia, a thin woman with perfectly smooth blonde hair that highlighted her perfect cap, didn't plan to be a nurse for long. The first week they were on the wards together, she pulled Ruth into the utility room. "Look Ruth," she said, jabbing her finger at Ruth's chest, "I'm aware you're here from some spot on the highway up north. I imagine you want to get out of there. Just know that ANY doctor we see I get first dibs on. If I see you flirting with any of my men, I'll report you to the school. I mean to get out of here as soon as I can catch me one of them." She gestured at a group of medical residents across the hall. "So don't get in my way. Even if they seem to want to speak to you."

Ruth, appalled, stepped back. "I'm here to learn nursing. Nothing else."

Patricia looked her over, shrugged. "Yeah, you say that, but you are too pretty. They'll want to get to know you. Just let me try them out first." She shook her head. "You can't tell me you're not on the lookout for a handsome doctor to take you on. It'd be a perfect escape from what sounds like hell up north. All those children? And being a minister's daughter must be awful. No freedom at all." Patricia flung the door open, calling back over her shoulder, "I'm not going to hold your hand through your training, though. I had to teach myself, so should you. Only call me when you need me. I've got my own work to do."

Ruth controlled her feelings with difficulty. How dare Patricia comment on her family? And the rest didn't sound encouraging. Ruth knew she'd need guidance and the other staff nurses were too busy to offer much. It made trying to reach her goals for assigned activities difficult. Every time she wanted to try a new skill, she'd try to find Patricia, not find her, and then would have to ask one of the other nurses. Patricia seemed to be always either busy 'helping' a resident or in a bad mood. The staff nurses got cross with her, but she didn't want to try something and make a mistake, so she kept hanging about the nursing station. Eventually, one of the other graduate nurses would sigh and give up and go with her. It was embarrassing, but some things she had to do were so frightening. Even doing a bed bath on a sick patient could be scary for the first time or two.

Ruth sensed the glares from the senior nurses and so she ended up trying to do her tasks herself, opening her nursing textbooks in the utility room and reviewing steps before she went. It took far too much time, and the other staff gave the treatments to the other students. This was no good at all. The students all had a notebook of skills to learn while on the ward, and if they didn't complete them and have them signed off, they'd have to repeat the placement. If only Patricia would show up now and then! Ruth quailed at the thought of confronting her.

Back when Ruth was growing up in Napanee, her father had just started his work as a preacher. He'd returned from the Great War and found his calling. Initially, his sulfur and brimstone sermons drew people to the church, but as he got to know his congregation and their secrets, he started being too specific in his speeches. The local Reeve, in particular, found having his latest affair being brought forward on a given Sunday infuriating, when all his extended family was present, and his mistress was in the back row. He left in the middle of the service, face bright red, pulling his wife and children along behind him. His mistress, a young lass who worked at the bakery, left shortly after in tears. Ruth remembered the hush in the church, the way the supposedly friendly parishioners turned on them then, refusing even to say hello. People really liked the Reeve, it turned out.

After that, there were murmurings about how Minister Maclean needed to be brought down a peg or two. Soon the parish council gathered and, after a meeting full of angry words, sent them all packing to the church in Cloyne. Fortunately for the Macleans, the numbers in town grew on Sunday when people would come in from all over the area to attend church. The rural families seemed more religious than those in the bigger cities further south, came to church more regularly, and stayed for the socials afterwards. Ruth figured it was because there was nothing much to do but toil and pray. Still, the people in the area had no money, and the Maclean family income suffered a severe cut back. Ruth ended up doing a lot more drudge work for the parish and the families all over. She was asked to babysit practically the entire area. Her older brother, until he left for the army, went everywhere cutting wood and helping build things. Ruth's mother sewed and baked and knitted endlessly, selling her wares to support the church. Sometimes the Macleans would get her baking failures, but these didn't happen often, and it was heartbreaking to come home after a long day of volunteering to smell something delicious, only to realize it had gone out the door to some other family.

Meanwhile, her father, embittered by the demotion, used to test his arguments out on Ruth. She always seemed to be front and centre when he wanted to rant about young people or the dangers of movies or about the impending war. It got so bad that Ruth even preferred babysitting the toddlers in the town centre, who lived in such poverty they had one toy to share among the five of them, and who endlessly wanted to be carried so they could rub their snotty noses on Ruth's shoulder. It didn't endear her to the thought of having children of her own. Worse still, she couldn't take payment from the parish families—it was 'part of the church mission'. Which would have been be fine, maybe, if Ruth wanted any part of the church mission. She had lost a lot of her faith when she saw the people of Napanee turn on her father, saw how ugly supposedly moral God-fearing people could be.

Pastor Maclean told his daughter once she could do whatever she wanted, provided she gave a good enough argument for it. This seemed unfair to Ruth because her father was a professional debater, and he quoted the Bible at her as a trump card. She rarely won. Instead, she got regularly flattened by her father's logic. Or shouting, which also wasn't a lot of fun. He shouted a lot.

All of this made it hard for Ruth to step forward, to confront when needed. Patricia's telling her off in front of all the other nurses for something she, Patricia, left undone, hurt, but Ruth couldn't speak back. Her terror at being squashed and the rules of the nursing school made her mute.

Chapter Five

Trying to manage

Nursing technique has been defined as the skilful handling of the patient with the least discomfort, the skilful handling of sterile apparatus without contamination, and the elimination of unnecessary movements so as to ensure the maximum speed compatible with highest efficiency.

Nursing practice is to be carried out with the following points in mind:
1. Comfort of the patient.
2. Accuracy in detail.
3. Neatness and finish.
4. Economy of time, effort and material.
5. Technique and dexterity.
6. Therapeutic effect.
7. Simplicity and safety.

Textbook of Nursing Technique, p. 19

H er first weeks on the wards weren't all bad, though. She enjoyed being helpful to the patients, loved making them smile or feel easier. One evening shift, on the surgical unit, she managed to get all the dressings done and sort all her patients into bed with a back rub and proper positioning. She felt good as she saw her patients settling to sleep, even if she wasn't allowed to manage the IVs or anyone truly sick yet.

The next evening, though, she had a patient who developed sepsis and ran a high fever after surgery. Ruth was assigned to bathe him with alcohol and cool water and try to keep his temperature down with ice packs that would keep melting. It wasn't easy—she had to maintain him between being too hot and being so cold he started shivering. She spent the entire shift managing his fever, but that meant her other patients ended up with their bedsides still a mess and looking all untidy at bedtime. Patricia stormed into the room, swore, and rushed around, tidying up everything.

"Miss Maclean! Did you at least manage their dressings?"

"Most of them," Ruth admitted. "I didn't get to 34B. Would you mind?"

Patricia growled but headed over to do the dressing. Ruth, watching, felt guilty—the wound had soaked through and even stained the sheets.

Patricia smoothed clean sheets over the patient after she finished and as she pushed by Ruth, she whispered, "Utility room, now!"

Ruth crept after her. When they got to the utility room, Patricia shut the door and turned on Ruth.

"You can't leave the beds like that! And the dressing soaked through—it might have picked up an infection. How do you explain yourself?"

"It was my patient with the sepsis. I had to keep bathing him to keep him cool, and I barely had time to breathe. His temperature just wouldn't stabilize."

"You need to learn how to prioritize. The patient with sepsis likely won't make it to morning. Yes, you kept him comfortable, but meanwhile the patients who might actually survive were put at risk. Think before you act, sort your patients into risk categories, organize your care. The dressing you left is important, as is the general tidiness of the ward. Good thing the head nurse didn't come in, or you'd be in real trouble."

Ruth hung her head.

"And now you owe me. I covered for you, so you'll have to cover for me. I'll let you know when." Patricia smiled. It wasn't a friendly smile.

"But..."

"Not now. I will let you know. I might need to take a longer coffee break one day, or you can watch my IVs, do a dressing change or whatever." She smirked. "I might be talking with someone important. In the meantime, clean up and restock the utility room. You'll have to run down to the autoclave and pick up supplies. Don't stop for anything—you're already behind."

Ruth fled with an inwards wince. She sensed that owing Patricia anything wouldn't be a pleasant situation.

As she worked through her shifts, she also noticed a few of the medical residents seemed to follow her. Ruth felt a thrill at the thought of one of the laughing fellows maybe wanting to date her. They seemed so comfortable with themselves and each other. She did long to meet a man who wasn't as driven as her father, a man who could enjoy himself, even as he worked. An educated man, unlike the farmers and hunters back home. She wouldn't compromise her goal of independence for anyone less.

Unfortunately, she learned fast that the residents were just as or more browbeaten than the nursing students—with one difference—they could pick on the nursing students. The nurses couldn't pick on the residents. Nurses had to stand when the doctors entered the room, listen silently, take their orders. Some residents hanging around Ruth turned out to be doing so because they wanted to get her to do extra tasks, tidy up after them, bring them supplies they'd forgotten, even take their washing to the laundry. The other nurses refused. It didn't help Ruth's confidence that Patricia would watch the residents, glowering, whenever they stopped to talk to Ruth.

Then there were her 'outbursts', as the head nurse called them. One day, as Ruth redressed her tenth patient that day, tidying up all the old dressings the doctors had left thrown all over the bed, she complained to Patricia, "Do they always have to leave such a mess?"

The head nurse just happened to pass the room and overheard. She swept into the room in a state of electric dudgeon that positively frightened the patients. One of them pulled her sheets over her head in terror.

"Miss Maclean," she said, in icy tones. "I hope I don't hear you criticizing our physicians. As a nurse, and especially, as a probationary student, you have no right to comment. Your duty is to obey without question. I'm afraid I will have to record this on my report."

Ruth cringed. She'd already been written up for another comment, but that time Patricia had started it. That day, while they made a bed, Patricia was gossiping about the residents to the patients and said, "That Dr. Blythe needs a good slap. He keeps touching me."

"Don't you like him?" Ruth had asked. "He always seems to want to work with you."

"Not him. Ugh. He has these long disgusting nose hairs." She waggled her fingers in front of her nose.

Ruth and the patient burst out laughing. Ruth asked the patient between giggles, "Wouldn't you think a doctor could figure out how to tend nose hairs? Or eyebrows?" She waggled her eyebrows at the patient, who was waggling hers back when the head nurse stormed in. That time, the frown on the head nurse's forehead forced her own eyebrows into a mono brow, which did not help the patient stop giggling. To be fair, the patient was on a bit of morphine at the time. And Ruth didn't think a bit of laughter hurt anyone. Unfortunately, the head nurse disagreed.

One more comment reported, and Ruth knew there'd be a report made to the head of the school. She immediately resolved to be quiet. But it wasn't always easy.

She found the discipline challenging. She sometimes forgot to let senior nurses enter the cafeteria before her or didn't stand as quickly as she ought to when a doctor or the head nurse came by. She found it hard to understand why she had to stop everything the minute the doctor entered the room, even if she was in the middle of a treatment or a bed bath. It seemed rude to the patients. And having to be in perfect uniform shape whenever she wanted to do anything, even take things to the laundry, was annoying. She went through stockings like crazy as she dashed around to keep up and that got her into trouble, too.

"Just play along," Betty counselled her one night over dinner. "Pretty soon we'll be senior nurses and get to lord it over the next group."

Chapter Six

October

If you find it helps to note down such things on a bit of paper, in pencil,
by all means do so. Perhaps it more often lames than strengthens
the memory and observation. But if you cannot get the habit of
observation one way or another, you had better give up being a nurse,
for it is not your calling, however kind and anxious you may be.

Nightingale, Notes on Nursing, p. 117

Mistakes seemed to follow her around. One night, Betty came in after her shift and knocked on Ruth's door.

"Ruth—you forgot to do your evening vitals! I did them all for you, but they are going to see my signature, and the senior nurses were mad. How could you forget them?"

Ruth bounded off her bed in shock, walking back and forth around her room. "I don't know," moaned Ruth. "I got busy with the dressing changes and the shift just seemed to get away from me. And then the doctors pulled me out on rounds last thing...."

"I covered for you this time, but if they catch you—and worse still, if the patients developed an infection and no one was aware! Can you keep a list of what you need to do?"

"I try. But yesterday I got completely soaked when I bathed that big man in 405 and my list...," she reached onto her dresser, "got all like this." It was a mangled mess. "And then the ink leaked onto my dress. I've been hours trying to wash it out." She gulped back a sob.

Betty frowned. "Well, you're a mate, so I don't mind covering this time, but you'd better watch out. I know Patricia won't be so generous, and she's watching you like a hawk."

"When she isn't flirting with the residents, you mean. I never see her when I need her."

Betty made a face. "She checks your work. I've seen her. Be careful."

Ruth spent an eternal night that night, wondering if she'd made the right decision. Why did she think she could be a nurse when she couldn't even keep track of stitches when knitting a sock? Maybe she should go home and marry Chuck, the plumber who used to follow her back from church and who kept writing her sweet letters. She never wrote back. At first she liked the attention he gave her, but when he mentioned wanting a family like Ruth's, all she saw ahead was diapers.

It didn't help that her father thought Chuck was a perfect solution. "A God-fearing man, always at church. Makes a good income, and we could use his skills around the house. You should at least think about him, Ruth. A dutiful daughter serves her family by adding good men to it. You could do worse."

She could do better, too, she thought mutinously, as Chuck sat beside her in church. Everyone in town was already talking about them, and she hadn't even said anything encouraging to him, just tried not to be mean. They had nothing to talk about, except the weather. Surely a relationship couldn't be built on that.

That previous August, as she hopelessly tried to darn a sock, her mother coughed to get her attention, and summoned her into the kitchen. She spoke quietly. "Ruth—I believe Chuck is going to ask your father for permission to marry you. How do you feel about that?"

"Does it matter?"

Her mother frowned at her. "Is there something wrong with Chuck? I'm aware you don't want to end up like this," she gestured around the kitchen at the mess and untidiness of a large family, "But it's not the worst thing that could happen."

"No, Mother, I know. But we have nothing in common. And I hate housework." Ruth put her hand over her mouth in shock, realizing she might have hurt her mother's feelings.

Her mother laughed, quietly. "Yes, I have noticed you don't seem very enthusiastic about following in my footsteps. But your father wants you settled. I think he's afraid you are going to get into trouble. And he really likes Chuck. They talk bible teachings all the time."

Ruth visibly shuddered. She saw the long evenings being berated by father and husband over her faulty remembering of bible phrases.

Mrs. Maclean smiled. "Have you ever considered starting a career for yourself? There's always school teaching, but I think you may have had enough of children for the moment."

Ruth nodded. She'd just come home from helping care for a family of six, all with croup.

"I hear they are recruiting nursing students in Kingston. Surely your father can't object to you doing that, especially after Billy..." She swallowed. Ruth's older brother left for the front more than two years ago, over his father's objections. They had heard nothing from him for ages, and everyone feared the worst. The family still wasn't really allowed to mention his name. Billy was meant for the priesthood, her father had argued. But he'd gotten out, and now Ruth was being offered an exit, too.

She hugged her mother. "That's a wonderful idea! It would give me a challenge. I'll look into it," she said. She didn't mention how it would be an excuse to get out of Cloyne for good, before despair and proximity made her give in to Chuck's advances.

"I've already written to Pastor Neely—he'll write a recommendation for you. Your grades were good, so that shouldn't be a barrier. We can let your father know once it's all set up. Then he can't say no, can he?"

Ruth stared in amazement at her mother. Who was this woman, so perfect at wifely duties and still with time to think about her children's needs? And plot to defeat her husband?

"Besides," her mother added with a smile, pulling the offending sock out of Ruth's hand, "I do so hate having to redo all the things you do...."

Ruth was grateful to have an alternative. Chuck and the other boys had mocked Ruth's hair and clothes, which Ruth hadn't told her mother about. In grades five and six, they'd made her life hell, and even in grade eight, when she'd had a crush on a boy in her class, the pack found out and followed her around shouting things at her until the boy avoided her entirely for the rest of high school. Chuck didn't remember his role in the bullying she endured. When she grew up and became more attractive, all of a sudden, he decided he wanted her. Ruth hadn't forgotten his cruel behaviour, and every time Chuck smiled at her, she saw the evil laughter he'd showered her with. He might have grown up, she thought, but he's still the same person inside. She would not tie her heart to him, or to any of the other boys in Cloyne. They'd all been a part of the torture to some extent. She'd hated them all, while still yearning to be someone's girlfriend. It was confusing.

She knew she had to get out of town to survive, to reinvent herself, away from the aches and pains of the past. So it was begun, in secret at first and with growing excitement as the paperwork was done and Ruth was accepted to the nursing program. She simply must not fail.

Chapter Seven

Getting in trouble again

The most important practical lesson that can be given to nurses is to teach them what to observe—how to observe—what symptoms indicate improvement—what the reverse—which are of importance—which are of none—which are evidence of neglect—and of what kind of neglect.

All this is what ought to make part, and an essential part, of the training of every nurse.

Nightingale, Notes on Nursing, p. 111

B ut it was so hard. Everything was more difficult than she thought it would be, and Patricia was never around when Ruth needed her. Once she was struggling to bathe an overweight woman with too many tubes, and got them all tangled, pulling one of the IVs out. She'd had to bring in staff nurses to help her with tasks more than once and they didn't like it, and this time they refused.

"Where is your mentor?" they asked. "We've got our own patients to care for."

Patricia was nowhere to be seen. She also vanished after she made Ruth assist her first feeding tube cleaning. It got blocked and Patricia jerked it around, trying to unblock it. By the time Ruth got it flowing again, fluid had dripped down the patient's damaged throat, setting him to coughing. Patricia left the room, saying she needed to get something. When the nurses came in, the only person they saw who might be responsible was Ruth.

"Why were you fiddling with it? This is beyond your scope of practice as a student!" The head nurse was enraged. "You aren't even through your beginner checklist and here you are, trying a tube feeding? What were you thinking?"

Ruth wanted to tell them Patricia was doing the feeding, but as she started to explain, Patricia appeared, arms crossed over her chest, frowning. "So, there you are," she said. "I've been looking all over for you. The beds in 312 need changing." She turned to the head nurse. "I can never find her when I need her." When she got Ruth out into the hallway, she whispered through gritted teeth, "Not one word. I'm in charge of you, remember."

The patient, a sad-eyed man with severe pancreatitis, ended up with a lung infection as well.

This time, Ruth was called into the school head administrator's office. Miss Lukowski, another ex-army nurse, was built like a refrigerator and just as hard to move. Terrifying. And yet she had to report. She dragged her feet down the hallway to the head nurse's office, wishing she'd stayed home. How bad could marriage to Chuck be? After all, they'd always have adequate plumbing. Ruth smiled at that, thinking of all the crashing and banging the facilities at the nurses' residence made with every flush.

The smile didn't last. Miss Lukowski was waiting for her, sitting behind her desk, glowering like the cumulonimbus that hovered over Ruth's home much of the summer.

Miss Lukowski glared at Ruth over her eyeglasses. "Do you sincerely feel nursing is the profession for you?"

Panic overwhelmed Ruth. She felt tears starting. She must not cry. "Oh, yes!" she said. "I love nursing."

"And yet you don't seem to pick up the most rudimentary things. You don't see what your patients need. Other nurses end up picking up after you. You broke three thermometers this week alone, you backtalk to the residents, you almost killed Mr. R. with your feeding tube failure, and," she waved her hand to indicate Ruth's appearance, "you don't seem to want to look like a nurse."

Ruth blushed. "I've just finished three bed baths and an enema. And I tried my best with poor Mr. R. I'm so sorry. The tube wouldn't clear."

"This is what I mean—no talking back! You should accept what I am telling you. Surely Miss Brannigan is there to help you. Why aren't you using her guidance more often? And you should be able to manage looking clean and together even after all that. What in the name of all that's good and holy happened to your apron?"

Ruth looked—her apron was crumpled on one side, and she hadn't even noticed. It must have happened when she was rolling over that enormous patient to change his bed.

"I'm sorry. I'll fix it."

"I'm afraid it simply isn't enough to be sorry." Miss Lukowski sighed. "Miss Maclean, your heart is in the right place, and you seem smart enough in your academic studies, but you seem careless, and you miss things. You are slow with your assigned duties, and you are risking making serious mistakes. I think maybe you should choose a less demanding profession, one where you can do less harm."

Ruth panicked. She'd already proven a disaster at housekeeping. She wouldn't go back home in disgrace.

"I can give you one more week to pull up your socks—or stockings, in your case," said Miss Lukowski, pointing at the offending garment. Ruth sighed. As always, they had bagged around her ankles and there was, of course, a tiny run up one calf. She couldn't seem to stop catching them on the hospital beds.

"After that," Miss Lukowski continued, "we will have to look at returning you home."

"Oh no, Miss Lukowski! I know I can do better! I just need to be more organized. I know I can. I don't go out, I study hard...."

Miss Lukowski templed her fingers together. "Yes, your grades are fairly good. Not the best in your class, but it is obvious you are trying. And the residence don says you are in every night." She paused. "This IS very important to you, isn't it?"

"Oh, yes. My family...well, there are a lot of them. I hoped to work and send money home, help out—and there's no room for me there anymore. My mother is expecting another baby...."

Miss Lukowski frowned at Ruth's open file. "It does seem there are rather a lot of you for one minister to support. And in Cloyne, too. Lovely spot, but not, I imagine, much fun for a person of your age."

Ruth nodded, torn between misery and hope. Miss Lukowski sounded like she might even understand.

"Still, we aren't running a shelter here for women. You've got to pull your weight. And we can't let you continue to make mistakes. Why you even forgot to take your evening vitals the other day."

Ruth swept a tear from her eye. She would not cry. If she cried when arguing with her father, that meant he'd won. "I know. I can't believe I did that. Thank heavens Miss O'Donnell caught it." She wrung her hands. "I am trying. I seem to be clumsy or something. And too slow, I know, but I want to get things right. I'll get faster, I promise."

"And from what I hear, Miss Brannigan is not overly present. I am speaking with her next about her role."

Ruth squirmed, knowing that would not play well with her mentor. She saw a lot of bedpan duty ahead.

Miss Lukowski looked at her sympathetically. "There is one other option."

"Yes? Oh, I'll do anything to stay!" Ruth blurted out in excitement.

"You see, this is what I mean. Speak less, listen more, Miss Maclean." She clasped her hands together. "There are a few openings in the Veteran's Hospital, on the TB ward. It might be a suitable area for you. You could work there, even earn a bit to send home."

"The sanatorium? But doesn't everyone there...die?"

Miss Lukowski allowed herself a short laugh. "Well, at least then, if you kill them, they won't have lost much...." She cleared her throat. "No, in fact, we are having a lot of successes of late with the new surgical approaches, and there is talk of medications that may help. The key thing is, Miss Maclean, it would allow you to build up competence in basic nursing care. Most of the patients only need bed baths, skin care, vital sign monitoring."

"And spit bottle cleaning," moaned Ruth. "I hate spit."

Miss Lukowski looked at her over her glasses. "Be that as it may, there's a need there and you aren't quite ready for here. Would you take the position, or shall I write to your father to pick you up?"

Chapter Eight

Decisions

And I could honestly assure any young lady, if she will but try to work; she will soon be able to run the 'appointed course'. But then she must learn to work, and so, when she runs she must run with patience...I would also say to any young ladies who are called to any peculiar vocation, qualify yourselves for it as a man does for his work. Don't think you can undertake it otherwise...

...if you are called to do a man's work do not exact a woman's privileges, the privileges of inaccuracy, of weakness, muddleheaded. Submit yourselves to the rules of business as men do....

Florence N, Oct 27, 1868, as quoted in Crothers, p. 10

Ruth paused. She didn't want to leave. She'd lose the friendships that had just started to form, miss the friendliness of the nursing program. But maybe, if she played along and worked at the other hospital, she could reapply and might be able to keep up. Would they ever let her back in? She didn't know. But if they failed her now, it was back home for sure, and facing the scorn of her father. She shuddered. "No, please. I'll take the position. When would I start?"

"We can use you as soon as we can get organized. You won't need to go to class anymore—in fact you won't be allowed to as you may become infected yourself and risk passing tuberculosis on to your fellow students. You'll have to move.

There's a residence right at the hospital. It is quite comfortable, and this means you can get to the wards easily without having to pass by patients sick with other issues."

"Won't I be able to see my friends?" Ruth felt a whine starting, but she bit it back.

"In between, I suppose there is nothing we could do to stop you. Bear in mind, though, you may harbour tuberculosis. Have you had the TB test?"

Ruth nodded, glad she had passed the strange test where they injected a tiny bit of tuberculin under her skin to see if she reacted. Her arm had remained blissfully clear, no sinister raised lump.

"In some places, they give their San staff a vaccine against TB. We don't do that here because frankly, Dr. Hopkins doesn't feel it is safe, and the vaccine also makes it impossible to repeat the test you had. The test would be positive after the vaccine, and we'd have no way to tell if you'd been freshly infected. Does the risk of tuberculosis worry you?"

Ruth shook her head. "I hear there's more risk with all the other things the boys are bringing back. Tuberculosis seems not very infectious."

"Well, it isn't, provided you are very careful about aseptic technique. Don't let them cough on you. Be sure to wash your hands often. And stay well back as much as you can." She smiled. "And stay away from those boys with the 'other things'."

"Am I to go now?" A tiny candle of hope shone in Ruth's heart. She could still stay in Kingston, still do some work that didn't involve the parish of Cloyne. She wanted to get out of Miss Lukowski's office before she changed her mind.

"If you would. There's no time to waste. We are filling up quickly with patients. You won't be alone—we will send your mentor over with you. Miss Brannigan has some advanced training in TB treatment and will continue in that role in the San."

Oh great, thought Ruth, more time spent watching her flirt and doing all her work and mine, too. Outwardly she said, "Oh, that's good news. I'll be glad of someone to show me the ropes."

"Best thing is, you will get a really good grip on basic nursing skills, Miss Maclean. Perhaps as you get more confident in those, the added things for a full nursing role will come easier."

"What will I tell my parents, though? They think I'm in nursing school!"

"Do you need to tell them? After all, this is a short-term secondment, similar to the usual rotation you would otherwise have later in your training. You will just be at a slightly lower level. More of an aide. You will be paid, too, of course. It's not much as if you were a full nurse, unfortunately, but there will be some. You can continue to wear your probationer's uniform and will be called a Nurses' Aide. You could always sell your nursing textbooks, though I would keep them until you are sure you don't want to come back." She pushed her glasses up on her head, rubbed her eyes for a moment. "Perhaps you can keep your mailing address at the Nurse's House until we know where we are at? That might be easier all around. We could forward your mail. We often ship mail from this site to that, lab results, etc. We could tuck any letters for you in with the regular courier."

"Have you met my father? He'll be furious if he finds out we are tricking him."

"Yes, ah... I met your father when you first applied. A man of decided opinions. Therefore, I suggest you maintain this light falsehood. You are still a student here, just in a different focus. It will give us both time to decide and re-evaluate. By next fall, we'll know where you are."

Next fall? That was so far away! Ruth drooped. An unworthy thought crossed her mind. She'd heard about a big influx of TB patients, and maybe Miss Lukowski's suggestion had less to do with her than with the need for another warm body. A cheap warm body. Still, it meant she could stay in Kingston, in nursing, so she went back to the nursing residence and packed her bags for the move to the building on Park Street, just off Princess. It would be a bit of a walk to meet up with her friends, she thought. She wondered how often they'd be able to get together. If they could. Would she be terribly lonely? And what about the Halloween Dance? She'd made plans to go with the girls on her residence floor, but they seemed less keen when she told them she might have been at the sanatorium for a week before then.

She ran her news by them over their usual tea and toast snack in the common room.

"What if you're infectious?" Gloria, one of the students, asked. "And then we might get TB."

"We'd lose our year!"

"Or they'd send me home! I'm sorry, Ruth. You'd better plan to stay home instead of coming to the dance."

She could see their point. But was she to remain in isolation for her whole time at the San?

Chapter Nine

Halloween

To learn to cope as a nurse, you've got to have the ability to forget about yourself. You have to strengthen that ability to focus on the people you're looking after. I still take that rule. If you dwelled on your own feelings, you'd be overcome.

Jude Rogers, 24 June 2018

Her transfer delayed for some administrative things, Ruth was able to make it to the Halloween Dance the weekend before she had to move. The soldiers at Barriefield were holding a dance with some of the Navy men stationed in Kingston, and they sent a bus around the nursing residences to find partners for the men.

"I'm so glad you can come with me! It's a masked dance," Betty said with glee as she read the invitation. "We'll have to get some masks to wear!"

They hunted downtown Kingston and eventually found some stiff fabric they cut into masks. The nights before the dance were spent in hurried sewing and attaching of beads and buttons to the masks. They didn't have a lot of those, so some decorations consisted of kidnapped supplies from the hospital, which made for an interesting selection. Betty's mask was garlanded with gauze. Another student made hers out of tongue depressors. Ruth pulled an old newspaper from the waste pile and folded it into flowers that she stuck around the mask.

"How'd you learn how to do that?"

"One patient on my ward knew how to do origami. He showed me how the other day after rest period. They still don't look right, though."

"Well, it is hard to make flowers from newspaper."

"I tried to pick pretty pages and the comics—tried to keep the news out of it."

"Good plan. The news never seems to be good!"

The afternoon of the dance, everyone ran about, bathing and doing their hair, trying on dresses and makeup. By the time the buses arrived, the entire residence was in a tizzy. The bus went past the Veteran's Hospital and several of the staff jumped aboard. Ruth peered out at what would be her new home, a strange, cheap looking building just off Princess Street.

Ruth and Betty had promised to smuggle back any treats they could for the nurses who had to be on shift. The women all sang "I'll be seeing you" at the top of their voices as the bus trundled through the streets and across the bridge, puffing up the hill to the base.

When they got off the bus, the women were all herded into an enormous hall and left to stand in a row while the soldiers and officers came and picked them out for a dance, one by one. "This is horrible," whispered Ruth to Betty. "It's like being at a high school dance, waiting to be chosen. Let's go get a drink."

They turned and wandered over to the punch table, claiming a drink each. The choosing line was thinning out. Betty cried out, "Oh, there's Jack. I must go get him before someone else does!" She scampered off, leaving Ruth alone.

She wandered around the periphery of the dance floor, watching the others twirl and swing. Tapping her foot, she tried to look eager to dance, yet shy and not too bold. A difficult balance at the best of times, and she'd just come off a particularly gruelling week and was weary to her bones. Ever since the hospital had learned of her transfer, they'd stopped letting her do interesting things, and she ended up on endless bedpan duty, running errands all over the hospital, and cleaning, cleaning, cleaning.

Finally, a tall lieutenant walked over to her, and, frowning, said hello.

"I'm Bruce," he said. "And you are?"

"Ruth."

"Right. Well, you seem to be the only one left. Would you like to dance?"

Ruth nodded though she felt very tolerated and not appreciated, and they swung into the crowd. Bruce danced elegantly, light on his feet and good at steering Ruth, so despite her feelings she had a lovely dance, then two, then three.

"You dance well," Bruce finally said.

"You do, too. I imagine we should trade off for other partners?"

"Oh, why? I'm enjoying myself. Aren't you?"

So they danced another three dances before Ruth finally put up her hand. "I've got to get a drink," she said, stepping away from him.

"Don't go far," he said.

She smiled back at him. Betty sidled up beside her. "I see you've met Bruce."

"Yes. He's a wonderful dancer."

"Watch him," said Betty. "He isn't always a gentleman."

Ruth gritted her teeth. Couldn't she just dance without it being about anything else?

Apparently, seeing her dance encouraged the other men to ask her as well, and the rest of the party passed in a whirl of men and songs and laughter. It felt good to let go of the rigid expectations of the residence and work.

She was pink faced and warm when Bruce reappeared to claim another dance. This time he was drunk, and he gripped her a little too strongly. His hand traveled to places it shouldn't, and he held her tight against his chest until she could barely catch a breath. When she leaned back, he breathed alcohol into her face. She extricated herself after one circuit around the room. "I've got to go," she said. "Early shift tomorrow and the bus is here." He made a face but released her.

She wasn't sure about the bus, but she needed an out and it was about the time they had to be home, so she hastened to get her coat. Betty waited there, too.

"We've got to hurry—the bus is outside, and they don't always wait. I don't have the money for a cab, do you?" Betty looked at her, hopefully. "We could stay longer if you did."

"Are you kidding?" Ruth laughed. "Let's dash!"

The bus was filled with cheerful laughter and a thin haze of alcohol. Many of the nurses were a bit worse for the wear, but who would blame them, thought Ruth. Every day seeing death and pain. They needed an outlet sometime.

The next day at breakfast, though, everyone was talking about Ruth and Bruce and whether they were an item. Ruth kept her head down and didn't encourage the talk. She was glad she'd be leaving the gossip mill. Maybe at the San she would be able to focus on her nursing skills.

Chapter Ten

Off to the Sanatorium

Remember, every nurse should be one who is to be depended upon; in other words, capable of being a "confidential" nurse. She does not know how soon she may find herself placed in such a position; she must be no gossip, no vain talker; she should never answer questions about her sick except to those who have a right to ask them; she must, I need not say, be strictly sober and honest; but more than this, she must be a religious and devoted woman; she must have a respect for her own calling, because God's precious gift of life is often literally placed in her hands; she must be a sound, and close, and quick observer; and she must be a woman of delicate and decent feeling.

Nightingale, Notes on Nursing, p. 133

The Veteran's Hospital and Sanatorium was located in two H-huts built for Alcan when they first needed to house female employees during the war. Hastily built, they were planted at the end of a long U-shaped driveway, with a large lawn surrounding them. Each building was white with green trim, two stories high and had clapboard siding, already weathering badly. A linking building stood at the top of the Hs to hold a lounge, dining room, canteen auditorium and offices. It didn't look as if much had been spent on making it nice or secure. Ruth was astonished to see long metal tubes stretching from the second story of the building to the ground and stopped a moment to gaze at them in confusion. They looked like elephant noses, pointing to the ground. Wasn't that bad luck? A soldier walking by saw her and said, "Those are the fire escapes. The patients can't walk, so if there's a fire, they all will get shuttled to the verandahs and slid down the tubes."

Ruth couldn't imagine what it would be like to be short of breath, sick and coughing, and be shoved down these things that looked like they were for construction waste. She wondered what the rest of the building was like. Walking around to the front entrance, she saw gaunt patients in lounge chairs, wrapped up in blankets, set all around the front porch. Some of them called cheerfully to her, but most were silent. Some appeared asleep, despite the October chill. As she stepped up the entrance stairs, she turned her head away from the coughing, dreading the scene inside. Would there be beds everywhere filled with skeletal patients?

The interior of the building was painted in military tones of dark green and buff, which didn't lift Ruth's gloom. Still, the dining hall was open and light and cheery. In a corner, one patient was playing the piano—a sad rendition of "I'll walk alone." Despite this, Ruth could feel her heart lifting after the sinking she'd felt as she was sent away from the nurses' residence. A few patients looked absolutely cheerful. She so hoped this would not be a scene of endless suffering and death. Some of them must get better, surely?

She followed the signs up the stairs to the residence area to an even bigger surprise. The upper floor of one of the H wings was allocated to the nurses and students and it was decorated with fine furniture and pretty curtains. Apparently, the Alcan workers had made it look like home while they were there, and they'd left their furnishings after they were shifted to other residences or returned home. Ruth couldn't believe how lovely it was after the spareness of the nursing residence at KGH. She had a beautiful high bed and her own sink and dresser. The closet was huge. She unpacked quickly, scanning the rest of the room while she did so. The final touch was spreading her mother's quilt over the bed. Her mother had made it of pieces of the children's pyjamas, and every square had a memory attached to it. She traced the squares with a finger, remembering her siblings.

How would she explain her transfer to her parents? They'd be so disappointed. She hadn't even told Meg yet.

She was to share the room with another student, this one from the Hotel Dieu Hospital School of Nursing. She must be Catholic, Ruth thought, looking at the crucifix hanging above the bed. Sure enough, there was a catechism on the bedside table, marked with a bookmark, and a rosary hung from the bedpost. She was gazing at a rather florid picture of a painting of the Sacred Heart when her roommate bounced in.

"Hi! You must be the new nurse's aide? I'm Mary, of course. Most of we Catholic gals are Marys. I'm Mary Lavoie, or you can just call me Mary L. There's only two Mary Ls." Mary laughed, plopping herself down on her bed. "Weren't you a nursing student before? Why are you here as an aide? I love your uniform—nice stripes. Will they let you keep that? Mine is so boring, and it never hangs well. I hear you were at KGH? How was that?" She stood and undid her apron, hung it up. "I'm so glad to just have to think about one thing during this rotation—I'm a nervous wreck when I have to float all over the hospital. Is that why you came here?"

Ruth finally got a word in. "Yes, KGH was terrifying. They told me I should start over here to 'learn basic nursing skills'. I kept making mistakes. Everyone works so fast."

Mary L peered at her. "Hmm. I'll bet they were looking for staff for here. They are SO cheap! We're getting all these soldiers and TB patients in from all over, and this place is paid for by the good citizens of Kingston, so they are trying to cut corners as much as they can. You'd be good cheap infill and I'll bet you know more already than people the pull in off the street—and, I'll bet, most of your classmates. Fast isn't everything. And they can skip the training that they usually give the nurses' aides—they've just started a new program, did you know? It will be good to have more hands to help but training them will take time." She kicked her shoes off, swung onto the bed with a sigh, rubbing her feet. "Still, our hospital could be worse. Over in Hastings, they refuse to pay for a sanatorium at all. Imagine! We get some of their folks here, but they have to pay, poor things. Most of the time they haven't got two bits to their name. Some of the other nurses make stuff to sell to help fund the patients' stay here—rather than send them home to their families to infect even more people. I'm hopeless at it. Here—let me show you—do you knit? I'm making some absolutely terrible socks. I simply can't get them straight." She leaned over and pulled a tangled mess out from under the bed. "I don't think I'll be able to sell these, and I can't imagine they'd wear well on long hikes. I'm much better at scarves. Short scarves. Otherwise, I get lost."

Ruth couldn't help laughing. The tangle looked hopeless. "My mother forbade me to knit at home," she said. "I doubt I'd be much help to you. Maybe I can do something else."

"Well, you'll need a hobby, and you get extra bonus virtue points if you make something and give it away to the cause. I suppose you can always roll bandages. We usually get together in the evenings to do that. It's pretty jolly here, but they don't like us to go out much in case we're harbouring the Dread Disease. So, you'll need something for the quiet hours. Do you know what floor you'll be starting on?"

"Not yet. My residence mother just gave me my suitcase and directions here."

"How very mean. No weepy goodbye?"

Ruth shook her head. "I think they'd already filled my bed. I barely had time to get my uniform from the laundry."

"Well, good riddance, then. We nurses are meant to be treasured. We may as well find out where you are going. Let's go ask the supervisor."

"Won't she hate being disturbed? Ours used to make us make appointments a day ahead."

"You're fresh blood. She'll be overjoyed. Oh—should warn you though—there are all these luscious soldier boys here recovering. This has been a veteran's hospital for a while. They are only now changing it to focus more on TB, now that the demobbing is over and most of the boys are home. The men are terrible flirts. Haven't seen many women while they were away, and we're the only ones they can see now. The powers that be discourage 'fraternization'. Which is pretty hard to avoid when we're washing their bums. But be careful! They fired a gal for being caught kissing one of the lads the other day. I personally see NO attraction in kissing someone with TB, but I'm fussy. The doctors though...." She fanned her face with a hand. "Handsome!"

"Oh, oh. My assigned mentor is a real flirt. She used to spend all her time all over the residents at KGH."

Mary L made a face. "Do you like her?"

Ruth wrinkled her nose. "Not much."

"Well, let's don't warn her then. We can watch the fun."

Mary L slipped on her shoes, grabbed Ruth's hand and they went out into the hallway. "Miss Baumgart's office is down this way. She insists on living with us, but I think she just wants to be close in case any untoward fraternization happens." Mary giggled. "Of course, there's the entire city to 'fraternize' in. We go out when we can. The patients sneak out half the time. And the doctors go anywhere."

Ruth shook her head. Inside her heart, a little song was beginning. Mary L seemed like good fun and already she liked the atmosphere of the place better than she'd thought. It didn't seem depressing at all.

"Don't you find the patients sad?" she asked.

"Oh yes, of course. We cry buckets all the time. Especially when the good-looking ones come in and we have to cut them all up."

Ruth stopped short. "Cut them all up?"

"Well, I mean when they have their surgeries. They don't look quite the same with ribs and half a lung gone. But we try to be jolly to help them along. There's no point in making them any sadder than they are, away from family. And it really is good fun here most of the time. They've been places they are glad to get away from—this is like a holiday for them. They might have ended up in a grave in Dieppe or somewhere else shot to death or taken prisoner. I imagine a warm bed and regular food has a cheering effect, even if they are dealing with TB or war injuries." She laughed again. "Why, some of the men have formed a branch of the 'half-lung club'—and they hang out all the time playing cards. And some of them are taking art classes once they are up for a bit. You'll see." Her face darkened. "If only the surgeries had a better result."

Ruth turned to her, a question on her face, but Mary L. had stopped in front of a half-open door and tapped on it.

"Here we are," Mary said, waving Ruth in with a wide wave. "Miss Baumgart, here's the new girl!"

The supervisor was younger than the head nurses Ruth had been working with at KGH, and she stood, smiling, with hand outstretched. "I'm Angela Baumgart. How lovely to meet you! You've come highly recommended. I'm looking forward to working with you."

Ruth paused. She didn't know quite how to respond. Wasn't she here for punishment? Why the recommendation?

Miss Baumgart continued, "Oh, I hear you have a mentor coming over with you—Miss Brannigan, I believe? I think, however, we'll partner you with someone who has been working here more recently. There's a senior nurse, Miss Dennison—she'll start you off. You will start with her on the day shift tomorrow. First floor, ward C. It's a men's ward. You are fine with that, I presume."

Ruth nodded her head. Better and better. "I have quite a few brothers, so they don't frighten me. What will Miss Brannigan be doing? Does she know she won't be mentoring me?"

"Really, none of your concern. For your information, however, I've started Miss Brannigan on the women's wing, ward D, right across the building on this level. I hope she'll be happy there."

"Oh, that's where I am," Mary said. "I'm so sorry we won't be working together yet!"

Miss Baumgart continued. "I thought you might be of more help to orient Miss Maclean to our lives here, so instead I've scheduled you on the same shifts for a while. You can trade notes after work."

Mary giggled behind her hand as soon as they left the office. "And," she whispered, "I can keep you up to date on your 'mentor'. I get the feeling she's in trouble."

"Watch your back," Ruth added. "Mistakes seem to happen where she is, and you can bet she won't take the blame. Be careful."

"Oh, I'll be fine. Remember, I've got God on my side," she added, with a big smile. "Let's go see if we can find some food, shall we?"

Chapter Eleven

Orientation

"There was nothing to recommend (the sanatorium building) archi-tecturally and internally it was the most dismal depressing unat-tractive dark building one could imagine. It was ultra-Institutional, being decorated from one end to the other with dark green and buff paint."

Dr. Hopkins, as quoted in Barton, pp. 27-28.

Her new mentor, Beth Dennison, showed Ruth and Patricia all over the hospital the first day, pointing out all the dirtiest spots. "We actually have cleaners here," she explained. "Thank God. They are all past patients and so don't have to worry about getting TB—they already have had it! We need to be more careful. Catching it means the end for your training."

The building had recently been bought by the Department of Veteran's Affairs. Its focus was treating the men and women returning from the war. As the men came back, it became apparent that tuberculosis was rampant in the returning forces, so most of the wards changed to TB treatment. Dr. Hopkins was pushing to make the entire building a TB sanatorium as there was so much TB in the general population, and so, gradually, non-military patients were admitted. At present, there was one woman's ward and a ward of children, one residence of female service members, the nursing residence, and the rest were all military men, most of them with lung disorders.

The floors were broken up into sets of four-bed wards and a couple of private rooms. The nursing station was on one side of one H, along with the utility rooms, clean and dirty, where the treatments and supplies were stored. Every room was overcrowded, with extra beds pushed into the wards and doubling up in the private ones. Ruth couldn't help thinking there would be a lot of walking here, with only a few nursing stations for the whole hospital. The utility rooms were organized but full, needing more supplies than the administrators at first expected. As they toured the various wards, Beth explained the treatment room, the kitchen, and the laundry. An x-ray room filled part of the basement, and double doors there led to a small surgical suite. The furnace and incinerator opened out to the back, as did the coal chute. Everything seemed cast off, though Beth assured them the operating rooms had the newest equipment. The beds and tables looked older, like remainders from the main hospital. Some of them had chipped paint.

Ruth gasped to see a patient in the treatment room, hung from the ceiling on bandages. "Getting a body cast," Beth explained as they walked away. "The doctors don't like an audience for that. The patients often panic if they see they are being watched."

Ruth winced. "Don't blame them. Looks like torture."

"It's a way to immobilize bones that are breakable because of TB. It can really help with pain. Looks worse than it is, I think. But then I haven't been in a body cast."

"Ooh," said Patricia. "Would they cast one of us? For the experience, I mean? Maybe one of the residents would like to practice on someone?"

Beth made a face. "Yes, I'm sure they want to waste a bunch of bandages for 'experience'." She snorted and led on. Ruth tried to smother her grin.

Beth explained the windows of the sanatorium ward were always open, even in the winter. The fresh air was supposed to be good for the patient's lungs, but they were also wrapped in heavy blankets. "It's always cold for us, but it helps if we keep moving," said Beth. "And we aren't allowed sweaters." She scowled. "I'm sure they keep it cold to keep us working, too. Sometimes at night I wrap a

Johnny shirt around me, but you've got to be quick to take it off if anyone comes around."

Beth handed Ruth and Patricia folded over pamphlets, entitled 'Rules of the Sanatorium'. "Learn these well. The doctors expect us to enforce them, and the patients are always trying to push the rules. The most important things are taking temperatures and the rest periods. No talking, reading or exercise of any sort during them. Every day from 08:30 to 09:30, 13-1500, 16:30-1700, 1800-1900, and lights out at 2100. It's posted on the wall here for the patients. There's a sheet in every ward."

"How boring!" Patricia grimaced. "They must go mad."

"If their temperature is down, they can read occasionally during the quiet periods. And we're hoping to let them listen to the hockey if they are well. It's really hard on the ones who are running a fever to miss out on the games," Beth continued. "We also have to keep an eye out for the men sneaking out after curfew. The other patients seem to be more obedient, but the men...." She sighed. "I wish they'd realize it's for their own good. Plus, they're infectious. Honestly!"

"Can they have visitors?" Ruth knew that cheered up the patients in the hospital.

"Only for an hour in the evening, and preferably in the salon downstairs so that others on the ward can rest. That's provided they are off bedrest. Few are. They really are very sick, most of them."

As they toured the rest of the hospital, they came past Ward C, where several children lay in leg casts. They chattered away in a language Ruth couldn't understand. A gaunt man in the ward with them rose slowly to introduce himself. Dark-skinned and obviously in pain, it took him a few minutes to reach them at the door of the ward.

"I'm Pauloosie Angmarlik," he said. "I help in this ward." He smiled. "New nurses? That's good. It's getting busy in here!"

"Why are the children in casts?" Ruth asked Beth, who shrugged. Pauloosie answered.

"It's helping them heal."

When the women still looked puzzled, he continued. "They were taken from their families—they are from up north. They don't speak the language, so didn't understand they needed to stay in bed. The nurses in Montreal used to beat them if they put their feet on the floor. One doctor took pity on them and cast them so they wouldn't feel tempted to get out of bed. They're still kids, though," he added, as one boy threw a stuffed animal across the room at another. "Stop that!" Pauloosie said, followed by a command in another language. The boy fell back onto his bed, sulking.

"Casting seems a bit extreme, doesn't it?" Ruth asked.

A shadow fell over her shoulder. "Not if they need to be immobile to stop the disease, Miss...?"

Beth turned and curtseyed to a bewhiskered, heavyset man. "Dr. Rosen? I'm sorry, we're just touring the ward to get oriented. This is Miss Maclean, our new nurses' aide. And Miss Brannigan, a new nurse, fresh from KGH."

"Well. Perhaps after your tour of the wards you could review the current treatment protocols for tuberculosis, hmm? Particularly before you question our methods in front of our patients, Miss Maclean." He turned and left the room. Pauloosie wiped a hand across his forehead and winked at the children. They laughed, one or two of them ending their laughs with bouts of coughing. Ruth ran to bring them tissues and hold their backs while they coughed. Beth and Patricia held back.

Beth looked daggers at Ruth. "Miss Maclean. You stepped in without putting on a protective apron. You'll have to change your uniform now. Or at least you should. I don't have time to wait for you. We must get back. For now, here's the utility room. Wash up well and cover yourself with an apron. After we've got caught up, you can head upstairs to change."

Ruth's head hung. She so hoped this placement would go more smoothly and here she had made a mistake already.

"Never mind that sad face," said Patricia. "We're on to the military ward next! Come on! I heard they had a lot of new admissions today. I'm sure we can help."

Ruth glared at Patricia's receding back. Or maybe you can help yourself to a soldier, she thought, mutinously. She dashed into the utility room and scrubbed her hands hard, draped a surgical apron over her uniform. Cleaner and chastened, she met up with the other two. They stood in the lounge with the new admissions.

The room was full of slouching male bodies. Ruth gasped at how many crowded into the space. Would there be enough beds for everyone? The men all passed smokes and coughed at each other, and she thought she spotted a mickey being passed from hand to hand.

Everyone went quiet when Mrs. Graham stepped into the room.

"Oh no," Ruth whispered to Beth. "I worked with her at KGH."

"I heard about her," Beth whispered back. "Rumour is she's strict."

"Attention! I am the new head nurse here. They thought my military training might be handy to keep you boys in line. Served overseas in the last mess. Now, cigarettes out. You can have them later. We know they help TB, just not all at the same time inside. And do I smell alcohol?"

The 'boys' cringed and there were some furtive movements, but as Mrs. Graham walked around the room one soldier couldn't stand the pressure and handed the bottle over.

"No alcohol. The occasional beer with dinner, but none of this," she held it at arm's length with two fingers grasping the neck, "Miss Brannigan, will you dispose of this, please? It's likely contaminated."

Patricia stepped forward and took the bottle as the men moaned. At the door, and behind Mrs. Graham's back, she turned and winked at the room. The men stopped groaning and smiled, but by the time Mrs. Graham smelled a rat, Patricia had fled the room. Mrs. Graham focused on Ruth.

"I see you have arrived. Time to get to work. What in heaven's name are you wearing? Go upstairs and get a clean uniform right now and then get started doing intake on these men. They'll all need temperatures, weights, bottles, tissues. And you men all should be sorted into bed, now." She turned to the men. "The doctor will be by shortly to see where you should be in terms of activity, but for now all of you need to be on bed rest."

Ruth scampered up the stairs and stripped quickly, tossing her soiled uniform in a pile on the floor. She had one left that was not completely wrinkled, and she put that on. When she returned to the ward, Mrs. Graham glowered at her, but soon they were both too busy to worry about uniform pressing. For the next several hours, Beth, Ruth and Patricia worked hard getting everyone's name and details, placing them into the wards. It was made more difficult because the men kept pretending to be one another like a bunch of schoolchildren and eventually Ruth lost patience.

"Get back to your bed," she shouted at one man who clowned around after Patricia. "Let us get this done!"

She yelled loudly enough that Mrs. Graham poked her head in the door, looked about and nodding, satisfied, withdrew. One triumph at least, thought Ruth.

Chapter Twelve

Meeting the boys

Most authorities agreed that, until something better turned up, the rational management of the disease would have to rest on two pillars. The first was the sanatorium regime...The second (which came a little later) was collapse therapy.

Sanatoria represented a somewhat ill-defined way of life, an attitude rather than an activity. Collapse therapy was an invasive surgical procedure. Yet they rested on the same underlying principle...To combat active disease—or rather, to let the body combat active disease with its own resources—the diseased part has to be put to rest.

The White Death p. 249

Over in the corner of one of the soldier's wards there was a fellow who wasn't playing around. Pale and thin, he coughed repeatedly, covering his mouth with a tissue that showed a red tinge. Ruth went over to him. "Hello. Mr....?"

"Just call me Jerry. Bousquet, that is."

"Oh. Is that a French accent I hear?"

"Mais oui. I am from St. Hubert, Quebec. I hope they send me to Montreal where I be closer to family, but the sanatoriums there were trop full." He coughed again. "I am hoping for a transfer, but they say I'm too sick."

"Have you been coughing long?"

"I don't know, really," he said. "These men and I were all stationed at the naval base in Bermuda together. We sleep in a hut where we were all crowded together. One man, Jack, started coughing, and then we all did. And voila, here we all are."

"You seem to be much sicker than your fellows," Ruth said.

"Well, Jack had the cot next to mine. The rest were further away. We all got it. It's just the Navy docs didn't notice until Jack died. Then—panic! Prochaine, we were all on the plane to Kingston."

"Nurse, don't listen to him complain. He's an old sad sack, aren't you, Jerry?"

"You are correct. I am a sad sack." Jerry waved at the man sitting on the bed beside him. "May I introduce mon ami George, Miss?"

"I'm Miss Maclean." She bent over and whispered, "Ruth, since we are all first naming things. Let's get you two settled in beside each other so you can gossip as much as you want." The two men laughed, and Ruth set to work tidying their beds, taking intake temperatures and blood pressures, weighing them, and in the end, tucking them in. She had trouble at first opening the disposable sputum cups and fitting them into the brass holders, but eventually got the hang of it. Looking around, she wondered where they were to be disposed of, full of TB bacteria as they were. Wouldn't they risk being spilled?

"We use sawdust from the bucket in the utility room to soak up the excretions and then place them carefully in the bags. They all get gathered in the dirty utility room and taken to be incinerated," Beth explained to her curious glance. "Be very careful about handling them and be sure they don't fill to overflowing. It keeps us busy."

The settling in took quite a time, but finally Ruth finished arranging the sheets at the bottom of George's bed. He lay back, sighing luxuriously.

"Oh, that is lovely, that is! You can tuck me in anytime, nurse," said George. "Will you be regularly putting me to bed? Because that would make me very happy." He winked. His blue eyes sparkled. Ruth felt a thrill.

"Lay off," said a corporal down the ward. "She's got a dozen better-looking guys all lined up around the room."

Ruth blushed. As she looked around, she dared to differ. George was a slim but well-built man in his 20s. The war didn't seem to have damaged him at all—he looked well-nourished, not wasted by TB like some others, and no injuries, unlike most of the rest of the men. He wore his wavy brown hair longer on top than most of his fellow sailors and it gave him a rakish, movie-star appearance. His blue eyes had a shine in them that seemed healthy, rather than feverish. His temperature supported this assessment—he didn't have the usual late day fever the rest of them were showing.

Gathering up their charts, she looked over to see where Patricia had gone, only to see her sitting on a bed and laughing with an army sergeant in the next ward. She hustled over. "Miss Brannigan, remember—no sitting on the beds! If Mrs. Graham should see you!"

"Lighten up," said Patricia, pulling Ruth's arm so she had to sit beside her. "There. They can't possibly fire both of us. Not with this lot to care for." She chortled and smiled at the man in the bed. "She's a Goodie Two-shoes," she explained to the corporal. "Never have any fun, do you, Miss Maclean?"

Ruth ducked her head and tried to stand up, but Patricia held her arm tight. "I have fun," she muttered, to gales of laughter from Patricia and the corporal. It felt like grade eight all over again. Her face turned crimson, and she struggled.

"I'm sure you do. She's a minister's daughter, you know. Better watch your language around her. She'll report you to God." Patricia laughed, the men joining in.

Ruth slumped, trapped.

"Nurse? Nurse Maclean?" A voice broke Ruth's misery. It was George. "I wonder if you could help me over here."

Ruth tugged her arm out of Patricia's, hard, and hurried to his bed. He whispered to her. "I don't really need anything; just thought you'd like an excuse to get away from them."

She smiled, rearranged his pillow. "Thanks!" She whispered back. The smile he gave her warmed her heart.

"Good for you," said Beth, coming by the bed. "Don't let the men think they are in charge, or they'll run all over you. Miss Brannigan, please stand." She raised her voice. "And if the men know what's good for them, they'll behave. After all, we have ultimate power! Want dinner, boys? Better be nice."

The men laughed, several of them dissolving into coughs. Ruth was alarmed to see that Jerry had turned away toward the wall and pulled his blankets up over his shoulders. She made a mental note to check on him often.

Beth summoned the two nurses to the front of the room. "I see you both need a refresher about TB care. Let's review how to keep from getting TB yourselves before it's too late. It's a good teaching moment for the patients, too. Listen up!" She shouted to the men, who gradually quietened down. "I'm going to read to you from the guidebook. Please pay attention." She opened the book and began.

"Patients must cover his nose and mouth with a paper napkin without contaminating his hands. This should be done whenever he coughs or sneezes and at all times whenever a nurse or attendant is giving bedside care or is in the room. In this way, if he coughs suddenly and unexpectedly, the droplets of sputum will be caught on the paper napkin and not sprayed about the room. Coughing is exercise and should be controlled whenever possible. It may be helped or relieved by taking a sip of water."

Beth demonstrated.

"Disposable paper napkins, which can be used once and then placed in a paper bag at the bedside are to be preferred to cloth handkerchiefs which have to be laundered. The patient should only expectorate into a paper sputum cup, which will be disposed of by burning. We will show you the best method of handling such cups. When out and about, sputum bottles must be used. Expectorating on the grounds will not be tolerated."

She continued reading. "Patients are not to offer food, candy, or fruit to employees or visitors and should not accumulate food in the room to attract mice, cockroaches, and other pests. The patient should clean his teeth at least twice daily with a brush and cleanser. After use, the brush should be rinsed, wiped as dry as possible with a paper napkin, a clean paper napkin folded loosely around the bristles, leaving the top open so it can dry, and then placed in a clean mouthwash glass, brush part up, and placed on the bedside table. Artificial teeth should be handled with paper napkins and the fingers never allowed to touch the teeth. At night, they should be removed, placed in a glass of water or antiseptic solution, or else wrapped carefully with paper napkins and placed on the bedside table."

"This is worse than the Navy," grouched George. "At least there we could go out and shoot at things when we were fed up with the rules."

"Shh." Jerry said. Ruth gave him a tiny smile.

Chapter Thirteen

First loss

The physical difference of death-beds by different diseases is little observed. Patients who die of consumption very frequently die in a state of seraphic joy and peace; the countenance almost expresses rapture. Patients who die of cholera, peritonitis, etc., on the contrary, often die in a state approaching despair. Their countenance expresses horror.

Notes on Nursing, p. 110

B eth took the two women aside. "Now it's time for your X-ray."

"What? We've both been tested!"

"I know. Policy. You get an X-ray when you start here, and every three months afterwards. TB is, unfortunately, a communicable disease." Beth glared at Patricia. "Yet another reason not to do too much fraternization. The X-ray department is in the basement. They're expecting you. I'll see you when you are done."

Patrician and Ruth headed for the stairs.

"Dried up old bat." Patricia muttered.

"Old? She can't be over 30."

"All the rules. It's so stupid. It's not like I'm going to be snogging any of the guys. Trying to cheer them up, that's all."

Ruth kept her mouth shut. She disagreed. She knew Patricia had her out route planned, and it would mean snogging someone.

The Radiology department was in the sanatorium's basement and Ruth shivered with anxiety as they walked through the gloomy halls. "I don't really want an X-ray," she told Patricia.

"Why not? It's the best way to see inside."

"I know. My parents had me get my feet X-rayed the last time I went for shoes. But there are all the reports of burns, aren't there?"

"I imagine this machine is up to date," said Patricia, smiling at the doctor who was sitting by the machine.

"Well, it's not the latest model. That's at the main hospital. But this one is perfectly safe. No burns happening here. Who are you two, please?"

"New staff," said Patricia. "We're to get our initiation X-rays, apparently."

"Yeah, they tell you it's to protect you, but really, we're only making sure you aren't carrying TB yourself. Who's going first? Names and birthdates, please."

"I'll go first," said Patricia. "I'll write my birthdate. No reason to share it around, is there?" Patricia looked at Ruth. "You should step out until I'm done, right, doctor?"

"That's correct, Miss," he peered at her name tag, "Brannigan. Now, if you'll step right this way. You, stay behind the wall. It will protect you from any wandering rays."

Ruth couldn't help but wonder if, if she needed protection, was the procedure itself safe? She stepped behind the wall and prayed it would all be okay.

Patricia was done in a moment, and it was Ruth's turn. "You'll have to take off your uniform and any underthings," the doctor said. "You can change behind here."

Ruth warily stripped. Who knew if he was looking with his machine at her right now? She wrapped a gown tightly around her and stepped out from behind the curtain. The doctor pulled her none too kindly over to a vast machine. "Sorry to rush you, but I've got another ten films to get to today. The main hospital lost power because of an accident, and they are sending patients over here."

The cool of a glass plate behind her made Ruth shiver again as the doctor arranged the machine just so.

"Don't move, or we'll have to do it again." He stepped behind a glass partition. "When I tell you, take a deep breath. Now, take it in and hold it."

The machine whirred and clunked. Ruth felt nothing.

"There—we're all done. That wasn't too bad, was it? I'll develop this and call upstairs if you have to come back for another film."

"Oh, I hope not," said Ruth. "Um...thank you!"

"Don't forget to get dressed," the doctor laughed. Ruth had headed out of the room in her panic. She blushed and ran back behind the screen, pulling on her uniform without even pausing to adjust her hair. She fled.

"You look a mess," said Patricia. "Better tidy up before we go back to the ward. I'm just going to grab a smoke. Meet you at the stairs. There's a ladies' room right around the corner. I spotted it on the way in."

Ruth swooped into the room, gazed at herself in the mirror. Her hair was mussed, her uniform astray. And a run had started in her stockings. Why did they always catch on things, she asked herself. She looked at her hands. Hangnails again. Looking at herself, she sighed. She really didn't look like a nurse, as Mrs. Graham had said. Would she ever? She tucked her hair into place, turned her stockings so the run was less visible, tugged at her hem.

A wash of anger passed over her. She would not let little things like runs in her stockings defeat her. She chuckled, seeing suddenly the ad for Penman's 95 Underwear—"Correct Underwear is 'Health Insurance'" it said. Well, the same could be said for correct stockings. She vowed to take Betty downtown on their first day off to Jackson-Metivier's and buy herself some decent stockings. And some Pacquin's Hand Cream.

Feeling cheered, she headed upstairs in search of Patricia.

As they returned from X-ray, Beth was at work bathing one of the soldiers. She called through the curtain to Ruth and Patricia. "I'm about done this side of the ward. Can you start the baths on the other side? Don't forget to check for lice."

Ruth hastened to one of the semi-private rooms and started taking out the bed bath equipment—the basins, the orange soap, the facecloths, and towels. Most of the men they were responsible for were still on total bedrest, which meant they needed everything done for them, all to rest their lungs and allow recovery. Ruth quickly tidied away her first patient and pulled the screen around the second one in the row.

"Fast worker," said the man in the bed. "I'm glad of that."

Like Jerry, he was gaunt, pale, but unlike the others he was already lying flat in his bed, gasping for air.

"Let me raise your head a bit," said Ruth, reaching for the bed crank. As she turned it and the head of the bed elevated, she heard the soldier's breathing get a bit easier. "What's your name?"

"Seaman Les Howie, miss. From Cape Breton, Nova Scotia."

"Your family must be worrying about you. Do they know you are here?"

"Not yet. We were shipped out so quickly we didn't have time to write." He paused, turned his head away, managed a feeble cough. "They think I'm still in the hospital overseas." He thumped the bed in annoyance, but he was so weak it barely dented the covers.

"Let's get you settled in and then I can get you some paper and pen so you can write to tell them. They might be able to visit."

"I doubt it, Miss. There's the farm to manage."

They began the bed bath, Ruth moving the sailor's wasted body carefully, trying not to add to any pain. She saw every rib moving under his waxy skin. She almost wept as she washed his head, his skull so close to her fingers, his hair sticky with sweat. He was burning up, and she hoped the bathing would cool him down a bit. He breathed shallowly, trying not to cough. As Ruth turned him to wash down his back, he dissolved into a spasm of coughing long enough the other man in the room called out to ask if he was okay.

"I'm sorry, I'm sorry," whispered Ruth. "Did I move you too fast? I'm so sorry!" He was left gasping, clutching the bedsheets in an attempt at control. Ruth was frantic, trying to support him, holding his back, raising him up to sitting, but he simply couldn't get a breath in.

"Get the doctor," Beth called. Ruth leapt to do so, but the soldier grabbed her hand.

"Don't leave me," he wheezed. "Please?"

"I'll find the doctor," said Patricia. It took her a few minutes to return, laughing doctor in tow, obviously not knowing of the emergency. By that time, the soldier had stopped coughing. Breathing, too. Ruth stood, holding his cooling hand, as tears ran down her cheek. He'd slipped away as she stood there, helpless. Beth stood beside her, sober faced.

The doctor put a stethoscope on the soldier's chest, shook his head. "Why did you wait so long to call me? We might have done something. Too late now."

"He's just arrived," Ruth choked out. "I was getting him settled."

"And you know we can't resuscitate TB patients...," said Beth. "Not without doctors present."

The doctor looked at Ruth, seeing her tears. "None of that. You'll see many more deaths before this week is out if I'm reading things right. Let's move this bed. These other pour souls doesn't need be frightened. At least it wasn't the usual bloodbath." The three of them unlocked the bed's brakes and Ruth lowered his head to flat. They covered his face with the sheet and pushed him, bed and all, out to the hallway. The soldiers in the wards looked on, silent.

"Sucks to survive the war and then get here and die," said one.

"Language," said Beth.

The men muttered amongst themselves.

"I'll call the orderlies to take him to the morgue," said Beth. "After they take him, sterilize this entire bed. Use the weskadine and then the oil solution. Miss Brannigan, you know what to do. Don't bring the bed back in until it is spotless."

The doctor leaned over to Ruth. "When they contact the commanding officer, you may want to add a note to the letter home—the families like to hear their sons weren't alone."

Ruth quickly wiped her eyes.

The doctor looked at her sharply, spun on his heel and headed back into the ward. "Now boys," he bellowed cheerily, "let's examine how well the rest of you are doing."

Orderlies arrived and lifted the man easily onto a stretcher. He was so light and wasted, they barely needed to make any effort. They covered him up and set off, the wheels making a mournful squeak as they rolled.

"New nurses," one said.

"Yup," laughed the other one. He turned and gave them an extravagant wink and bow. Patricia pointedly ignored them.

That left the bed.

Patricia and Ruth spent the next half hour stripping the sheets and washing down the bed with iodine and wiping it with a foul-smelling oil solution, supposed to make it easier to clean the bacteria away. Ruth was grateful for the distraction. The sudden death of the patient had rocked her. She couldn't help the tears falling, but at least while bent over the bed, scrubbing, no one else would notice. By the time their work was approved by Beth, they were tousled and spotted with cleaning solution. Getting the springs underneath had been the worst bit.

"He wasn't even in the bed for half an hour," grumbled Patricia. "How would he have soiled the springs?"

Ruth shrugged, but Mrs. Graham was nearby, so she made sure not to comment in reply.

Eventually they were done, and, making up the bed with fresh sheets, rolled it back into the ward. There was a man waiting for it, sitting patiently in a chair. He crept toward it and sighed audibly as he lay back.

Matching his sigh, Ruth gathered a blank chart and a thermometer and stepped toward him.

Chapter Fourteen

At work

One of these is the method for reducing dust and bacteria in a patient's room by the oil treatment of the floors and bed clothes as advocated by the Commission on Air-Borne Infection in collaboration with the Commission on Acute Respiratory Diseases. The oil treatment of the floors is accomplished by adding two and one-half gallons of pale paraffin oil to each one hundred pounds of reasonably fine sawdust. This makes a sweeping compound which when properly used leaves a slight amount of oil on the floor, and thus reduces the dust content of the air.

Marriette, p. 825.

The days on the ward followed one on the other in a sluggish dismal stream. A lot of the work was plain drudge work—cleaning and tidying, mopping up messes, running back and forth with urinals and bedpans, tissues and bags. Ruth and Beth would start at one end of a ward and work their way through, gathering bottles and bags and wipes and changing bedding. They'd leave everything spick and span, smelling vaguely of antiseptic. Occasionally, they'd get an orderly to come help with the heavy bed washing, but often it was just one of their assigned duties. Ruth thought miserably that her mother would be thrilled at how good she was getting at washing down floors. Fortunately, Patricia had been shifted to the women's ward, and they didn't have to deal with her flirting on the ward.

They'd load up a cart as they went, and it would be full of dirty waste halfway down the room. Ruth would have to roll it off down the hall to the utility room and empty everything, restock with fresh supplies, and roll it back while Beth 'entertained the troops' as she called it, cracking jokes and singing with the men. The men loved it and even Mrs. Graham got into it occasionally, singing old WW2 tunes with the best of them.

"Good for their lungs," she explained, a twinkle in her eye. She seemed to be in her element, working with the soldiers. She'd even relaxed a bit and could be seen joking with some of the doctors.

Ruth and Beth would finish at the end of the wards, and by then it was time to run around with the meal trays, cleanup and more quiet time for the patients. This meant the nurses had to tiptoe around in monk-like silence, carrying urinals and boxes of tissues. The designated rest periods chopped into the days, and at first Ruth got hushed a lot by the senior nurses. Eventually she started whispering, changing her voice to match the patients'—they had the rules down pat. She struggled to remember to call everyone by Miss and Mister, especially when she tired, and got glares if she didn't stand up quickly enough when the doctors came to do rounds. But they seemed less strict here, and so Ruth felt less nervous and gradually learned what was expected.

The worst part of the job was that once in a while a patient she'd looked after would be missing when Ruth came on duty. There hadn't been a death most days she worked at the big hospital, and here it was eerie to say goodnight to a fellow and never see him again, whisked off to the morgue as he was. Initially, Ruth mourned each patient, but their bed soon filled and, except for a few of the men, they all started to seem alike after a bit. It seemed the supply of soldiers with TB was endless.

Every day or so, the doctors would come by with another treatment for the patients. These varied, from potions to needle aspirations to inhalants. Nothing seemed to slow the disease. Every new treatment meant new learning for Ruth as she tried to assist the patients, positioning them to drain secretions or breathe in powders or receive oxygen.

"What does any of this matter, anyway?" Ruth asked Mary as they chatted one night in their beds. "They seem to either get better or not, no matter what we do."

"Don't let the doctors hear you say that," Mary cautioned. "They really trust in all their treatments."

"But what about your patient the other day? She had so many surgeries and still got it in her spine. I heard she fell, too."

Mary made an angry noise. "That was Patricia's fault. She ran off to do something over your way and she left her sitting on the edge of the bed. Honestly! I saw her beginning to slip, but I was in the middle of repositioning Mrs. S. and couldn't let her drop. Terrible. She screamed. Heartbreaking."

"Oh, no! Did the head nurse see?"

"Of course not," grumbled Mary. "Patricia only slips out when she's not around. When Mrs. Conley is on the ward, she's as sweet as pie. I hate working with her."

"Come over to our ward," said Ruth. "We have chocolate!" She pulled the two chocolate bars George had smuggled into her pocket out from her bedside table. "Want one?"

Mary grinned and took it. "I wish the women were as generous as your fellows," she said. "They just seem to expect us to look after them."

"Well, I'm getting a little worried about George. I'm afraid he's flirting with me."

"How exciting! Do you like him, too?"

Ruth blushed, covered her face. "No! I'm not allowed to have any thoughts like that. My father would kill me. He'd call me home in a minute if he thought George was sweet on me."

"My lips are sealed—as long as he keeps providing tasty things to eat, that is."

They laughed and settled in to sleep.

As the weeks passed, the long-term men became friends with each other and the staff. Now and again there'd be a scattering of arguments among them, mainly over conscription and the Quebec unwillingness to be involved. If things got ugly, Jerry would turn to the wall and pretend to be asleep, but the other French-Canadian soldiers enjoyed the argument. Mrs. Graham would have to come in and explain that everyone in the ward had gone to do their duty and shouldn't have to suffer any prejudice.

"That's just it, Matron," one soldier argued. "Their duty!"

And the arguments would swing in again.

"How about him?" one man asked one day, pointing at George. "He showed up so late he might as well have not bothered."

"I had to help with the farm," George replied hotly.

"That's not what they told me," said the soldier, but he burst into coughing and the argument was forgotten.

Ruth looked over at George, but he blushed and turned away. She wondered if the gossip was true. He did seem much healthier than the other men.

If the men survived the first few days on the ward, they stayed around, healing slowly. The wards became more and more filled, new beds being squeezed in-between the old ones. Every day the nurses monitored their temperatures, hoping for the end of the late day fever that meant the disease was still active.

Just as it seemed some of the men might be improving, the winter influenza crept into the wards. This pushed many of the sicker patients into the serious category. Despite the new vaccine, the patients were still at terrible risk. Not everyone could get the vaccine, due to short supplies, and some patients were too sick to form any sort of protective response from it. Often the doctors refused to operate on the patients who got the flu, arguing that scarce resources should be saved for those with the chance of survival. Influenza attacked the lungs, too, making breathing even more difficult for those with TB lesions. Part of every day now involved rotating patients out of their wards to an isolation ward, where masked and well-covered nurses cared for them. Tuberculosis and influenza together could mean the patient only had a few days left. The morgue was hectic in those days, the orderlies becoming more and more grim as the weeks passed and they came back and forth.

Soon, even in the regular wards, the nurses wore protective equipment. At least it kept them warmer.

Chapter Fifteen

Routines and surprises

Used sputum containers are removed using special forceps and incinerated. During collection of soiled cups the nurse wears a gown and rubber gloves. She places the cups in a location for specially trained porters. The nurse then washes the gloves and boils them, discards her gown, washes and dries her hands.
Gloves are boiled for 2-5 minutes and then dried, powdered, and put away.

Eyre, 1949, p. 56

The nursing work didn't stop at the end of the shift. Many of the patients at the San weren't getting better, losing their battle with the tiny foe TB. It seemed so unfair after their fighting in the war. In their hours off, Ruth and the other nurses wrote to families, telling pretty stories of their family member's last moments. They'd sit around a big table, sharing ideas and stories, passing inkwells around.

"Glad I'm not Catholic," Ruth said to Mary. "I'd feel terrible about all the lying I'm doing."

Mary put her pen down and stretched her hand. They were sitting in the common room, writing together. "Well, I know I am keeping the priest busy in confession. But I can't honestly say I'm going to go and 'sin no more' when the next group of patients are being wheeled onto the influenza ward. And no one needs to know how their son really died."

Ruth nodded. "I can't wait until this flu is over." They bent to their task again.

Suddenly cheery, Mary piped up. "They've got roast beef for dinner again tonight. At least that's heartening."

Dinners at the hospital were almost always good. Tuberculosis wasn't called 'consumption' for nothing—those with it lost weight dramatically, and it looked like the patients consumed themselves as the disease progressed. It reminded Ruth of the patients with cancer she'd nursed back at KGH. It all was a game of trying to get in enough calories to prevent the body from totally wasting away, all presented in a form that it wouldn't take too much energy to eat. The kitchen prepared three hearty meals a day for the patients and several snacks, and this meant the nurses' meals were equally good. Breakfasts of oatmeal and eggs, lunches of rich soup and bread, suppers of meat and potatoes. Plus, the desserts, concocted to encourage those who with no appetite. They tasted delicious. Ruth was finding her uniform getting a bit snug already and tried to get out for a walk every day. Mary often joined her, and they'd fast walk down Princess Street to the downtown and back—always tough because the return trip meant one long slow uphill from the lake. Add in a little snow and the ever-present wind and the walks became faster and shorter as the fall progressed.

They started to walk earlier in the day, allowing a stop at Morrison's for a warming cup of tea. Everyone treated them well when they saw their uniforms and capes.

"I used to hate having to wear our uniforms everywhere," said Mary, biting into a teacake. "But I like always being able to get a table in here. And they save us the best treats!"

"Not much help for our slimming plan," said Ruth, "But I'm not complaining. This is so much better than the stuff we got in the nursing residence!"

Ruth always felt a little guilty buying treats at the coffee shop. Her income wasn't much as a nurses' aide, and she didn't send as much home as she'd like. She'd make a point of only getting one treat a week, telling herself she deserved at least that after a week of gruesome fetching and cleaning.

Gradually, the ward filled up with longer-term patients and the routine became easier to follow. Some men graduated from 'absolute rest' to 'on basins', which allowed them to wash themselves and go to the toilet by themselves. Some were allowed to get up for longer periods. George was deemed well enough to be up out of bed for an entire hour, though Jerry remained stuck at basins and had to mostly stay lying down. George would use his up and about time to get treats from the dining hall for them both and some of the other lads. Sometimes he'd bring Ruth a chocolate bar, smuggle it into her pocket as she rearranged his pillows.

"You are so naughty!" Ruth grinned as she sensed the weight of the chocolate bar slipping into her pocket.

"Sweets for the sweet," George said with a wink. Jerry groaned.

Jerry and George were Ruth's favourites. She tried to always end up at their corner so she could spend a little extra time with them. George would flirt outrageously, Jerry would join in a more civilized way, and soon all three would be laughing. Ruth told herself it was because of her worry about Jerry, but she found herself thinking about George more and more as the days went on.

Chapter Sixteen

Disasters

I am on 'basins'. Everyone is 'on' something. 'Absolute' is entirely in bed, 'basins' is getting up to wash in own room (mine is a basin and taps) and go along to the toilet, 'OTW' is out to wash, through 1 hour up, 2 hours up to 4, and then 'exercise', 1 round, 2 rounds up to 6, and then 'grades', which is work, graded upwards. All very interesting. Spoke to one other person in the weighing room—seemed pleasant and serious—only allowed to whisper or, as she puts it, 'I'm on whispers'. 9.30 pm lights out. Thank goodness windows were wide open.

Hurt R., p. 351.

Ruth was walking down Princess Street in search of even more stockings a few days later when she spotted Betty at the door to their favourite coffee shop. She was peering in and when she saw Ruth, she waved urgently at her. Ruth joined her, starting to give her a cheery hello until she saw the tears in Betty's eyes.

"What's up, Betty? Let's get a table. Are you all right? What's happened?"

Betty sat, wringing a handkerchief in her hands, her nose red from weeping.

The waiter came by. "Two coffees, please, with sugar," said Ruth. She leaned forward. "What's wrong?"

"It's Derek." Betty sniffed. "Remember the other night when I told you he was a keeper? Well, he isn't."

"Oh no," Ruth said, hoping they wouldn't be overheard. "What happened?"

"Well," Betty began, "it happened after the dance last Friday. He said he was going to drive me back to residence. You know how all those guys have cars, right? And it was so cold out. I didn't think it would do any harm."

She stopped and sobbed. "He was always a perfect gentleman!"

Ruth's heart sank. "Shh. People are looking. What did he do?"

"So, we stopped in this parking lot and started kissing a bit. He told me he really cared for me and everyone else was kissing. When I said no, I wanted to go home, he said all sorts of things to me, but he apologized so sweetly, I thought it wouldn't hurt just to kiss him a bit...."

"Oh Betty," Ruth groaned. "I'll bet he didn't stop there."

"No," she sobbed. "Before I knew it, he was on top of me and ...."

"Did you fight him off?"

"I tried, but it sort of was nice, you know? Until it wasn't. He kept telling me how much he liked me, how he wanted to see me again." She sobbed again. "And after that, he drove me home and dropped me like a sack of potatoes. He hasn't called since. I've had Ann taking all my messages and phone calls when I'm off and not a word."

Ruth put her arms around Betty. "Are you okay?"

Betty gathered herself. "I hope so, but he didn't use anything...and I can't tell anyone except you—they are already threatening to throw me out because I've been caught out late a couple of times."

"What are you going to do?"

"Well, I can't report him. It would be an enormous scandal and you can bet I'd get the worst of that. I am never dating a soldier again!"

Ruth thought privately that Betty must have had some prior experience. She seemed more worried about people finding out than the loss of innocence that Ruth herself would have felt.

"But what will I do if... if ...anything happened?"

"We'll have to figure that out, I guess. Let's hope nothing took. When are you due for your monthlies?"

"In a couple of weeks yet," she said. "I should find out soon. I've been doing vinegar douches, but I'm afraid someone will notice the smell in the bathroom."

"My mother tried those. Of course, she told us it was just for cleanliness, but I've always wondered. I hope it works better for you than it did for her."

"Really? Oh gods! What else did she try?"

"She used to have some sort of herbal pills she took—said they were supplements—but they didn't seem to work very well, either. But you probably don't need to worry about that. What are the chances? I mean, your mother isn't like mine, popping babies out every few months. There's only you and your sister, right? Maybe you aren't very fertile."

Betty nodded. "Right. I'm sure it will be all right."

Ruth peered into Betty's face. "Are you okay, though? He didn't hurt you?"

"Not much. He was a bit rough, but I'm not hurt badly. Just somewhat bruised. And mad."

"You're sure you don't want to report him?"

"Oh no. Can you imagine? I'd never live it down."

"But you weren't...."

"A virgin? No. And that would make reporting things even worse." Betty shook her head. "It was a boy in my high school. We were planning to get married. And then he went off to the war, and...came back in a box."

Ruth hugged Betty tight. "Oh, how terrible! How are you managing to keep moving?" She took in a deep breath. "I'm sure you'll be fine. Just go home and get a good rest."

Betty smiled through her tears. "I'm up for my rotation to Rockwood, you remember, that creepy psychiatric hospital down by the lake. They say hard work can help get rid of...anything I don't want. And if not, the ghosts there might scare it out of me!"

"Well, if that doesn't terrify anything away, nothing will. Rockwood is not my idea of a fun rotation. But at least it's a change—it will provide distraction, anyway. Don't you have to move over there?"

"Yes, I've got to get packed up this weekend. I hear the rooms are freezing, too. I'll just have to endure." She sighed extravagantly, hand to brow. "But when that's done, I'll get my cap! Can you come and make sure I don't faint? I'm so afraid they'll decide I don't deserve one at the last moment."

Ruth's heart twisted. If things had gone better at KGH, she'd be getting her cap and bib soon, too. "Of course, I'll come, Betty. I want to cheer you on." Her stomach rumbled. Practical thoughts over regrets, she told herself. "Would you like something to eat? I could use something before I get my stockings."

"Again? You must spend half your salary on stockings!"

"And they are hideous. Can't wait for my whites, if I ever get back to school."

"You will. I believe in you." Betty smiled, and they ordered soup and bread rolls. Comfort food. They talked about other things and gradually Betty calmed down. She left, bouncing briskly out into the evening.

Ruth shook her head as she started her walk home. She vowed to study harder and avoid any men entirely until she graduated. Especially soldiers.

Over the next few days, things smoothed out. Ruth was getting faster at her tasks, and Patricia was still assigned to the women's ward, which made life easier. Often, over dinner, she'd spot Patricia glaring at her, but despite rumours that she'd asked for a transfer, she remained far away from the men's ward. Mary would report Patricia's missteps and the two of them would giggle over them late at night.

One evening, as Ruth was studying in her room, she heard a banging on her door and shouting. "Come out, come out!"

She pulled the door open. Betty was outside, her hair blown into wild curls, all in a flutter. "What? It's my friend," she explained to the other nurses, who had stuck their heads out into the hallway.

"Tell her to be quiet. Some of us are trying to sleep." The doors slammed.

Ruth stepped outside her room, and Betty grabbed her arm.

"It's freezing out! I ran all the way here and I'm still chilled to the bone."

"Come sit by the fire," Ruth said. "It's down the stairs in the common room."

Betty gaped as they entered the room. "Wow—this is nice! Better than the old nursing residence, that's for sure. I can't wait until my rotation here!"

"Why did you run over here? What's happened? Are you...? Is it my mother?"

Betty stopped gaping at the room and instead gaped at Ruth. "Oh no, I'm fine. Really. All clear, thank God. No—it's your dad! He's here!"

"He's here? What? How? Why?"

"I'm so sorry," Betty said, almost in tears. "I've been picking up your letters, but we've been so busy I haven't had a chance to bring them over to you. I guess this one was where he said he was coming." She handed Ruth an envelope.

Ruth tore it open, read the brief note. "Oh heavens! He's here for the Interdenominational Conference. He always gets into a tizzy at those. He wrote he wants to meet with the dean and see how I am doing."

"Oh, I'm so, so sorry. What are you going to do? I told him you were on the ward, and I had to go get you—he doesn't know you are way over here."

Ruth paused for a long, slow breath. "I guess I'll have to meet him. Let's go."

"Are you sure? I'd hide. Or pretend. Want to pretend my room is yours? You didn't tell him you were transferred, right? Is he going to be angry? He looked scary."

"Betty, you are not helping. There's no point in panicking. He can sense it, like blood in the water." Ruth paused for a minute, then shook her head. "He'll figure it out. I could never lie to him. Why do you think I never snuck out at night with you girls? I'd end up telling Matron as soon as she asked."

Betty laughed, quick. "I'm glad you didn't come out with us, then! You're coming for the Christmas dance though, right?"

"I'm not sure. If my father takes me home...." Ruth cringed. "I should have explained this to him. He's going to be furious." She wrung her hands. "We'd better get moving. I'll go grab my coat."

"And your hat and gloves, too. It feels like snow."

Chapter Seventeen

Fighting with Father

Treatment

It almost didn't matter which modality a patient chose; they were all useless in the face of tuberculosis. Chopin, writing to a friend from the island of Mallorca said, "I have been sick as a dog the last two weeks. I caught cold in spite of the 18 degrees heat, roses, oranges, palms, figs, and the three most famous doctors on the island. One sniffed at what I spat up, the second tapped where I spat it from, the third poked about and listened how I spat it. One said I had died, the second that I am dying, and the third that I shall die."

Wallace, p. 19.

It was unreasonably cold, and Ruth shivered as they started out, but she wasn't sure if it was the weather or fear of trying to explain things to her father. She couldn't remember the last time she'd lied to him. The most recent one that came to mind was when she was in ninth grade and she'd gone to a friend's house after school so she could skip chores, telling her parents she had to help at school. Her mother explained later that he'd been worried she'd gotten lost, but that didn't help with the initial terror. She'd never dared disobey again.

He wasn't an easy man to explain things to. He growled first and blustered, and then maybe, maybe, after a night or two, he'd settle down enough to have a civilized discussion. Ruth didn't have time now for him to ease into understanding. Her thoughts scurried around her head, searching for an explanation he might buy. None came to mind. Clinging to hope, she told herself perhaps he'd just be glad to see her. She was afraid that wouldn't be his reaction, though. Yell first, care later....

But first, she had to get to the residence. Slipping on the damp road, they hustled on.

As they sped along the streets, climbing over snow hills, Betty said between gasping breaths, "He won't take you home today, will he? You are still working as a nurse, right? How can he object?"

"Well, remember even though I'm getting paid, I'm barely able to send anything home. He might tell me it's better if I come home and marry Chuck and...," Ruth gulped back a sob. "I can't, I just can't."

Betty pulled at Ruth's arm. "What's this? Is that guy still writing to you? Did he propose? And you didn't tell me? Why are you here?"

Ruth tugged her arm away. "I'm not engaged. Chuck keeps saying he wants to get married, but I don't answer. I don't want to just marry and be a pastor's wife like my mother. I'd be no good at it, anyway." Betty looked like she wanted to ask more, but a glance at Ruth's face made her hold back. Despite their fast pace, the walk from Park Street to Union seemed to take forever. Ruth began to cry as they walked along, Betty holding her hand for comfort.

Finally, they walked up to the nurses' residence, dread slowing their last steps. A familiar car was parked in the drive. They stepped carefully up the stairs, Ruth shaking with fear. She squeezed Betty's hand, used her other hand to wipe away her tears. It never paid to show weakness in front of her father. Never.

A tall, familiar person was standing inside the lobby, waving his arms and shouting at the student nurse in charge of the door. "But she lives here. I know she does. I left her here not two months ago!"

"Father," Ruth cried, then stepped back as her father turned his blazing eyes on her.

"Where were you? What have you been doing? What is all of this about? She says she hasn't seen you!"

The nursing supervisor appeared in her office doorway, and for once the girls were grateful she was there. She seemed to have a soothing effect on the minister.

"Come now, Reverend Maclean. Let's go in and share a cup of tea and I can explain everything. Miss Maclean and Miss O'Donnell, you wait in the kitchen. I'll call for you when it is time."

She led the still gesticulating man into her office, and they shut the door. The supervisor poked her head out briefly. "Miss Maclean—make us a pot of tea, will you? And bring some of those biscuits, will you?" She actually winked at Ruth before the door closed again. Ruth and Betty stared at each other in astonishment. They scurried off to the kitchen to gather tea makings.

"Maybe he'll let you stay. Miss Connor always says nice things to the parents. I've heard her. She'll sing your praises."

"But I'm not one of her students. She doesn't even know me," Ruth moaned. "He's going to be so angry. The last time one of us lied to him, well...it was the strap and prayer duties for a month. I even had to dust the underside of the pews. He'll want to drag me home for sure."

"Is Chuck looking like a better option?" Betty teased.

Ruth threw a potholder at her. "You are no help at all. Don't you have studying to do? I'd better face this alone."

Betty frowned. "There is a big exam tomorrow. Are you sure you'll be okay? I can stay...."

Ruth shook her head, and Betty made a grateful retreat, waving as she went around the corner.

She made the tea and gingerly knocked on the supervisor's door to bring it in. Her father seemed unusually quiet, sitting somewhat chastened in one of the hard steel chairs. "That will do, Miss Maclean. Please join us," Miss Connor said. She poured the tea, adding extra sugar to the reverend's. "For the shock," she said, when he raised a hand. He sat back.

"So, Miss Maclean, I've explained the situation to your father. I've told him, also, that you so far are an excellent student within your capability and that you have never caused us any concern. Well, except for your tendency to state your opinions." Miss Connor frowned. "I did also tell him of my concern about you being friends with other students caught out after curfew and in the company of several soldiers from the army base. You haven't been out with the girls, have you?" Her eyes bored into Ruth's.

"No, Miss Connor, never. I am too tired after my duties and studying."

"Yes, that's another thing. Reverend Maclean—although your daughter has been found unsuitable for the full nursing program, I hear she has continued on her own to study the materials. I am certain she will be an acceptable student one day soon."

"What? Unsuitable? How dare you? She's every bit as bright as the other girls."

"Now, now. It has nothing to do with her intellect. She just needs to grow up a bit. Perhaps life in Cloyne left her somewhat behind the rest of her peers...in certain skills." Miss Connor raised her hand to block another explosion from the reverend. "She is doing excellent work in the Veteran's Hospital, however. She's just begun, but already her charge nurse speaks highly of her. And we need her there."

This puzzled Ruth. She wasn't sure she'd made any impression. She noticed a twitch in Miss Connor's mouth. She was lying for her, but why?

"But isn't that looking after all the military fellows back from the war? Should a young impressionable girl be exposed to that? Their behaviour?"

Ruth spoke, despite Miss Connor's warning frown. "Oh, Father, they are all so sick. They need so much care. And I think they enjoy having someone their age to speak with while they are trapped here. So many of them will never go home, and their families are far away. And if you suppose, heaven forbid, that I might want to get romantically involved? Well, you've never had to care for a TB patient, obviously. I take as good care as I can, but sometimes even I have to leave the room until I can settle my stomach."

"That's enough, Miss Maclean," said Miss Connor, sternly. She slapped her hands on her desk and stood. "Well, are we all squared away? I really must see to my work, and Miss Maclean needs to get back to her ward."

"No. Wait. Are you telling me she is just doing grunt work? Work she might just as easily do at home? That she's not learning anything? What about her fees?

Can we get a refund? I'm not made of money, you know." Reverend Maclean was spluttering in all directions, his outrage making his face bloom red.

Ruth felt her stomach tighten. Trust her father to focus on the money. She ducked her head, embarrassed at his display.

"I'm afraid her fees were already spent on her uniform and books. She'll be able to use them later, perhaps, or can sell them to another student. She is being paid as an aide in the hospital. It's lower pay than she'd get as a nurse, as the skill set isn't so acute. With practice and continued application, she will be able to rejoin the program."

Ruth kept her face turned down and gritted her teeth. How much more application would she be expected to do?

"In any case, it's between you and Miss Maclean to decide if she stays or returns home. You should be aware that she is doing vital work. We've had so many soldiers come back from the front with tuberculosis. We can't simply abandon them to their fate after what they have done for this country. Many of them don't have suitable homes to recover in, and many are too sick to be without twenty-four-hour care."

Reverend Maclean sat, index finger stroking his moustache, thinking. Ruth held her breath. Finally, he spoke. "Perhaps I could visit the ward to say hello to the men? Then I can decide what to do with my daughter. I'll have a better idea of what she's been doing, and the potential risk she is under from these men. I remember well what it was like when I was at war...." Ruth took a deep breath. Was there hope? Please God, she thought, don't let him get lost in reminiscence. That might go on for hours, and she could see the supervisor was already getting impatient. Being an administrative burden wouldn't make them more likely to take her back.

"That will be fine, though it is after visiting hours. The men might enjoy a chance to speak with a minister. Many of them don't have long in this life and might be glad of some spiritual guidance. I must get back to my work. Miss Maclean, can you take your father over to the ward?"

Ruth nodded, though she was terrified what her father would say when they were alone. Sure enough, he turned on her as soon as they stepped out of the door.

"How dare you lie to me? It's bad enough you have failed at your studies, but to lie about it to me, and your poor mother. I don't have any idea what to say to you, except you better be ready to pack up and come home with me this instant. I knew that once you were away from home, you'd slip into evil ways."

Chapter Eighteen

Proving herself

"I have never been able to join in the popular cry about the recklessness of soldiers. On the contrary I should say...that I have never seen so teachable and helpful a class as the Army general. Give them opportunity promptly and securely to send money home & they will use it....Give them a book & a game & a Magic Lantern & they will lay off drinking. Give them suffering and they will bear it. Give them work and they will do it...If Officers would but think thus of their men, how much might not be done for them."

Florence Nightingale, as quoted in Gill, p. 396.

"No, Father." Ruth sensed her spine strengthening, though her stomach still swirled. "I'm doing good things. Come and have a look at the men on the ward. You will see how I am needed here."

He shrugged, unconvinced. "Marriage is where you should focus your efforts, not this nursing. And your mother needs you at home." He stuck his chin out, beard bristling. "You were once a dutiful daughter. And Chuck is heartbroken."

Ruth ignored this, adding, "And I didn't fail. I just have had a delay. I still mean to be a nurse."

He grunted at that, and after a sullen, silent drive across the now snow-swept streets, they arrived at the newly named Hopkins Institute. Ruth took his arm and walked him to her ward, peeked through the doors. She so hoped no one was bleeding out at the moment. Or naked. But she knew how impatient her father could be and she wanted to show him, quickly, before he grew even more determined to take her away. She glanced at the men. Good. Everyone lay, tidied into bed, and no one was using a urinal or anything. She breathed deep with relief.

"Miss Maclean!" a cheer rose from the men.

"What are you doing here? Aren't you off for the day?" asked George.

"I am. This is my father, the Reverend Maclean. He's here to visit and check out what I've been doing."

Ruth turned to her father, who stood frozen in the doorway, staring agape at the men. She suddenly viewed them with fresh eyes. Non-nurse eyes. They did look ghastly. A few seemed relatively healthy—playing cards at a table in the corner of their ward, but the great majority were pale, gaunt, breathing with difficulty. One lay crookedly, swathed in bandages after a rib removal. Ruth hastened to straighten him in bed, and he thanked her in a soft voice.

Other patients had tubes coming from their chests, draining into large bottles set in buckets of sand. A couple looked even worse, completely slumped over, most of their ribs and lungs gone. Their skin tone almost matched their sheets. Despite this, they raised a hand to wave to Ruth. Ruth, used to the sight, smiled back at them. Her father glanced at her and shook his head.

A moment passed. Finally, Reverend Maclean rubbed his hand over his eyes and stood straight. He reached into his pocket and brought out a bible and a notebook. "Hello, boys. Can I pray with you?"

Then it was Ruth's turn to be amazed as she watched her father travel from bed to bed, speaking to each man softly, writing down their names and addresses, blessing many of them. She'd seen him often in the pulpit, but not so often in his one-to-one sessions with parishioners. He was surprisingly gentle with them, his voice lowered from his usual fierce growl. By the time he had finished circling the ward, though, he looked almost as pale as the men. Ruth saw how ministry wore on her father and felt a stab of guilt. Was she being horrible not wanting to go back and help him?

Ruth, abashed, joined the other nurse on duty and they made the temperature rounds while her father prayed. At last, he finished, and he and Ruth left the ward. Reverend Maclean shuffled down the stairs, groped his way to a nearby bench, almost fell into it. Ruth, startled at the change in her father, ran to get some tea. When she returned, her father's colour had improved, and he was sitting up straight again. He smiled at her, reached for her hand. "I'm fine."

He exhaled. "What a reminder of the last war! I hoped never to view such carnage again. The stories they told me! What happened to all the boys wrapped in bandages? Had they been shot? Those are hideous injuries. Some of them could barely breathe."

Ruth leaned her head on her father's shoulder. "No, father. That's part of their treatment. The doctors here collapse the lung with the tuberculosis in it, to keep it from spreading until the rest of the body strengthens. Sometimes, when the collapse works well, it cuts off enough oxygen to the infected area that the cells stop growing. The tubes and bottles beside the beds are from when the doctors create a pneumothorax. That's when they put air or something else in to collapse the lung temporarily. If that doesn't work, they take out ribs or lung sections even, all to control the disease. They've had good success." And some horrible failures, too, she knew. She hoped there wouldn't be too many more of those. It was hard enough to take when the men just wasted away.

Her father stared at her, not comprehending. "They take out their ribs? How do they walk?"

"We work with them, teach them how to hold themselves upright. I do exercises with them every day."

He stared at her, a tear in the corner of his eye. "Where will it end?"

Ruth stood up. She thought of something that might cheer her father up.

"Come over here, Father—there's a children's ward."

They entered the ward and peeked at the children, most of them sleeping. One or two gazed wide-eyed in silence. Two younger ones were crying, and a nurse sat between them, stroking their heads. "They miss their mothers," she explained. Reverend Maclean walked over and blessed them, making them go quiet as they stared at this tall stranger.

Ruth waved thanks at the nurse, and they left. Outside the building, the reverend stopped to wipe his eyes.

"Such suffering. Those poor children with the broken legs...."

Ruth tried to explain but gave up. It was too complicated. "Father," she asked, hesitant, "Now that you have seen what is here, might I stay? I believe I am doing good work here."

Her father looked at her through his eyebrows. "Where are you staying? I only approved of you coming here because of the supervision you had at the nursing residence."

"Oh Father," Ruth laughed. "It's so much nicer living here—we've got our own floor, away from the patients, and the supervisor stays on the floor with us." She laughed and pointed up at the second-floor windows, where curtains modestly covered the windows. "No one is creeping out after hours from here." She crossed her fingers, realizing she shouldn't have mentioned that possibility, hoping she could pass the lie. The truth was a goodly number of patients and nurses snuck out after hours, and they even had a special system where one door was jammed just the smallest bit open. When she'd first arrived, she'd mistakenly shut it and there was all sorts of trouble that night.

Reverend Maclean frowned at her. She'd forgotten how terrifying his eyebrows were. He said nothing for a long time. Ruth held her breath until she thought she might faint. Finally, he sighed.

"Ruth, I had hoped to bring you home. Your mother needs your help, too. As you know, she's expecting again."

"Father! Why? That can't be good for her."

He had the good grace to blush. "Hmm. But she will need help."

Ruth waited. She would not give him the answer he wanted.

"And it seems like you may have learned some useful skills here that would be a help to her. The boys said you gave them excellent care, kept them tidy, and so forth."

Ruth's heart sank. Surely, she hadn't made her own bed to lie in, had she? She'd die if she had to go back to Cloyne. On her days off, she'd walked all over Kingston, been into the little shops and seen the boats, met up with friends, even danced once or twice. She loved it here. She couldn't tell her father that, of course. And what about Chuck? He'd never let her go if she moved back.

He gazed at her again. "I note you've learned to keep your mouth shut when it needs to be, too," he said, gruff, but with a twinkle in his eye. He shook his head. "I don't know what to do, my shining girl. I want you home. I miss you around the place."

Ruth could feel tears starting. She swallowed them back.

"But I saw how happy the boys seemed when you went in—and how efficient you were at looking after them. I think they do need you. I hope that Bill, er, other veterans would have such caring attention if they needed it."

She breathed. She hoped.

"I'll give you another six months. If you haven't proved yourself by then, I'll expect you back home. Understood?"

"Thank you, Father! I'll work so hard!" Ruth hugged her father tight. "I miss you, too, and all of them back at home—but I want to do this work. You can understand, Father? The need to do good?"

"As long as that is what you are doing." He hugged her back. "Keep those boys' hands off you. Are you going to church?"

"When I can," said Ruth, crossing her fingers again. "Mrs. Graham makes us pray every day and I still have Aunt Doreen's little blue book for reference." She pulled it out of her pocket.

Her father took it from her hand, flipped through the pages, grunting approvingly. "Your aunt was a good, good woman. Think of her if you get in trouble." He handed it back to Ruth. "Six months. Be good! I'll write to these boy's parents, tell them I visited." He slapped his hand on his chest pocket. "At least perhaps I can help in my small way." He smiled. "You're so professional in that uniform and cape. All you need is the cap."

He turned away and strode to the parking lot where the ancient Ford stood. It would be a long ride home at his usual slow rate. Ruth waved and tried not to cry as he pulled out of the parking lot. She missed him, brusque manner and all. But she had a reprieve! Heart soaring, she danced back to her residence.

Chapter Nineteen

Ikiaq

Persons afflicted with tuberculosis have been subjected to more un-scrupulous treatments and fake "cures" than any other group of individuals. Nostrums and quackery have cost consumptives huge sums but positive proof has never been given to show that they have cured a single case of tuberculosis. In all instances time and money have been spent and not infrequently the patient's physical condition actually worse. Only the time-tested regime of bed and fresh air, supplemented by modern collapse therapy in selected patients has proved effective in the treatment of pulmonary tuberculosis.

Wherrett, 1941, p. 291

At the end of her days, Ruth often was exhausted and sad. Such sickness everywhere. She was missing her little brothers, too, so, after changing out of her uniform to a fresh one, she would often go to the children's ward to read stories. She and Pauloosie would get the children giggling as they tried to distract them and keep their casts clean and dry. It seemed to cheer everyone up. Pauloosie had taught Ruth a few words in Inuktitut that she tried to say to the children, leading them to laugh at her pronunciation. Sometimes the doctors would come in and ask for Ruth's help in re-casting the children.

Near the end of November, though, things didn't go as planned. Ruth was reading to the children in one corner. Pauloosie was working with the ward nurse to position an eight-year-old Inuit child, and as they turned him, she heard a terrible crack and the child shrieked. They called in the doctors and after one look they sent the child off for X-rays. Ruth fled back to her room. She had already had too much sadness that day.

Ruth checked the next day on her way back to her ward, only to find Pauloosie sitting, slumped down, in a chair in the hallway.

"Hello, Pauloosie. What happened? Are you not well?"

He looked up at her, tears streaking his face. "That boy, Ikiaq, he has TB in his hip joint. When we turned him...well, his cast must have gotten damp, and it didn't support his hip anymore. His hip bone just degenerated. They are looking at amputation."

"No! But that's so serious!"

"His family are all hunters near Sturgeon Bay. It means he probably can never go home."

"How terrible! How is he doing?" She made to go into the ward.

"Don't go in. The children are all afraid that they will be next and don't want to see either of us. Ikiaq is over at the hospital being operated on. The horrible thing is he's not likely to survive even with the surgery. They might as well have just sent him home to die." He wiped his eyes. "He'll be on the paediatric palliative ward now, and all alone in the regular hospital. I wish they hadn't operated on him, though I know they are trying to figure out ways to help. More practice with these surgeries would be good, but not on these children. Maybe we can get him moved back after he recovers from surgery?" He looked at her, eyes brimming with hope.

"Oh, I hope so! He'd be much more comfortable here."

Later, Ruth and Pauloosie went to KGH to visit the poor child, who turned away when he spotted them. They tried to communicate with him, in English and his own language, but he kept his head turned away. He pushed away the book and toy they brought with them.

"He blames us," Pauloosie explained as they left, both deeply saddened. "He's not wrong. He never should have been taken from his home. Now he must die here, alone." He sighed. "I wish he'd respond to me, at least, but I think he's already gone in his heart."

Ikiaq died the following day, and the crying in the children's ward was long and loud. Even the soldiers were subdued. A few of them had had lung resections, but no one had had limb amputations yet and it was a very great fear. They figured they could still work with only one lung, but losing a leg or an arm meant they'd be dependent, and the thought of dying in surgery was always in their minds. They grieved the boy's loss, too—several of them had spent their active time crafting little children's toys for the ward. The patients who were allowed out for short walks always brought back stuffed animals and treats for the children.

Ruth and Mary spent the evening over their toast and jam in the common room, talking about all the heartbreaking results they'd seen. The other nurses joined in with their own sad stories.

One sighed. "Does any of it make sense?"

"I wonder," admitted Mary. "But we can't just do nothing, can we? It's so hard, though."

Mary, in particular, wasn't having a happy time with her assignment. She had spent a lot of time with one woman who was near delivery time and whose TB was quite active. Somehow, they kept her well until delivery time, and then there was great excitement when she went into labour. She gave birth to a healthy boy, who was whisked away to relatives to avoid contagion. She was barely able to hold her baby before they were separated. That was one of the times Mary cried buckets, sitting on the side of her bed while Ruth brought handkerchiefs and tea.

The woman was recovering slowly, but the spirit seemed to go out of her, and Mary was trying to figure out a way to keep her feeling positive. One day she arranged for the patient to stand by the window as her husband and family stood with the baby outside on the grounds. It was too cold for them to linger, though, and it didn't seem to help cheer the woman.

"I won't see him for years," she'd wailed to Mary. "My cousin in Newfoundland still hasn't held her baby, and he's three!" She wept and seemed to get weaker by the day. She stopped eating and refused to do her exercises. The nurses were at a loss. The doctors wouldn't let her go home because of the risk of infecting the baby, and they had no timeline for when she'd be better.

Ruth had an idea. Would the mother on Mary's ward feel better if she could help with the children at their hospital?

"Good idea," Mary said. "Though it might make her miss her baby more. I could ask her, though. I hope she isn't one of those people who thinks Indians aren't worth looking after."

"Ugh. I hope not, too. I have to keep controlling my slapping hand when I hear some of the talk."

"And you'd think the soldiers would be more understanding. After all, they've heard about the snipers, right?"

Ruth nodded. Native sharpshooters were in high demand in the Great War and their skills made them even more valuable in the latest one.

Mary stretched. "Right-o. I'll run it by the head nurse and see how it all feels. I know it would cheer me up to be of help, anyway. It must be deadly having to lie about and do nothing all day."

"I agree. The men play cards and such, but they need more to do, too. They are getting restless, and all the news about the economy isn't helping. They worry about their families."

"Maybe we could set up a rota for the children's ward!"

Ruth shook her head. "Remember Pauloosie, though. If he has nothing to do, they might send him back to Montreal."

"They'd still need him to translate for the children, right? I understand a bunch of the men are translating for the French Canadians, too."

"Yes. It sure helps. The French nurses are spread thin. I wish I'd paid attention in French class."

"Speaking of being over tasked, I've got two post-ops tomorrow. I've got to get some sleep." They said goodnight to the other nurses and headed to their room. In no time, they were tucked in.

"Goodnight, sleep tight...." Ruth pulled her covers up and rolled over.

"Don't let the...."

"NO! Don't even say it." They'd had a bedbug infestation a few weeks before and no one wanted to joke about it even now.

Chapter Twenty

Armistice Day

If a patient is cold, if a patient is feverish, if a patient is faint, if he is sick after taking food, if he has a bed-sore, it is generally the fault not of the disease, but of the nursing.

https://blog.nursing.com/florence-nightingale-quotes

A rmistice Day celebrations were held in Kingston the eleventh of November, and after the parade and church services, the entire hospital organized special events for the military patients. Each patient received a ditty bag full of puzzle books, magazines, new games, and toiletries from the Women's Auxiliary. It was like a mini-Christmas. Everyone shared their goodies with everyone else, and the atmosphere brightened for a while. Meantime, the nurses spent the evenings finishing their hand made socks and hats and got them ready to send to local charities. Every evening, the students and staff would gather in the dining hall and pack everything up, tossing in bars of Lifebuoy soap that the local drugstore had donated. A volunteer from the Salvation Army would come by every few days and pick up the parcels to send them somewhere.

"Wish we knew where these were going," said Mary one day. "It would be nice to know if the people getting these actually need wool socks or if they are sweltering in Africa or someplace."

"I don't think a home-made wool sock can ever go wrong," said Mrs. Graham.

"Unless I make them," whispered Ruth to Mary.

"Or me," Mary whispered back. They'd eventually been assigned to scarves, many of which turned out rectangular. "At least they are warm," Mary sighed, as she folded up another trapezoid.

Meanwhile, the Nuremberg Trials filled the news. Another revelation was reported every day, and the soldiers and staff listened, quiet, horrified at what they had been fighting. A few patients slipped some rum in past Mrs. Graham and one night the men held a morose party where quite a few of the lads got blind drunk. After that, Mrs. Graham had the nurses do a bed check every evening. Ruth suspected Patricia of smuggling contraband, often seeing her leaving the ward with bandages or other supplies, pretending she was on a proper errand.

It didn't help that this winter was becoming one of the coldest on record. Bermuda, where many of the seamen had been stationed, seemed like only a wonderful memory as they sat by an open window, swathed in blankets, icy sleet blowing over them. On December 14th, the entire city shut down after a huge snowfall. Cars and horse-drawn vehicles were storm-stuck for hours. The resident nurses at the sanatorium had to cover for all the staff who couldn't make it in. Everyone pitched in and helped each other and they found time to hold a round of Christmas carol singing in the afternoon to cheer everyone up. Mrs. Graham relented and let the staff close a few of the windows. She even let them play a little music on the CKWS radio and stay up after lights out to hear the hockey game.

"Life has to be worth living for them," she argued, but Ruth suspected she just enjoyed having someone to listen to the hockey with. The Montreal Canadiens and the Toronto Maple Leafs were causing shouting matches across the wards. A few men dared to declare their support for the Boston Bruins, which led to more bellowing.

Some of the men took to putting their thermometers in water so their temperature would be down for the evening check, and they'd be allowed to stay up for the games. As the season played on, Ruth was sure she overheard betting taking place between the beds, but Beth told her to ignore it. "Gets their blood moving," she said. Ruth disagreed. A few men lost a lot of money, and she worried about fights breaking out.

Mary's patient had been delighted at the opportunity to help on the children's ward and she popped over whenever she could. She was sick enough that she only managed a visit once a week, despite asking almost every day. The children enjoyed her visits, and it took a bit of the weight off Ruth and the nurses, who had been trying to get in to read.

Meanwhile, the therapists had started classes for the men—drawing, painting, some were even writing their memoirs of the war. This wasn't always a good thing, however, as it sometimes caused the men to revisit horrors and get them overexcited and tired. Often at night the men would wake, shouting and screaming. It set everyone off.

"We need to keep them calm, remember, girls," Mrs. Graham kept saying, even as she turned up the hockey on the radio to loud cheering.

The nurses also were assigned to mail out envelopes for Christmas Seals. Funds from the program last year had been used to do community TB screening. Even the patients offered to help, though of course they couldn't lick the envelopes. The nurses gave everyone a sponge and some water, and they sealed the envelopes up that way.

One day in mid-December, as Ruth was washing out the spit jars, one of the regular medical staff, a young doctor, came to the door of the dirty utility room. "You, there. Come here—I need help," he called.

"I'm not a full nurse," Ruth answered, seeing he was in his operating room apron. "I can't help with procedures."

"Never mind. I just need help to hold things. You can do that, can't you?"

"But I'm needed on the ward."

"No, you aren't—I've just been there, and all your patients are asleep. I need help more than they do."

Ruth thought of arguing, but remembered in time that good nursing students didn't question the doctors. She nodded, washed her hands, and headed out.

Chapter Twenty-One

An expanded role

Consumptive patients often put their heads under the bed-clothes, because it relieves a fit of coughing, brought on by a change of wind or by damp. Of all places to take warm air from, one's own body is certainly the worst. And perhaps, if nurses do encourage this practice, we need no longer wonder at the 'rapid decline' of some consumptive patients. A folded silk handkerchief, lightly laid over the mouth, or merely breathing the steam from a basin of boiling water, will relieve the coughing without much danger.

Nightingale, Notes on Nursing, p. 88

After telling the head nurse where she was going, Ruth followed the doctor downstairs to the treatment room, an all-white space surrounded by stainless steel shelves. Bandages and basins were stocked on the shelves, and a rolling table was in the middle of the room, filled with more bandages, scissors, soft lining cloth, and cotton wrap. There was a sink in the corner of the room, and the doctor was running the water to warm it up. A young woman stood in the centre of the room, bandages wrapped around her jaw and tied to a hook on the ceiling, holding her upright. She moved slightly on her feet—they seemed almost not to touch the ground. Her eyes were wide with terror, and she was breathing fast.

"So, you're Miss Maclean, right?" the doctor said, peering at her name tag. "Dr. Anderson."

Ruth nodded.

"Well, we may as well get started. This patient has spinal involvement. We are going to cast her in a double shell to give the spine a chance to rest and hope that the lesions will heal on their own." He saw Ruth looking at the patient's feet. "We extend the spine through this traction," he gestured at the bandages holding the woman upright, "before casting, to ensure the vertebrae aren't impinging on any of the spinal column."

Ruth tried to make eye contact with the woman, but it appeared she wasn't seeing anything. She didn't respond to Ruth's smile.

"We've had to sedate her pretty heavily," Dr. Anderson explained. "She was quite frightened."

It didn't surprise Ruth—the rig the patient was in looked like she was about to be hung.

"Now, first we are going to wrap her head to ensure we can support her properly. We're going to wrap the head with gauze first, then plaster wrap. Can you help me as we go around?"

Ruth held and wrapped bandages around and around the woman's head, under her jaw, and even over most of her face.

"We'll trim that back when it hardens so she can see better, but we need to be sure there is adequate support for her cervical spine. The TB lesion is just below there at T1, and we don't want any movement around the area. The first thoracic vertebra, right at the base of the neck," he added, seeing Ruth's puzzled expression.

After half an hour, the head was done.

"There, that should be somewhat easier for her. She can relax into the neck support."

"Can't we get her a chair? She must be exhausted."

"No. We need to keep the spine at full extension until we finish wrapping."

Ruth again tried to reach the patient with a smile, but the woman now had her eyes closed. They checked her respirations.

"Good, she's asleep. That will make the next bit a little easier." They removed the woman's gown, draping her with blankets to keep her warm and somewhat covered. Dr. Anderson started wrapping the woman's chest. "It can feel compressing, as if they can't breathe," he explained. "We want to make it tight enough to support the spine but allow some chest expansion. We'll cut away a bit in the front once we get the frame assembled so she can expand her abdomen forward. I may need to split the cast in half, but I like it to dry fully first."

They worked quickly now, doubling the plaster cloth to add additional strength around the sides and back of the body cast, putting extra padding over the woman's almost visible hip bones to support the created brace work. She was so gaunt it took hardly any gauze to cover her entirely. Ruth kept trying to cover the woman, but eventually the blanket she had wrapped around her fell away, and the poor patient was left standing, almost naked except for the plaster.

Ruth ran back and forth to warm the water for the plaster, worked at smoothing things to match what the doctor was doing on the other side. After they got the abdomen and back finished, he stepped away to inspect her work, smiling with approval. "That looks excellent, Miss Maclean. She'll be comfortable with that. Well-done."

Ruth felt a wash of pride. "I've been assisting with the children's ward, helping to replacing their casts when they get damp."

"So I heard. Good practice for this sort of thing."

"But they seem so uncomfortable. Does the casting help?"

"I see your skepticism, Miss Maclean. It doesn't seem very comfortable, does it? It does help, though. Movement in spinal tuberculosis is excruciating. As the spine collapses from the holes left by the TB abscesses, the spinal column gets pinched, sometimes even severed. The nerves send pain signals down the patient's legs. Patients tell me it's like fire all down their legs—and none of our medications seem to help it unless we knock the patient right out." He sighed. "And of course, being unconscious isn't good for anyone. Other problems occur. They can't clear their lungs effectively, they get bedsores. Mind you, that's a risk with the casting as well. They must be carefully positioned. The casting should help the spine stay intact until the bones re-knit."

"How long will that take?"

The doctor shrugged. "Depends on the patient, how well they are otherwise." He stepped behind the patient to where she couldn't see him and frowned at Ruth. He gestured at her emaciated arms. Ruth understood. It would be lucky if the patient lived long enough to experience the spinal recovery.

"It's really the best we can do," he added. "At least she'll be a bit more comfortable. Now, we've managed to secure the cast to the hips, and it all seems to be drying well. Let's cut some holes and trim around the face before she wakes up fully."

They carefully cut back the plaster around her face so that she was left with a solid cap and chin strap, the chin cut back enough so she would be able to eat and talk. As they were trimming a hole in her abdomen to allow for her lungs to expand, the patient woke up and started screaming.

Dr. Anderson nodded at Ruth to do something, his hands busy with the trimming. She didn't know what to do with this immobilized patient, but she tried. She put her hands on the woman's cheeks where she could touch her skin and looked at her directly. The woman stopped screaming, but her pupils were dilating with shock.

"What's her name?" she asked.

The doctor shrugged, looked around for her chart. "I cast so many...."

"Miss, ma'am—look at me. Look at me?" The woman's eyes moved, fixed on Ruth's.

"You remember you are in the San, don't you?"

The woman tried to nod, couldn't.

"You are in a cast. It must seem strange. The doctor has put it on to help your spine heal. You won't be able to move much, but we are here with you and will take care of you. Right now, the doctor is cutting a bit back so you can breathe easier. That will help."

The woman blinked. A tear ran down the side of her face.

Ruth wiped it away with a tissue. "It is very hard, I know, but you'll feel so much better once your bones heal."

The woman closed her eyes. At least she wasn't still hysterical, Ruth thought. She couldn't imagine what this would all feel like from the inside.

"There," the doctor said. "All done for now. She will have to stay here for another hour or so until the plaster hardens fully, then we can cut her down and take her to bed. Ward D, nurse. You can stay with her?"

Ruth nodded. As if she'd leave the poor woman alone in this state. Besides, she had to tidy up the mess of dressings and plasters all over the place, and that would take at least an hour. Ruth doubted the doctor ever had the experience of clearing up after a casting. He had flung things far and wide, as doctors always did. She quickly covered the woman with a gown and placed a blanket over her shoulders. The poor woman was shivering.

"Good work, Miss Maclean. Would you be willing to help me with my other castings? We have another two this afternoon."

"You'll have to check with my head nurse—she'll need to get someone to do my other duties."

"Right, of course. I'll do that. Back soon with number two." He waved, smiled, and was gone.

Ruth didn't know what to think. It sounded like she'd be tied up for longer than she thought, though at least not as tied up as the patients. Did she want to spend the day in here with screaming patients and paste? She wasn't sure. Still, she'd calmed the woman, and the doctor had admired her casting technique. That had to be a good sign. And it would make a change from bedpan duty.

Maybe. The woman started looking agitated and Ruth realized that washroom duty was still going to be a component. She worked a urinal into place and the woman emptied her bladder. She blinked at Ruth, even tried a small smile.

"Thanks," she whispered.

Ruth was just washing things up when Mrs. Graham appeared at the door. She came in, inspected the work done on the casting, asked Ruth where she'd helped. The patient watched it all in silence.

"That's good, Miss Maclean. I'll get someone to cover your patients." She looked about. "What a mess! You should clear it up while you are looking after this patient. Can you manage that?"

"I already am, Mrs. Graham. I don't want to leave the patient alone, though, so some of it has to just wait on the table."

"Understood. Well, carry on. I'm glad Doctor Anderson has help. It's a long procedure, especially if you don't know how it goes."

Ruth was glad she'd had the practice of replacing the leg casts on the children earlier. It was less involved, but she'd learned how to handle the plaster wraps.

"She's ever so nice," added the woman in the cast.

Ruth smiled, as did Mrs. Graham. "Glad to hear it," she said, and exited.

Ruth was feeling a glow of accomplishment when suddenly Patricia was behind her, whispering in her ear. "Remember, doctors are mine, right? Don't you get any ideas. You should let me do this and get back to the ward. I'm senior to you, don't forget. You know I can make things bad for you."

Chapter Twenty-Two

Lies and more lies

If a nurse declines to do these kinds of things for her patient, "because it is not her business," I should say that nursing is not her calling. I have seen surgical "sisters," women whose hands were worth to them two or three guineas a-week, down on their knees scouring a room or a hut, because they thought it otherwise not fit for their patients to go into. I am far from wishing nurses to scour. It is a waste of power. But I do say that these women had the true nurse-calling—the good of their sick first, and second only, the consideration what it was their "place" to do—and that women who wait for anybody else to do what their patients want, when their patients are suffering, have not the making of a nurse in them.

Nightingale, Notes on Nursing, p. 32.

Ruth jumped and turned around. "Hi, Miss Brannigan. Um, I don't know why he chose me—probably thought I looked easy to boss around. Besides, I did a bunch of casting before—maybe the doctor wants experience." She knew Patricia avoided the children's ward. "You could talk to him. I'm sure he'd ask for you if he wanted you."

Patricia actually hissed at her and left. There would be trouble, but at this moment she couldn't care less. She could do a specialized skill, and the doctor had asked for her by name. It felt good.

From then on, she became the casting nurse. She still had her regular duties as people weren't put in casts every day, but when she'd see Doctor Anderson in the doorway to the ward, apron in place, she'd join him and be there while some poor patient was wrapped like a mummy.

She learned that casting was used primarily when there was bone involvement, but sometimes also after rib surgery. Some of the new techniques involved removal of bits of lung and several ribs and there needed to be a cast applied while things stabilized a bit. Initially, patients had been maintained in frames, pulled apart in traction, but it was an unsteady position and patients hated it. The casts seemed more secure.

Ruth had wondered at the crumpled-up people she'd seen on the streets of Kingston. Now she understood why they hunched. Some of them were missing half a lung, most of their ribs, and even the muscles supporting the ribcage. Though they would do exercises with them on the ward post-operatively, the practices didn't seem to stick, and so many were lurching around, bent over.

"I suppose they must be glad to be alive," she said to Betty when they had a chance to meet up and compare notes about their experiences in their different locations, "but it must be so uncomfortable. How do they manage to work?"

"Often they don't," said Betty. "People suppose they still have active disease, so don't want to hire them. I often see them in the hospital—they can't work, they drink, they are so poor some other disease moves in on them. Miserable, really. I doubt I'd have that surgery myself."

They were talking at a Christmas social held in the Princess St. United Church for the staff and some of the healthier veteran patients. Betty came along with a tall, mustachioed artillery captain on her arm. She looked so happy. Ruth hadn't seen her in a few weeks, so they left the men to chat among themselves and wandered off to catch up.

"Who's this one?" Ruth teased her friend. "This must be number six, right? How do you keep their names straight?"

"Hush!" Betty looked around. "This one may be a keeper. He's RCHA. Very dashing when he gets all dressed up in his mess kit. He's officer material for sure."

"So, what's the plan? Are you considering leaving nursing?"

"Not yet. He hasn't quite bitten the hook. But the security! It IS tempting. And wouldn't we have handsome children? I mean, look at him!" They turned and waved at him—he smiled and did a little bow back.

"Such a gentleman," Betty sighed. "Say what you will, but the Royal Military College teaches them how to care for a woman. He's going to graduate next year."

Ruth had heard differently. She thought Betty might have remembered her experience with a soldier and rethought things. Some of the men in the ward had told unpleasant tales about how the cadets behaved, but she held her tongue.

"What about you and that George fellow? I hear he follows you around like a little puppy."

Ruth laughed. "He does, doesn't he? But he's a patient. And I am loving my work. I don't want to have to leave just when I finally get some recognition."

"Putting casts on dying people? Cruelty, I'd think. When are you coming back to the fold? We miss you at the nurses' residence. And in class. I have no one to cheat from now." She screwed up her face.

"That's up to the supervisor, I guess. I'm hoping that if I do well with the special duties, she'll let me come back."

"What else can you do? Other than the regular care and casting, that is? Will they let you come to our capping party? Can you get a cap? Or a bib? You must be tired of looking like you are on probation all the time."

"No changes in uniform until I get back to school, they said. That's why I'm trying to get as much experience as I can—so they'll have to let me back in! And I'm hoping to help with some of the actual surgeries here. We've got our own OR at the San, you know. Not as grand as you have, but maybe I can get some experience."

"That would be so exciting! I'll keep my fingers crossed for you. Oh, see, the boys are lonely. We'd better get back to them."

"Yes. I see Patricia has found your fellow."

"That witch," said Betty, speeding up her steps. "You heard she is telling everyone that Indian kid died because of you, right?"

"What?"

"No one believes her, but you know how she is, whisper, whisper, whisper. She's poison."

Sure enough, by the time they got back to the men, Patricia was laughing with Betty's friend, her arm through his and gazing up at him. Some rumpled-looking veteran patients stood nearby, one or two on crutches.

"Patricia! I didn't realize you were off duty today," Ruth began.

"Oh, I'm just on break. Had to check on these boys and make sure you weren't inflicting your nursing on them. I must go back. Sorry to go!" She left, waving a toodle-oo with her fingers.

Ruth turned to one patient. "You seem a bit pale—are you feeling all right?"

He smiled at her. "I'm fine. Just need some of that dinner."

"Well, let's go eat then. Betty, you coming?"

The group headed toward the buffet. The veteran was looking at her askance. Was he just tired, or did he listen to some of Patricia's lies? She didn't want to ask. Honestly, Ruth muttered to herself, this is as bad as being in Cloyne. Everyone talking about everyone else.

Chapter Twenty-Three

Christmas at the San

As Christmas neared, the patients in the hospital grew considerably more morose. One day one man got out of bed, stumbled over to the radio, and shut it off with a vengeance.

"If I have to listen to that 'chestnuts roasting on an open fire' song one more time, I'll...," he broke off, sinking back onto his bed. It squeaked in agreement.

The other men clapped.

"They're playing it non-stop. Jack Frost can go nip someone else's nose!"

"Total sh...garbage, that song. Where's the real Christmas music?" said another.

"What, you mean, like hymns? They aren't any better."

"Still makes me wish I was home," said a third. Everyone went quiet for a while after that, and the staff tried to be cheerful without being too sunny. After all, most of them could go home at Christmas.

Ruth had offered to work on the holidays. It meant extra pay, and she wouldn't have to put up with all the church services at Cloyne. Besides, she thought to herself, other nurses really wanted to get home. She didn't.

Mrs. Graham planned to work the holidays as well, as did Patricia. Ruth winced when she saw the duty roster. No chance to relax, of course.

Three days before Christmas, Mrs. Graham popped by the ward with news. "The Salvation Army is coming this afternoon, with their band. Isn't that exciting?"

There were alternate cheers and groans.

"Now, I want good behaviour. Who brought you your supplies when you froze out in the field? We are grateful to them, always. Why, my Bob counted on them when he led his battery." Ruth stared in amazement as she wiped away a tear. "When they arrive, I expect you to make them feel welcome."

Ruth turned to the soldier she was helping write a letter home. He'd had both of his hands burned badly, and the healing process was not helped by his TB. "What do you think, Lieutenant? It will be nice to hear some Christmas carols, surely?"

"Yes, Miss Maclean. I just hope they keep the tuba downstairs. It'd be awfully loud in here. Like when they play bagpipes at mess dinners."

"I'm not sure if they will come up to the ward. Maybe they'll play downstairs instead—that way the people who need rest won't be too disturbed."

"And the ones who hate their preaching can skip it," growled the private who shut off the radio.

"Who's a grumpy Gus?" The sergeant in the next bed poked at him.

"Piss off," the private muttered, rolling over towards the wall. Ruth stood to go over to him, but the head nurse shook her head. Later, in the utility room, she took Ruth aside.

"He's just had a Dear John letter," she told Ruth. "Probably best to let him get through it."

"Oh, no! That's the third one already this month! These women...why can't they wait until the men get better?"

"Wish they would. It would be better to hold off until they were stronger. Though, to be fair, it will be quite a wait. Time and tide wait for no man, right?"

"And no woman, I guess." Mary had told Ruth similar messages arrived for the women on her ward, too. The closer they got to Christmas, the faster they seemed to arrive. It added to the pre-holiday gloom. Everyone was already missing their family for the holiday. Finding out their family wasn't missing them seemed particularly hard.

Surprisingly, the angry private joined the group that came down to the concert. Well, perhaps not too surprising, thought Ruth. He spent much of the time in a corner laughing with one of the female patients. She'd have to monitor that. He obviously wouldn't be alone for long. Fine, she mused, but the powers that be didn't approve of patient-to-patient relationships developing. It got messy, especially with the long-term stays.

That wasn't the only concert. The nursing students from KGH and the Dieu both came by to sing in the doorways. They got a better reception, though not always an appropriate one. Still, it brightened the days.

Santa Claus visited, too. Apparently, several Santas had agreed to go through the halls of the hospitals, bringing cheer. They stayed out of the wards where tuberculosis was active, but even waving from the door brought excited squeals from the children and some laughter from the soldiers. Mary's patient had told the children all about Santa and they all hoped for goodies.

The weekend before Christmas, Ruth, Beth, Mary, and the other nurses spent whatever spare time and money they had putting together stockings for the patients. The biggest ones were for the children, of course, but everyone had something—hand creams, little vials of toilet water, fresh toothbrushes and razors, the occasional lipstick. And oranges for everyone, stuffed in the toe. The ones who could knit made up the stockings and put the second one, rolled up, inside the one they would hang. Mary wrote out bits of a Bible verse onto little scrolls of paper, "for encouragement," she explained. Ruth had written to her brothers for some funny jokes and limericks and wrote those out as well. It took a lot of time to assemble them all, including some stockings for the female military members staying in their own wing.

"These stockings still look pretty thin," said Beth.

"Let's do a chocolate run," said Mary. "I just have time before I have to head home."

"Oh, I wish I could join you," said Ruth.

"You stay here to hold down the ship," she said. "We'll be back in a jiffy."

It was hard to find chocolate in the almost empty stores—rationing was still going on, especially for sugar—but Beth and Mary made a diligent hunt and came back with enough to break up for the patients' stockings.

"There," Mary said, satisfied. "That should cheer them up."

Late Christmas Eve, while most of the patients slept, the nurses tiptoed around, attaching the stockings with ribbons to every bed. For the children's ward, they left them outside the door since they would wake up at the slightest noise and would spoil the surprise for everyone. They added a plump one for Pauloosie to find when he arrived in the morning.

As Ruth finished her ward, she noticed Jerry was awake, peering at her under his eyelids. She put a finger to her lips, and Jerry smiled.

All the nurses, when they got upstairs, were in fine fettle. "Merry Christmas!" echoed down the hallways. It felt good to do this little thing for their patients. It was some good they could see the effect of.

The next morning, they heard shouts of glee from everywhere. Everyone smiled, even when the priests came by offering Communion and blessings, and the priests seemed to enjoy the jovial attitude. Ruth took a few minutes off to make a call to her home, but of course the line was down. She'd have to write to tell them all about the day. She couldn't wait.

Chapter Twenty-Four

Ward E

The said book of rules begins by saying that 'It is expected that any patient that cannot adapt herself to these necessary restrictions will inform the Medical Superintendent and make immediate arrangements for transfer to an institution more suited to her tastes', and that 'she will not endeavour to make herself more comfortable by lack of discipline which can hinder the staff and make matters more difficult for fellow patients'. It goes on to say that two rules are absolute—1. 'No alcoholic liquor may be brought onto the premises or consumed on or off the premises by any patient', and 2 'No patient may have any communication with patients of the opposite sex', and Dr Morris tells me that means if one passes a man in the grounds one may not say 'good morning'!

Raymond Hurt, p. 351.

L ife on the TB ward was both easier and more challenging than Ruth had been told to expect. Yes, the daily routine of temperature checks, bed baths, sputum bottle collecting could be a bit boring, but there were often sudden catastrophes that kept her jumping. They were exciting to write about, but she only sent those letters to Meg. Her parents wouldn't have liked the gruesome details.

Meg had been impressed by her story about one of the older women in Mary's ward who sat up one day, started to cough, and before the nurses could get to her, had sent blood all over her bed and the floor and even her next-door patient. It took hours of carbolic and oil washings to get that cleared up. The woman died in that hemorrhage and Ruth, sent over to help, was amazed she'd still had that much blood in her given how pale and emaciated she'd become.

One day after Christmas, when the men were doing relatively well, Mrs. Graham came to Ruth and said she was needed on ward E. She cringed. While the soldiers were starting out healthy, if injured, when they got infected, and so were more able to battle off the infection, on the other wards were patients who had lived in poverty for years, the elderly, and the otherwise sick. They didn't cope so well and were often close to death.

Mrs. Graham saw her face. "It will give you some more experience. And they are very short-staffed today, and for the rest of this week. Remember to mask up and be careful of infection prevention while you are there. These patients aren't able to control themselves as well as the soldiers."

Ward E was made up of a four-bed ward filled with five beds surrounded by privacy screens. Despite using the screens to separate the patients, an odor blew through the ward, almost giving the air a greyish tinge. It reminded Ruth of the time at KGH that she had to look after a man with a wound contaminated with gas gangrene. She shuddered. She'd barely been able to look after the man, let alone his wound, open and gaping on his leg. When it was dressing changing time, two nurses would take it on, both masked, and each would flee the room every few minutes to clear their nose and retch. They didn't want to gag in front of the patient. The nurses on that ward took to sucking peppermints when going into the room, and that helped a bit. It got somewhat better after the patient's leg was amputated, but then it didn't heal properly, and they were all back to gagging and sucking peppermints again. Ruth wished she had some mints right now.

When Ruth reached to push one screen back, the other nurse said no. She gestured a cough and a spew of secretions, and Rose understood. Too much of a risk. The nurse, a tall thin blonde, introduced herself as Jocelyn Hannity. She wore a KGH pin and cap. Jocelyn walked Ruth through the ward, stepping between the beds, leaving the screens closed. "I'll give you a tour of the patients so we can figure out where to start. We're getting a new admission later today, too, so it's going to be busy. Remember your mask."

She continued down the ward, gesturing at one curtain. "This is Mrs. Smith. She's had a Semb's strip done."

Ruth looked at her, puzzled.

Jocelyn snorted. "I wish they'd give the float nurses some training before coming here. It's complicated nursing these patients. A Semb's strip is where the surgeons remove some ribs, stripping the lung from the connective tissue and the collarbone, and then they paralyze the diaphragm. It collapses the lung very effectively, but it's serious surgery." She pulled back the curtain. A gaunt woman lay curled up on her bed. "Let's get you more comfortable," she said, and she and Ruth stepped to each side of the bed and attempted to straighten the woman out on her bed. The patient moaned, and as soon as they put her in position, she started to curl in again. As they stepped away, closing the curtain, Jocelyn whispered in Ruth's ear.

"We should get her to do some physio, but she's not long for this world and she's in so much pain—it feels cruel."

They went to the next bed. "This patient was initially treated with an inhalation of brass and vegetable oil back in the 20s, if you can imagine! The things they used to do to TB patients! She's still dealing with that and now has TB in her larynx. She can't speak. She talks to us with a notepad and pencil. How are you today?" Jocelyn asked her, handing her the pad and pencil.

The woman, about 40, was barely present, she was so thin. Ruth could see every bone in her fingers as she wrote. "Bit sore."

"Would you like a drink?" Ruth turned to get a carafe. The woman's lips were cracked and dry.

Jocelyn shook her head and gestured at the IV drip in the woman's arm. "She can't drink anymore, isn't that right? I'll get you something for pain in just a moment." She turned to Ruth. "The TB has caused sores in her throat. It's too painful for her to drink. I'll run and get her a needle for her pain. I don't like to leave her waiting. I'll be right back."

Ruth stared at the woman, who reached out and held Ruth's hand in her bony one for a moment. She wrote something on her pad. "Not here much longer." She smiled thinly and closed her eyes.

Jocelyn came back into the room with the needle, a storm on her face. She gave the patient a shot and, as they turned to go, she whispered angrily in Ruth's ear, "Damn night shift didn't give her pain meds since midnight. 'A bit sore', she says. I'll bet she is in agony. Why they can't keep up with the meds, I'll never know. It's the most important thing on this ward."

The rest of the ward was filled with similar patients, one with a spinal fusion, and another with a phrenic nerve crushing, designed to collapse infected lung tissue or hold degraded tissues firm while they healed. One woman was recovering from a kidney removal and had a tube coming from her side instead of a catheter into her urinary bladder. Her bladder had also been removed, full of TB adhesions as it was. They emptied the urine bag and marked down her output, which wasn't large. "They would have emptied it on early morning rounds, so no need to worry yet. I just like to start with an empty bag."

Each and every patient looked consumed by their illness, barely clinging on.

After the first round, they stopped in the utility room to load up the cart.

"This is terrible," Ruth said. "They are all so sick. They even smell bad!" She stopped, shocked that she'd said that out loud, but Jocelyn didn't seem concerned.

Chapter Twenty-Five

January

The peak of thoracoplasty was reached by Carl Semb of Oslo, who in 1935 devised a manoeuvre, extrafascial apicolysis, which ensured that the lung was collapsed not only from the side (by removing the ribs) and below (by paralyzing the diaphragm) but also from above by untethering the upper lobe from its moorings to the spine and collar bone...

Despite all modifications and improvements, thoracoplasty remained a horrific operation; and it is not unreasonable to ask how it could have retained its popularity...it became in many countries the key to both charitable and official funding.

Dormandy, p. 358.

"**B**it of a change from the guys, eh? Yes, that's the rotting tissue in their lungs—once the TB gets settled in, it kills the cells off and the tissue starts to rot. It really is a terrible disease. All we can do by the time they reach this state is try to make them more comfortable." Jocelyn frowned. "You can't give meds yet, right?"

Ruth shook her head.

"Pity. This would be a good place to give you experience. They all need medicating every few hours, and you aren't likely to cause any harm. Okay, I'll go start drawing up the narcotics. You gather up sheets and bath stuff, and we'll start around in a few minutes once the shots have taken effect. In the meantime, better get gloves on to go with the gown and mask—when you get in close, they might cough at you. Can't help it, poor dears, but no point in you getting infected. It's a good thing you aren't capped yet. Those things are TB traps. I never wear mine when I'm doing patient care." True to her word, she unpinned her cap and placed it carefully at the nurses' station. "I'd leave it at home, but I have to put it on whenever a supervisor or doctor comes by. Totally annoying."

"But doesn't it make you proud?"

"No. I'm past that bit. Now it seems like a gigantic hassle. You wait until you have yours. It keeps falling off unless you pin it right through your scalp, and in a place like this, you need two or three so you can take them regularly to the Chinese laundry."

When Ruth looked at her, she added, "You know, where you take your cuffs and collar? Don't tell me you are washing and starching them yourself?" Jocelyn laughed. "I know, saving money. When you're a student, they pay for all that, of course, but I imagine they don't pay for you anymore?"

"No," said Ruth. "Not since I got sent here."

"I think you should ask about that. Infection prevention and all that. Would make sense to have them go through the brutal treatment they get at the laundry. No germ can escape that!" She added, "I can ask for you, if you like?"

"Would you? I don't want to seem demanding or anything."

"I imagine. I hear you are here on sufferance."

"No!" Ruth was indignant. "I'm just taking a break from the nursing course until I build up my skills."

"Oh." Jocelyn looked puzzled. "That's not what they told me. But let's see how you go."

The basic patient care was lengthy. Every patient was almost fully immobilized. Almost every patient they bathed had a bedsore starting where their hip and back bones jutted into the mattress. Some patients had sheepskins they placed under them but for the rest the best they could do was rub around the area gently with witch hazel and turn them slightly to each side.

"We'll come around in a couple of hours and move them again," said Jocelyn. "There's no excuse for bedsores if you are a decent nurse, even with these patients." Ruth wasn't so sure. Their bodies were so lacking in body fat there was little to cushion the bones. She vowed to be extra vigilant.

After they finished the pass through the ward and were emptying things in the utility room, Jocelyn looked at Ruth appraisingly. "Not bad. You seem to know what you are doing."

Ruth didn't agree. All the patients had new things to treat, and being completely gloved, gowned, and masked made her sweaty and clumsy. Still, at least she hadn't messed up yet.

"It seems a lot of work," she commented to Jocelyn. "Couldn't you use another staff person here?"

Jocelyn made a face, which Ruth only spotted by the wrinkling around her eyes. "No one wants to work here. The work's too hard, and the patients are too sad. I think everyone wants your ward."

Ruth suddenly realized how easy she'd had it, how fun it was with the men, who, despite their condition, were able to move around and in much less pain. She wondered if she should put in for a transfer to this ward. Would that mean she'd learn more, that she'd be more welcome back in nursing school?

"I sure could use you here," said Jocelyn, reading her mind. "Even a couple of shifts a week would be a big help. We had another nurse rotating through here, but she decided it was too much for her. It probably didn't help that I had to tell on her for skipping out and not giving the pain meds." She shook her head. "Some people just shouldn't be nurses. You seem to take it seriously, though—I'd be glad if you would come by. You're a hard worker."

Ruth didn't answer. She wasn't sure she wanted to make the change away from her boys, as she'd come to call them. She wanted to think about it.

The rest of the day was spent in the usual bedpan duty and turning the patients, but Jocelyn let her do a dressing change on one of the rib resections under supervision and then another without, nodding her head in approval when she checked it.

Chapter Twenty-Six

Seeking new challenges

Prevention and treatment of Pressure Sores (Bedsores or Decubitus ulcers)

Nature of a bedsore: Pressure on the skin can interfere with the circulation to such an extent that the tissue, deprived of nourishment, literally dies and becomes gangrenous or necrotic...

Bedsores, pressure sores or decubitii are caused by an interference in the circulation in a part, owing to pressure. This may result from the body's lying too long in one position, or from splints, casts, bandages, or bedclothes. The effect of pressure is frequently aggravated by heat, moisture, and decomposing and irritating substances on the skin, such as perspiration, urine, faeces, or vaginal discharge....

Prevention of bedsores is the responsibility of the nurse. As a student she should learn how to take care of a patient in such a way as to prevent bedsores, for with sufficient nursing care they can be prevented. The carelessness, neglect, and ignorance of one nurse may in a few hours undo the most skilled and painstaking care of another...the most important measure is the relief of pressure on bony prominences...

Harmer and Henderson, pp. 496-8

L ate in the day, the new admission came in. Jocelyn and Ruth had moved the patient with the laryngeal TB to a private room next to the ward, knowing that she wouldn't be using it for long. This left one bed in the already overcrowded ward free.

Unlike the others, Mrs. Henderson was a heavyset woman, suspicious of all they tried to do, and still strong enough to fight them as they tried to get her undressed and into bed. She had a productive cough, and the nurses made sure their gowns and masks were tied tight. It helped with the odour, as well. This woman hadn't washed in weeks. She lived up in the country somewhere beyond Northbrook and explained through her sticky gums that her well was dry.

"Never mind," said Jocelyn, in her most soothing voice. "Miss Maclean here will get you right tidied up and comfortable."

Ruth grimaced under her mask. "I may need your help...," she said to the departing Jocelyn's back. Jocelyn gave her a jaunty wave in reply.

Ruth started out talking about Cloyne and how they must live close to one another, but this only seemed to make Mrs. Henderson more suspicious. Eventually, they ended up working in silence except for the occasional grunt as they moved through the bath.

It took three wash basins of soapy water and a couple of sets of sheets and towels, but finally Ruth was able to get the woman clean. Almost. She refused to allow Ruth to remove her underwear. Ruth cajoled, insisted, tried to pull them off, but the woman resisted. Finally, she took the last basin off to the utility room to catch her breath and rethink.

"What's the problem?" Jocelyn poked her head around the door. "Not finished yet?"

"She won't take off her panties," Ruth growled. "And I'm sure that's where the smell is coming from."

"Wait—I have an idea..." Jocelyn trotted off. When she returned, she said, "I called Dr. Anderson. Maybe he can persuade her. Patients seem to do anything for him."

"Really?"

"You've seen him, right? He's quite handsome and smells divine. He seems kind, too. Married, though, more's the pity."

"Hello, Miss Hannity!" Dr. Anderson greeted them with a smile. "What's the problem?" He looked at Ruth. "Miss Maclean! Sharing your nursing skills in a new area? Aren't your persuading charms up to the task?"

Ruth shook her head.

"Give me a minute." He headed in to the bedside. They heard him speaking softly, laughing a bit. In a few moments, he came out again.

"She'll let you clean her up now."

Ruth sighed, picked up the basin.

"Not you," Dr. Anderson said. "She wants the 'real nurse' So it's up to you, Miss Hannity!"

Jocelyn grumbled but took the basin from Ruth and filled it with soapy water. As she left the utility room, Dr. Anderson turned and smiled at Ruth. "Seems fair, eh, Miss Maclean? After she left you to do the rest?" He winked at her and left. Ruth stifled her laugh.

Ruth ended up continuing with shifts on Ward E and on her regular ward, while still helping in the casting room. It was busy, and the shifts on the men's ward were often sacrificed for casting assisting. She never got re-tasked from Ward E. She was too needed there. Despite the challenging patients who interested her, Ruth still wasn't sure if she wanted to make a permanent transfer. She'd miss the jolly men who teased her all the time. It made the days less gloomy.

Despite her busyness, she craved new challenges. One day, Ruth was helping Dr. Anderson wrap a soldier with hip TB into a spica cast and put her desire for operating room experience on the line. Stomach knotting with anxiety, she started.

"Dr. Anderson—do you ever need help in surgery? The kind of help I could give, that is. I'm aware I'm not a full nurse yet."

He looked over at her, a spot of plaster on his eyebrow. She found herself longing to wipe it off, but refocused. He paused, wrapping the plaster cloth around the man one or two more times before he answered. He rinsed his hands and reached for another wrap, shaking his head.

"Miss Maclean, you're great here—I don't know how you keep everyone so calm when we are working so fast around them—but the OR needs fully qualified nurses. I'm not sure what you'd be able to do."

Ruth sighed. "I know. I'd like to learn, though. Perhaps act as a runner or something, or just observe."

"Hmm." He looked up at her. "I don't see what harm that can be. I'll see what I can do about having you observe. You might change your mind about helping when you see what it's like. Your colleague Miss Brannigan worked with us briefly. She couldn't stand all the blood and bits."

Ah, thought Ruth. So, this was how Patricia was trying to get around her with the doctors. "I'm not Miss Brannigan."

"True." He paused. "She told me you had failed the nursing program. Maybe it is better to stay where you are competent. You don't want to risk your job here, do you?"

Ruth felt herself turning red. How dare Patricia say such a thing? She started to answer, hotly, but controlled herself with an effort and said, "I didn't fail. I just wasn't ready. I'm working to get back into the program. Studying every night." She took a deep breath, tried to calm down. "The extra experience might help me get back in if I could at least observe in the OR. Plus, I could accompany the patients from the ward. Make them more comfortable, just as I do here."

"Hmm. Right you are then." He stood and went over to the sink to wash the plaster off his hands. There was a mirror over the sink, and he laughed, seeing the plaster on his eyebrow, wiping it off with a grin. "I seem to have made a mess of myself. You should have warned me, Miss Maclean!" He dried off his hands. "We're just about done here. Can you finish up?"

Ruth nodded, miserable. He obviously thought she was just meant for this duty and nothing more. Well, at least she could keep on casting. But she'd really like to see the operating room.

Dr. Anderson paused at the door to the cast room. "I'll tell the matron when my next surgery comes up. We'll try to get you in, once, at least."

Ruth felt her heart leap. With a smile, she proceeded to make silly faces at the patient until he laughed, cast and all.

Chapter Twenty-Seven

Rockwood

But in tuberculosis thick bands of scar tissue surrounding a lesion were capable of causing terrible deformities. These were most serious in the skin and around joints; but the consequences were even graver inside the body. Nobody knows the reason why tuberculosis scarring is so gross: only some burns leave comparable scars.

Dormandy, p. 220

At the end of a freezing cold week where many things had gone wrong, the woman with the esophageal TB had died, and everyone seemed grumpy, Ruth dragged back to her room, fed up with the world and everything in it, spit bottles and thermometers most especially. She found Mary sitting on the side of the bed, in tears.

"What is it? Are you okay?"

"Oh, it's just time for me to move. I was hoping all the extra men would mean I would stay here longer, but it's time for my psych rotation."

"Oh no! But we still need you here!"

"That's what I thought. But they will persist in trying to turn me into a nurse. You've got it easy, you know. Can settle in, can plan what you're up to the next day. They just sprung this on me. Apparently, one of the other nursing students had to go home sick, and they decided to patch me in. So, they are transferring me to Rockwood right away." She meant the gloomy limestone building on the shore of Lake Ontario that served as a mental hospital. "They're making me live there, too. They have some rather nastier student rooms over there, with a drafty view of the lake. I think I will buy myself one of those new chenille spreads from Shaw-Linton's. I'll need it to cheer me up. What will I do without my roomie?"

"Do you know what you'll be doing afterwards? That might help you, looking forward," asked Ruth.

"Not sure yet, somewhere back at the Dieu. But I have to get through the next six weeks first. And I'm scared. I never wanted to work in mental health."

"How bad can it be? They're likely all medicated, or sane enough."

"You just wait. One of my classmates had to change floors because one of the inmates on a locked ward decided he wanted to kill her."

"Yeah, but they can't all be like that. We've seen shell shock here—it seems more sad than dangerous."

"From your lips to God's ears," Mary said, making the sign of the cross.

"You'll be fine. You're so sweet and kind. Everyone will love you."

Mary winced. "Everyone 'loving me' might be worse. Hope they keep their hands to themselves." She slammed her suitcase closed. "I'm going to miss you—and this room! I hear it's freezing in the residence down there. Who will I laugh with at night? And I'm going to miss the food here! Bring me chocolates?"

Ruth gave her a tight hug. "We'll for sure see each other. Let's plan to get together in a couple of weeks and trade notes, okay? Oh, and my friend from nursing school should be there soon—keep an eye out for her—Betty O'Donnell. She's a hoot. She'll look after you for sure."

"Don't forget the chocolates, will you? I'll need it." She tugged her suitcase up and headed down the hall to shouts of farewell.

The room seemed vast after Mary left. Vast and silent. Ruth already missed her merry friend. She wondered how she would handle a psychiatric rotation. She'd had to calm a lot of men with shell shock, but that would differ from the long-lasting illnesses like schizophrenia. In Cloyne, one of her father's neediest parishioners was the mother of a schizophrenic son. She was beside herself with worry all the time. It didn't help that her son kept running away and being found by police somewhere far away, talking to invisible people. She shuddered. She hated the idea of losing her mind. How very scary that would be. She'd never been a good girl, physically. Clumsy since birth, she told everyone. She relied on her brain to carry her through. It wasn't great, but seemed adequate, anyway. If her brain didn't work...well, it didn't bear thinking about.

The serious shell shock was something she'd witnessed, too. Her father was an infantry corporal in the Great War, and he still had times when he would wake, shouting, in the middle of the night. He had black moods, too, when the family stayed quiet and away from him or risk being bellowed at—or worse. It helped that when he was well, he was a caring father, reading stories at bedtime to the little ones, joking with Ruth and her mother. When Billy had signed up for the Navy, their father disappeared into a very dark place for weeks. He wouldn't speak to anyone, just walked soundlessly back and forth to church, ate, slept. Ruth's mother tried to keep everything on an even keel, but the family was showing the strain by the time he resurfaced. Thinner, but back to his old self. He wouldn't talk about Billy, though. It was like he'd already given him up for lost.

Ruth didn't have long alone in the room, as while she was down for dinner, another Dieu nursing student moved in. A silent, shy girl, Theresa was a huge contrast to Mary. It didn't help that she had apparently never met a Protestant and was afraid of Ruth. When introduced, she stared at her as if she was an alien creature, and after setting up a little shrine to Mary on her dresser, she retreated into soft prayer with her rosary. More praying occurred after that was done, and Ruth, having given up on trying to make conversation, decided to spend more time in the common room with her other classmates.

In two weeks, Ruth met up with Mary. They headed out, shopping for soap and underwear, though the stores seemed bare. With so many soldiers in town for college, all crowded into tents on the Queen's campus or around the local high school, KCVI, supplies were scarce. After dipping into a few shops, they gave up and stopped for a hot chocolate downtown, chattering excitedly about everything while they waited. The patrons at the next tables smiled at them indulgently.

Ruth leaned forward, lowered her voice. "So, how is it over there? Are the patients as scary as you feared?"

Mary shrugged. "Some are pretty ...," she paused, "uneven. They seem fine one day, but when you show up the next, they don't remember who you are, or hate you." She sipped her cocoa. "It must be awful to be so confused. And the treatments aren't much fun, either."

"As bad as at the San?" Ruth whispered, looking around to be sure no one could overhear.

"Worse. I had to help with the electroconvulsive therapy yesterday. It looks horrible, but I guess it helps. Next week I'm assisting with an insulin shock treatment. That one scares me. What if the patient dies? Insulin is serious! And they require one-to-one nursing after the treatments to be sure they survive the seizures. But," she sighed, "That and ECT seem to be the only things that can treat schizophrenia. I wish we had better medications."

"Wow. I guess I'll have to see all that if I get back into nursing school. I hope I'll be able to handle it!"

Mary nodded. "Yes, the KGH students rotate through for about the same amount of time as we do. I end up praying a lot before my shifts. Hey, you know those kids at the San in their casts?"

"Yes, thank heavens they are reconsidering that now, after Ikiaq. They've taken the casts off most of them."

"Good! Well, there's a lady on my ward—a paranoid schizophrenic—and she has to wear arm braces all the time to keep her from harming herself. She's Dutch, so I'm not sure how much she understands, though. Earlier this week one of the other girls had to stop her from running into chairs. It's so sad."

Ruth gasped. "That's horrible!"

"Oh, and my new bed-making skill is figuring out how to put together the bed so that it ties the patient down." She laughed. "I suppose that would be a helpful skill for any of the stroppy patients—or children!"

"Like Mr. Hanover," laughed Ruth, mentioning a particularly grabby male patient that was exasperating the nurses.

"Shh," said Mary. "His relatives might be nearby."

Ruth put a finger over her lips. "Oops!" Kingston was still a very small town, despite its growth. Everyone seemed to know almost everybody else.

"And get this! We are assigned to take patients to church every Sunday! KGH students don't have to do that, but it's one of the big Catholic nursing student jobs. We go with them and sit at the end of the pews so they can't get away. They send one big orderly with us, but I still find it difficult to concentrate on the sermon."

"I'll bet."

"If it wasn't for the other nurses, I don't think I could bear the tension," said Mary, suddenly serious. She smiled. "But the hospital cooks make us fresh bread for our nighttime snack and it's so good. I ran into your friend Betty, by the way."

"How's she doing?"

"Fine. She was going to come with me and surprise you, but she had to work. She's enjoying the patients, but she really hates her dorm room."

"She told me. She doesn't like the drafts."

"We tease her because when she's off duty she wears her cape all the time."

"If I know Betty, she's probably getting ready to sneak out!"

Mary laughed. "There's a lot of that going on—but we're so far from downtown. I can't be bothered, myself. Especially in all this weather."

Chapter Twenty-Eight

February and capping

Deep Insulin Coma Therapy

Deep insulin coma therapy (DICT) was regarded as the only specific treatment for schizophrenia from the late 1930s until it was discredited in the late 1950s.

Comas were induced on five or six mornings a week. Typically, the dose of insulin was 10–15 units with a daily increase of 5–10 units until the patient showed severe hypoglycaemia. Treatment continued until there was a satisfactory psychiatric response or until 50–60 comas had been induced. Experienced therapists let patients spend up to 15 minutes in 'deep coma' with hypotonia and absent corneal and pupillary reflexes.... The hypoglycaemia made patients extremely restless and liable to major convulsions. Comas were terminated by administration of glucose via a nasal tube or intravenously.... There was a mortality rate of about 1% as well as a liability to permanent brain damage.

Jones, p. 148.

February crept in on icy feet, pushing cold into all the gaps in every building. Everything was still being rationed, so the rooms were kept at a chilly temperature, and the students and staff started to spend all their free time gathered in the social room, wrapped in blankets. It helped that one of the student's parents had sent lashings of peanut butter. Everyone stole rolls from the cafeteria and ate through the jars, speaking stickily to each other.

"Are you going to the capping celebrations?" Jocelyn asked Ruth, one night when they were sitting about in the nurses' lounge. "You must have mixed feelings about it all."

"I'm finding it a bit awkward," said Ruth, "but I promised Betty I'd be there. She's so looking forward to it. And it will be good to see the other girls."

"It's pretty special. Scary, too. We were called in one by one into the supervisor's office and they didn't tell us if we'd made it until right then. The girls who didn't make it just had to slink away. Fortunately, there aren't too many of those."

"Oh, that would be awful!" said Ruth.

"Padre Laverty and Miss Acton both said prayers for us, too. All extremely serious. They're talking about making it a full ceremony. I'm sure that would be better—then you aren't on your own facing judgement!"

"But wouldn't that be more embarrassing if you didn't make it?"

"Yes, but maybe they'd warn you and not make you go through it."

"And, after you got your cap, did you feel more of a nurse all of a sudden?"

"It did make me think hard about all the work I'd already put in and how much more would be needed before I progressed to this stage." She indicated her senior nurse's uniform and white shoes and stockings. "This is a serious thing we do," she added soberly. "Getting my cap was a reminder of that."

"Oh, I so hope I can get there next year! Do you think there's any hope?"

Jocelyn squeezed Ruth's hand. "Of course there is! I've been watching you. You're getting much faster and more organized, and you've been a big help on Ward E. Why you haven't spilled a pan in weeks now!"

Ruth dropped her head into her hands and groaned. "I didn't tell you about the one yesterday...I wish I knew why I am so clumsy!"

"I'll bet you're still growing. I always ran into things when I was."

"Oh, I hope not! I'm already too tall!"

"The military fellows like them tall," said one of the other nurses. "You'll be a great favourite, if you ever come out with us!"

Ruth shook her head. "Every time I try anything even slightly not allowed, I get in trouble. I'm planning to be completely saintlike until I graduate."

"Where's the fun in that?" one of the senior nurses scoffed. "I used to go out all the time, and I was okay."

"Yes, but you hadn't already failed once," said Patricia, coming into the room. "I'm keeping my eye on you, Ruth. We don't want failed nurses to ruin the reputation of our school."

Ruth tucked her head down. When she looked up again, she noticed the other girls had turned away and were chatting amongst themselves.

"Don't worry," said Jocelyn, in a soft voice. "I've seen your work. Patricia doesn't know how much you've improved."

"Well, thanks. Oh, look at the time! I've got to run if I'm going to make Betty's capping!" Ruth stood and, smiling back at Jocelyn, ran out of the room.

"No running," shouted Patricia at her back.

"No yelling," said another nurse. Ruth laughed. So she had some advocates, after all.

She dashed upstairs to get her cape. How she loved that cape. Soft, navy blue lined with scarlet, with a little pocket sewn in to put your key and mad money in. Ruth was so happy they hadn't asked for that back when she was transferred. Of course, it had her name embroidered on it, so it would be hard to give to anyone else. She vowed she would never give hers up. For a minute she had a vision of herself in nurses' whites, wrapped in the cape, lying in a casket, with a bunch of red roses in her hands. It was impossibly romantic.

Despite its glamour, she had to wrap the cape tightly around herself as she walked to KGH. This place was always windy, she muttered to herself. Impossible to keep warm. She walked faster, and as she sped along, her exertion warmed her enough that she was sweating by the time she arrived at the residence.

The student at the door let her in with a cheery hello, and she stepped quickly downstairs. Ruth didn't miss the door and phone duties. The students had to do shifts on each and it cut into their non-ward time. Ruth had always offered to staff the evening shifts, as they were usually quiet enough that she could get some reading done. The student at the desk now bent her head to her books as soon as Ruth passed.

Betty gave her a wink as she eased into the back of the room. There were a few other observers here, but not many. It was a semi-private occasion, not like the graduation, which was a much grander affair. Ruth watched, tears springing to her eyes, as Betty finally got called into the room and came out, cap in hand. This might have been her, she said furiously to herself. She had to be better. She was going to be a nurse or perish in the attempt.

Betty gave Ruth a big hug. "I'm so glad you made it! I wish you were getting yours, too. I'd never have gotten this far without your help with the classes."

"Sure, you would. And I'll be back before you know it."

"You'd better!" Betty frowned. "But not before our next series of classes. I'll sure miss you until then! Who will explain everything to me?" She whispered in Ruth's ear, "Don't tell anyone, but I'm on probation. They told me I go out too much!"

Ruth looked at Betty, saying nothing, but loudly.

"I can't help it. The boys just like me!"

"You could play a wee bit harder to get," laughed Ruth. "You don't have to go out with all of them. Haven't you read Dorothy Dix? She'd be scolding you for sure."

Dorothy Dix was the local agony aunt in the Whig-Standard newspaper. She didn't pull her punches, and the nurses frequently read her advice out loud in scandalized tones over snacks.

Betty grinned. "I suppose I should cut back. But, hey, a bunch of the capped are getting together. Going to join us? We're having a party in the lounge upstairs!"

"I've got to get back. I'm on nights." She hugged Betty again. "Congratulations! Have a wonderful time!"

She stumbled home, teary and sad. She really wanted to be going on with the girls she'd started with, but she was aware none of the others came over to talk to her. Probably felt she was a curse or something. Never mind, she told herself as she reached the San. All I can do is my best, and the people here seem to believe I'm doing a good job. Feeling somewhat comforted, she strode in and made herself a cup of tea. Her shift was coming up.

Chapter Twenty-Nine

Pneumothorax

"When patients have two hours chair exercise, they are given one, two, or three dining room privileges...Patients are expected to be properly dressed when they enter the dining room. Under no circumstances will patients be allowed in the dining room without their coats, collars, and ties. Take pride in your appearance."
Information and Rules for Patients, Ongwanada Sanatorium,
pp. 13-14.

Back at it, Ruth redoubled her efforts to be the best nurses' aide ever. She dusted the tops of the doorways with damp cloths soaked in Lysol, lined up all the beds whenever they moved, gathered things for sterilizing without being asked. She even stopped complaining about the spit jars, even if sometimes she had to control her retching as she emptied them.

Ruth's first chance at surgery came sooner than she expected. At the end of March, one soldier from her ward needed a pneumothorax procedure, and he asked specifically for Ruth to accompany him.

A new resident waited in the treatment room for Ruth and her patient. She'd seen the setup with others, so the strange machinery was familiar. Bottles, and tubes, a gas canister filled with nitrogen, syringes, and bandages. And a huge needle.

"I'll need you to set up the tray and cleanse the area. Then, can you hold him steady?"

The soldier, Wendall, was shaking, but he was having such trouble breathing Ruth didn't figure he'd put up much of a fight.

"Why are you doing this? I already can't breathe!"

Ruth, organizing the sterile equipment, turned to him to explain, but the doctor spoke first.

"Look, we know what we are doing, all right? Do you want to get better or not?" He tugged at the man's nightshirt and exposed his chest. Working quickly, he injected a local anesthetic in the upper chest area, moving the needle to a few sites and re-injecting more of the drug.

Ruth glared at the resident. She touched the patient's shoulder, felt the bones close under the skin. She said, gently, "Wendall, this is meant to collapse the lung that is infected. It's a way to protect your healthy lung. With the sick one closed down, the bugs can't get across to the healthy one as easily."

He still looked uncertain.

She continued. "You had to apply tourniquets in first aid, right? For injuries or whatever?"

Wendall nodded.

"Well, this is a temporary tourniquet for your lungs. TB, when it is trapped, makes a shell around itself. With enough rest, that shell hardens, and then the bacteria won't travel elsewhere. It's like keeping the snake poison away from the rest of the body."

Wendall nodded again.

"Ok, nurse," the doctor said, "Enough chatting. The numbing should be good now. I have four of these to do this morning. Put that pillow under his side so he's turned a bit this way. Now, get over here and clean the area."

Ruth swabbed the man's side with iodine and stood by to hand the doctor any additional equipment. She positioned Wendall's upper arm over his head and held it in place. The doctor leaned over and inserted a long needle into the man's side, between the ribs. She could hear a pop as the needle entered the pleura, and a whoosh of air as the pressure in the lungs emptied the air from the chest.

"Oh my God," cried Wendall. "It's like when I was kicked by my horse back home! That hurts like a bastard!"

"The worst is over now," said Ruth soothingly. She knew it might not be. After the anesthetic wore off, pneumothoraxes were seriously painful for a long time. She made a mental note to be ensure he had his medications on time. The senior nurses now trusted her to report patient pain and brought the patients' medication when she asked for it.

The doctor attached tubing with a three-way cock to the syringe and started the flow of warmed nitrogen into the lung cavity. Wendall sloped towards the needle.

"Hold him straight, nurse!" The gas trickled in, the doctor assessing Wendall every few minutes. It took a long time.

The doctor listened to Wendall's chest, nodded. He tapped over the lung apex and heard a satisfying echo. The senior doctor came by and double-checked, patted the resident on the back in satisfaction, and vanished.

"There," the resident said. "That should hold you for a bit. We'll do a roentogram in a couple of hours to be sure it collapsed enough of the lung. Nurse, please position him to ensure lung collapse remains." He left, leaving Ruth puzzled. What did he mean? While she was thinking, she busied herself applying a top dressing over the one the doctor had put in place to seal the needle entry point. She concluded she should roll the head of the bed up, and so she did so. If they wanted the top of the lung collapsed, surely gravity would help hold it down, and the gas up. She wasn't sure. More studying to do.

"I guess you're meant to stay here until they can take you for X-ray," she said. "He isn't big on instructions, is he?"

Wendall forced a weak smile. He still looked a bit shocky, Ruth thought. It wasn't uncommon for people to fail after a pneumothorax procedure. Just last week, one of the women who had had the procedure developed an air embolism and died before they'd even brought her back to the ward. She quickly took his blood pressure and pulse and was relieved to see it was normal, even if his pulse was a bit fast. She wrapped him up well in blankets and gave him a bell to ring. "I'm just down the hall, but I'll be in to check on you every few minutes. Don't worry. If you feel unwell or have any pain, ring the bell and I'll be here right away."

She turned to go, but at the door, she heard the bell. She spun around.

"Just testing," Wendell squeaked. "Sorry, nurse."

She spent the rest of the afternoon looking in on Wendell and the other pneumothorax patients, teaching them to cough properly, moving them a bit as they were allowed. The doctor discharged Wendell to the ward after his X-ray showed they had fully collapsed the top part of his left lung. The other men cheered when they saw him.

Ruth was cautiously optimistic for him. Even after a successful pneumothorax, outcomes weren't guaranteed.

"How's it hanging, Wendell?" one soldier shouted.

"Lighter," he joked. "At least I've still got my ribs!"

The next step after a failed pneumothorax, or if the disease spread further, was a lung resection. The doctors would remove several ribs from around the side of the chest, leaving the sternum attached to provide some support. Then they'd remove part of the lung, the infected part plus anything that looked potentially unhealthy. This would leave the patient with a permanent gap in their ribs and general slumping that required regular exercise to keep from becoming a hunchback. The streets of Kingston teemed with these men, and a few women, lurching up and down to the market or the bar. The nurses on the wards led all the patients in exercises to help them regain strength and hold themselves vertical, but they didn't always work. Or the patients didn't do them after discharge and ended up curved over. Because of this, their breathing got worse and over time work and even walking would become more difficult.

Ruth positioned Wendell in the prescribed high Fowler's position, the head raised up to over 45 degrees. She'd at last had doctor's orders, and he was to stay in that position for the next 24 hours. His breathing seemed easy, and his other vital signs had stabilized. She was always amazed at how the body kept functioning without such a vital part.

"Don't forget to cough," she reminded him. She said a prayer, knowing he might well have to endure more surgery very soon.

Chapter Thirty

In the OR

Several different surgical procedures are at our disposal. Some im-mobilized the lungs temporarily, some permanently. Sometimes only one lung is collapsed. Sometimes both lungs are partially collapsed...

Artificial pneumothorax

This is a procedure whereby air is allowed to flow into the thoracic cavity to collapse the lung. The degree of collapse is determined by the amount of air used. The greater the collapse the more the lung is put at rest. This type of collapse therapy is purely temporary. Unless refills of air are given regularly the lung will automatically expand. This is what happens when treatment is completed.

Instructions for patients, Ongwanada Sanatorium, p. 16.

She must have done something right with Wendell because the next day another resident came calling for her to help with a patient needing a rib removal. One of the older patients had had a lung resection earlier but needed to collapse more of the lung area, so they meant to remove several ribs. He was panicking, and the resident wanted Ruth to come along and help calm him.

That surgery was a real one, with general anesthesia and everything. The op-erating room was crowded with the surgeon, the resident, an anesthetist, several nurses, and Ruth. After the patient was anesthetized, she was released from her hand-holding role. Ruth stared wide-eyed at all the machines, the nurses and doctors moving smoothly around each other. The head nurse showed her how to do the scrubbing and gowning needed for clean surgery.

"Just stay back there and bring us what we ask for," the nurse griped. "Don't get in the way or ask questions. You are just here to observe. If you feel dizzy, leave the theatre."

Though Ruth spent most of the time in the back, getting supplies and handing them over to the graduate nurses and doctors huddled around the patient, she got to see the surgery itself, heard the saws, saw the blood, smelled the smells.

"Too shocking for you?" One of the operating room nurses peered into her face. "Not going to faint, are you? If you are, faint over there and don't destroy the sterile field."

Ruth growled to herself. Faint? Not her. She's seen her mother through quite a few births, and they were messy, too. She watched and cleaned and carried with nary a sound until the main OR nurse nodded to her approvingly. "Can you help with the bandaging, Miss Maclean?"

The doctors had done the sutures and as usual, left the rest of the mess for the nurses to clean up. Ruth stepped forward and, trying not to shake too much, did her first immediate post-op dressing with help from one of the other nurses. It helped that the whole patient was covered with sterile towels. Little chance of dropping the sterile dressing and contaminating it. The other nurses counted bandages and equipment, checking off long lists. At long last, both they and Ruth finished, and the senior nurse came over to inspect Ruth's work.

"That looks good. Well-done." The senior nurse smiled at her colleagues. "I think she'll do to assist, don't you?" They wheeled the patient out of the operating theatre to recovery and the nurses were left with the mess.

The other nurses smiled back, masks now off. "Welcome. It will be good to work with you. More hands will be a big help."

"She works hard, don't you agree?" Dr. Anderson stood in the door, hands raised, looking like he was getting ready for another operation.

"So far, so good," the senior nurse said. "We'll see. Remember, she's not a full nurse. She can only work as an aide here."

"I'll talk to Mrs. Graham," Dr. Anderson said. "We could definitely use your help. We seem to be missing staff everywhere. All the nurses are getting married and stopping work. I'll ask if I can get you off ward duty."

"Oh, but...," Ruth began, but he had left.

"It's much less grunt work here. You'll like it. Now let's get this room cleaned up."

An hour later, Ruth wasn't convinced about the 'less grunt work' aspect. Though they had cleaners on staff, it was the nurses' responsibility to gather up things to be washed and reused, and to set up trays to be sterilized before the next surgery. It took a long while and the blood from the surgery seemed to have gotten everywhere. The bone saws didn't half make a mess, spattering walls and the big surgical lights.

"No bedpans, though," the other nurses laughed.

"Normally," another said to gales of laughs. She described a bowel resection she'd assisted with over at the hospital that sounded worse than an entire morning's cleanup on the ward.

It transpired that much of the work Ruth was permitted to do occurred when there were no patients around. Later on that week, she spent her first night shift in the OR scrubbing and sterilizing instruments in the autoclave and setting up tables for the surgeries the next morning. Every doctor had his own preferences for the type of instruments, sutures, swabs, and more that he wanted to use.

"And don't you dare mix them up," warned the head nurse. "The doctors don't like that. One of them threw an entire tray of instruments at a nurse because there were the wrong sutures on it." She laughed, harshly. "So, if we seem to be double-checking your work, we are. None of us want all those pointed things thrown at our faces."

"Here," said one of the senior nurses. "We keep a list at the nurses' station. You can check it as you go. Of course, they will change their minds."

The rest of her job, in the surgery, was to count things going in and out of the patient. Sponges, wipes, sutures, instruments. She and a grad nurse checked everything together. "We don't want to leave anything in there by mistake," one nurse told her. "Once we lost a sponge and the poor woman got the most horrible sepsis. She had to be opened up again."

"Oh, no!" Ruth exclaimed. "What happened to her?"

The nurse frowned. "Sepsis causes a lot of internal damage. She never recovered completely. I think she might be still in the hospital."

Despite all the challenges of getting everything right, Ruth enjoyed her time in the OR. The nurses seemed a friendly lot, less involved in bickering.

Every night she wrote to her father, explaining what she'd been asked to assist with, though omitting many of the gruesome details. She couldn't help feeling proud of what she accomplished so far. Maybe she would get back into the nursing stream after all.

As her father would have said, 'pride goeth before a fall'.

Chapter Thirty-One

Shaming

"Let us be grateful to all those human guinea-pigs by whose sufferings and fortitude hope was kept alive which enabled surgeons to step up a ladder runged with blood and sweat and tears...bereft of many ribs, of phrenic nerves and vertebral transverse processes, padding out their vests to hide their scoliotic figures."

William Fowler, summing up three decades of tuberculosis surgery, as quoted in Dormandy, p. 360

Ruth got a shock when she arrived at her ward after her day off the third week of March. Mrs. Graham met her at the door, frowning so hard Ruth was sure the wrinkles would be permanent. "This way, please, Miss Maclean." She strode ahead of Ruth all the way to her office upstairs at the residence. It felt like the "walks of shame" the other girls had had to do when they were caught in a compromising position with a man outside hours.

But Ruth hadn't been out, except for cold constitutionals around the building with the men from the ward, following doctor's orders. Mrs. Graham pulled her into her office and shut the door.

"Miss Maclean, I am hearing some very disturbing things about you."

Ruth waited, heart pounding.

"I'm aware you've been assigned to a bunch of different duties, so I haven't had as good a chance as I'd like to assess you. I've heard from extremely reliable sources that you have been keeping company with one of the patients. Let me be clear—by keeping company, I mean conduct unbecoming. You've been seen violating your professional responsibility, and I've had reports of you even laying on the bed with him."

"What? Who?"

"Don't be coy with me, my girl. Everyone knows about your special friend in ward C."

"The children's ward? You mean Pauloosie?"

"Yes, I mean Mr. Angmarlik, Miss Maclean. And what's worse, he is not of our kind. Have you no shame?"

"I don't know what you are talking about!"

"You've been seen in the ward after hours. Do you deny it?"

"No," Ruth paused. "I go in sometimes to read bedtime stories to the children. They remind me of my brothers and sisters back home, and they are so scared."

Mrs. Graham snorted. "As if they understood a word you said."

"They are understanding, a bit, and I'm learning some of their language."

"They can't possibly understand. And it remains you were in there with Mr. Angmarlik, after bedtime for the children. What was he doing in there with you?"

"You know what he does, Mrs. Graham! He translates for the children. He came in to help with the stories." Ruth stood up. "I have nothing to apologize for, Mrs. Graham. I've done nothing improper and as for getting in bed with Pauloosie—Mr. Angmarlik—well, I never get into bed with patients, period. And he is just a colleague. There's always another nurse on the ward with us."

"You must realize much of what we expect is based on impressions. Our patients expect us to be intelligent, pure, devoted. If you appear to be an easy mark, you bring disgrace to the entire profession. You know this, as a minister's daughter. This shouldn't be unfamiliar to you."

"It isn't. I try to be proper at all times," Ruth muttered, adding under her breath, "not like some others I could mention." She wasn't sure whether to scream or cry. It was so unfair. She stood up. "Is that all?"

"Sit down. There's another thing. You are also accused of fraternizing over-much with the doctors. They have important work to do. You aren't to be distracting them or flirting with them. This is a workplace."

Ruth sat back. She was beginning to guess where this might all have come from.

"What? Who is telling you these things? None of them are true. I was in the company of the doctors more than usual, but they are showing me what I need to learn to be a surgical nurse."

Mrs. Graham templed her fingers together. "You were released from the nursing program, were you not?"

"Yes, but...."

"Yes, but nothing. I see my allowing you to help in the casting room and with a surgery here or there has gone to your head. You are not a graduate nurse and should not act as one."

"I'm not... I just want to learn." Ruth hated the whiny tone that came into her voice, but she couldn't help it. Her panic caused sweat to pour down her back. This was serious, she knew. If they believed she was flirting with the doctors, they would expel her right away.

Mrs. Graham tapped on her desk, undecided. Ruth dared to hope. Then Mrs. Graham stood, pushing herself up with both hands. She seemed weary; her shoulders slumped. "Nevertheless, I think we had better put you back to straight ward duties until you learn your place. Your mentor has been quite concerned about you."

"I'm sure she has been concerned, but maybe that's because I am being asked for, not her!" Ruth retorted, her face red.

Mrs. Graham slammed her hand onto the desk. "No back talk, Miss Maclean. She is assigned as your mentor. You should listen to her advice."

"Her advice? When? She's never on the ward unless she has a man she is interested in." Ruth slapped her hand over her mouth. She hadn't meant to say that, even though it was true.

"That's quite enough, Miss Maclean. You are to go back to straight ward duties with not another word of complaint. I'll increase your shifts on Ward E, as there are only women there. And stay away from the children's ward. If I see you in there again, we will be forced to take serious action. Mr. Angmarlik might be sent away because of this, you know. Think of someone other than yourself."

Ruth froze. She couldn't believe they were threatening Pauloosie over some made-up story Patricia was spreading. She vowed to speak to her as soon as she found her. She only hoped to control her anger enough to hold a civilized conversation. She stormed out of Mrs. Graham's office and back to the men's ward.

"Ooh, someone's got her knickers in a twist," said one of the other nurses, as Ruth banged in.

"Be quiet," Ruth said. "There's far too much chatter around here."

That evening, as she was clearing the dinner dishes and starting the evening rounds, Pauloosie came to see her. "Good evening, Miss Maclean. Are you coming tonight for story-time? The children are so looking forward to it."

Ruth looked around and spotted a nurse eavesdropping, her ears practically extending off her head. It was obvious that Patricia had been spreading lies everywhere when Ruth was tied up in surgery. She simmered.

"No, Mr. Angmarlik. It seems I may not go to the children's ward anymore, least of all with you." She leaned forward and added in a whisper, "Someone has been telling stories. They say we've been 'inappropriate'."

Pauloosie looked puzzled. "Romantic," said Ruth. "Boyfriend and girl-friend."

Pauloosie reared back in shock. "Oh no, Miss Maclean. If they think that, they will send me away, and who will the children have then? I can't risk that. I must go. Miigwech for all you have done."

Ruth watched him flee, sad to the core of her being.

As she stormed into the soldier's ward, she sensed a chill even there. She walked over to Jerry and George's corner, only to find them both unwilling to talk.

"What's up?" she asked, "feeling well, you two?"

"I hear you've been having a wonderful time," George said morosely. "You've forgotten about us all here."

"I have not! I've just been helping in surgery."

"Well, the doctors are a better catch, of course," George muttered.

"Right. This stops right now." Ruth turned and faced the ward. "Look. I'm not forgetting you all here, and I'm still working on this ward. I was helping with some surgeries, trying to learn more about nursing. You remember, Wendall? Didn't I help when you had yours?"

He blushed and nodded.

"I'm not, repeat not, looking for romance, nor am I involved in any. Now can we let it go? I miss working with you all."

There was an embarrassed shifting of bodies on beds.

"I'm sorry," George said. "It's just we heard all sorts of things, and you weren't coming by anymore."

"Well, thanks to the lies someone has been telling about me, you'll be seeing more of me again. I'm not going to be allowed to help the doctors anymore." Suddenly Ruth broke down, her composure gone. She ran out to the utility room and leaned against the wall, sobbing. She would be sent home now and be so embarrassed in front of her family. This was failure, total failure.

Somehow, she got through the rest of her shift, but her mood spread to the patients, and it was a gloomy, gloomy day.

Chapter Thirty-Two

A walk and a talk

Again, people often point to the frequency of consumption in some families to prove its "hereditary nature." Therefore it is "inevitable." It is, indeed, extremely likely that if one or two deaths occur from consumption in the family there will be many more; for the whole family has been so mismanaged, that it is very unlikely that it should not attack other members in succession, just as children's epidemics do. But because seventeen persons who eat poisoned sugar plums at Bradford, several out of the same family, all die, is that a reason for supposing their poisoning "hereditary," "contagious," or the result of a "family predisposition?"

Nightingale, Notes on Nursing, p. 46-47.

The next day Ruth was off, she vowed she would take the new ferry to nearby Wolfe Island and walk until all her angry feelings about the rumours were gone. She asked Theresa if she wanted to come with her, but she just looked at her wide-eyed. "On a Sunday? No, I couldn't. I only go out to Mass at home."

Shrugging, Ruth called on Betty and the two of them took a bus downtown from KGH and grabbed the morning ferry, the wind blowing tears from their eyes. For a change, the ferry was actually running. The government had just replaced it with a brand new one and the girls exclaimed over the shiny brass and fresh paint. The old one had been half-broken down for years. There wasn't much to see or do on Wolfe Island, but it had the benefit of isolation. Ruth felt she could talk safely there.

"As long as we go to the pub to warm up after," said Betty.

"I promise."

They disembarked from the ferry and walked on around Marysville until suddenly Ruth burst out crying.

"What am I going to do?" Ruth wailed. "Patricia—I'm sure it's her—has been going around spreading lies about me all over the San! I even yelled at the patients the other day."

Betty gasped. "You what?"

"They were all looking at me like I was acting like some Nathaniel Hawthorne scarlet woman."

"Have you been?"

"Betty! What do you think? Do I seem like the type to be lying about on beds with patients?"

"Nooo... but I did hear you are pretty popular with that young Dr. Anderson."

"He's married, you goose."

"For some, that doesn't matter."

"For me, it does. He just asked me to help him with a cast one day and he said liked the way I did the wrapping."

"I'll bet he did. You are a pretty girl, after all."

"Oh, be quiet. You are ruining everything. Now I'll feel so awkward working with him, and he was being so nice—and the OR nurses were so kind to me. Oh, it's all ruined. I doubt they'll ever let me go back to nursing school now."

Betty blew on her mittened hands. "Are we almost ready to go inside? It's freezing out here."

"Betty. You are not being any sort of help!"

"What do you expect me to say? I'd give my eyeteeth for the attention you've got from the docs. No one is offering to teach me new things or do in fact, anything with me. Unless it's downtown at the bars."

"Perhaps that's why they don't call on you?"

"Ooh, watch out—it bites. Look, Ruth, why not just let it blow over? You know it will. If the docs like working with you and the nurses are as friendly as you say, it will all be back to normal in a few days."

"But Patricia...."

"Do not engage Patricia. She's a viper. Some of the other nurses on my ward worked with her before. They were ecstatic when she was demoted to the San."

"Demoted? But wasn't she sent over as an experienced nurse to mentor me?"

"Oh, dear God, no. You really should gossip now and again. You'd learn all sorts of things. The nurses that worked with her used to hate being on shift with her. She'd let all her IVs run slow and then turn them up fast when she took off for dinner break. Everyone would have to restart them cos the veins would be blown. The poor patients ended up bruised and sore on both sides."

"Really? She's always nagging me about that."

"Just don't ever offer to cover her for mealtimes. And she kept going missing. She'd be nowhere to be found and her patients wanting pain medications and they'd eventually find her in the lounge laughing with some doctor. They loathed working with her."

"So why did she get assigned to me, I wonder?"

Betty laughed. "I imagine Mrs. Graham, in that devious mind of hers, thought you'd be an excellent influence, shining so angelically she'd hate to show up all dirty winged beside you."

Ruth stopped, waved her arms about. "It IS cold. Let's head back, shall we?" As they turned, she added, "Well, that explains a bunch of things. But now that she's told everyone I'm as 'dirty-winged' as she is, how do I get them clean again?"

"Time," said Betty. "There must be a scandal a week in the hospital. It is always forgotten quickly and replaced by the next one."

"But I was hoping to keep on with surgery. The new nursing intake is in a few months, and I so wanted to get in for it."

"Are you sure you want to put up with this ridiculousness? I'm beginning to long for gentle domesticity, a warm fire (especially now) and one day even a guy who loves me."

"Fat chance me finding that with all this hanging over my head."

"You want that, don't you? You aren't one of those women who doesn't like men, are you?"

Ruth laughed. "No. It might be simpler if I was. I admit that when George or Dr. Anderson look at me in a certain way, well, a lot of my drive goes out the window and lands in a little cottage with a white fence and babies in the yard."

"See? Maybe it's time to go home after all. You haven't had an easy time of it here."

"Home? No, no, no. Have I told you my mother is expecting AGAIN? I don't know why they can't stop making them but my heavens, if I ended up back at home the job would be the same, only without pay and no holidays or days off. No, thank you. And have you ever been to Cloyne?"

"No. Big city girl here. I couldn't survive where everyone knows everything about you. It was bad enough being a military brat."

"That's exactly the problem! And, of course, there's that foolish boy from my high school years who still carries a silly torch and wants me to come and marry him and help run his farm. Farm. Hah—it's all rocks out there. You'd get barely enough wood to keep a fire burning. And he will keep sending me letters! I hate the cold!"

"Speaking of which," Betty said, meaningfully. They looked out over the lake, where whitecaps were frothing about. "Time for the pub?"

"It's just around the corner—there—doesn't that seem cozy?"

The pub was in a ramshackle building that had definitely seen better days, but the lights shone through the windows in the early evening gloom, and they could hear the sound of laughter.

"Won't this ruin our reputations?" Betty asked, with a sashay that made her cape swing.

"You don't have one. But let's make a pact to sit together and not talk to any men."

"Done. I've had enough of men." She giggled. "For now."

"Are you okay, after all? No leftovers from your experiences?"

"Auntie Flo is perfectly regular! Can't you tell? I'm positively giddy! No more baby worries."

Soon enough, they were seated by the fire with a warm cider in their hands. The other patrons had stopped staring and were back into their own conversations.

"This smells heavenly," said Ruth. "Why don't we ever have cider at the residence?"

"Alcohol, silly. We might do something scandalous."

"Are you still sneaking in after curfew?"

"Oh yes, though it's harder down at Rockwood. You have to keep an eye out for the bus, unless some kind boy drives you home. Taxis don't like to go there. At least curfew is at eleven instead of ten, which means I don't have to sneak in so often. We have a whole routine set up, a rota system. Oh, I wish you were with us still. It must be so lonely where you are."

"Not really. The other nurses are friendly, and Mary was so much fun—just most of them are graduate nurses and look down on me a bit."

"They probably don't like you spending all that time with the doctors, leaving them the bedpans." Betty sipped her cider. "I like Mary," she continued. "She's got a good sense of the ridiculous. We keep getting scheduled opposite each other, though, so we haven't had much time to get together. We're both almost done our rotation!"

"That passed quickly. Where are you off to next?"

"Maternity. Should be an agreeable change."

"Better you than me. I helped my mother through a bunch of her deliveries, and I'd be glad to skip that rotation! I've just got to get back in, Betty. I can't go home with 'failure' stamped on my forehead. And I really like working in the OR. But my father barely let me stay as it is. I told you he only gave me six months to 'pull my socks up' before he comes to claim me. I'm afraid every day he'll be on my doorstep again." She tossed back the dregs of her cider, trying to look fierce. "I keep writing letters telling them all the exciting things I'm doing as if they were every day, trying to delay him. So far, he sounds positive, but I'm having to get quite creative."

"I doubt they'll send you home, Ruth. Mrs. Graham is a dragon, but I hear she needs all the staff she can get. It takes time to get someone trained and I hear we are getting a new shipload of Navy guys in any day now."

"Really? Oh, no. It's so sad, those lovely, sweet faces, their lives about to be ruined, or worse. Did I tell you about the rib surgery I observed? Brutal."

The afternoon passed in tales of nursing experiences and laughter over Betty's dates. It was so good to unburden to someone who understood. They rode back together on the evening ferry and walked home arm in arm, warmer in friendship.

Chapter Thirty-Three

Pressure from all over

Walking is the chief form of exercise. No other activity is to take the place of walking.

Ongwanada Sanatorium, p. 11

The next day, Ruth was nervous about going back to the ward. She wasn't sure how she would be greeted, after yelling at the men. When she arrived and was looking at her assignment for the day, there was a knock on the ward door. She stood, only to spot Dr. Anderson standing outside in the hallway.

"Can we talk?" he asked.

"Of course," Ruth said. "Where shall we go?"

"The hallway is fine. Best if we are out in the open."

Oh, oh, thought Ruth. He's been told the lies.

"Miss Maclean—I've been made aware of some disturbing comments about our working relationship."

Ruth looked down, gathering her thoughts. She wanted to be sure of a professional response.

"I have no idea who started these rumours—I assume it wasn't you?"

She shook her head violently. "I would never!"

"I thought as much. Look, I enjoy working with you and I really appreciate your technique. You seem able to calm the most excitable patient. It makes my work much easier. I've explained there is nothing going on to my wife. She trusts me, so I've decided to go to your matron and l tell her there is nothing to these ... reprehensible statements. Would you allow me to do that?"

Ruth looked up, tears shining in her eyes. "Oh, Dr. Anderson, I'd appreciate that so very much! I've tried to explain they weren't true, but no one seems willing to believe me. They might believe you."

"Besides," the doctor said, "I understand you are sweet on this Pauloosie fellow?"

"Oh, no! That's another of those rumours. We're colleagues, that's all. Sometimes I help in the children's ward, and we talk."

"Hmm. Well, someone has really been putting the rumour mill to work over you. Do you suspect who is behind it?"

Ruth bit her lip. "I have an idea, but if I tell you I'm just as bad as they are, aren't I?"

Dr. Anderson laughed. "Too right. Well, I'll go see what damage control I can do from my side of things. My wife was a nurse. She remembers very well the infighting that goes on. Keep your head down and I'm sure it will all blow over before you know it."

"With your help, I'm sure it will," Ruth said. "Thank you again. It means a lot."

Dr. Anderson was as good as his word and by the time the day was out there was a message from Mrs. Graham saying to resume her duties in the casting and surgical wings. Ruth almost wept with relief.

She would have to convince George and Jerry, though. And Pauloosie still wasn't looking at her when they passed in the hall. She didn't blame him. The outcome of a misunderstanding was too large for him. Ruth knew he felt responsible for every child in the ward as if they were his own, and if he'd been separated from them, it would be a disaster for him, and the children, too.

George was a different problem. Some of the ward patients were out on a brief, freezing exercise walk around the hospital when he came up beside her and took her elbow.

Startled, she pulled it away.

"Ruth, please, let me talk to you."

She slowed to let him walk comfortably while he spoke.

"Ruth, when I heard all those rumours about you and that Indian fellow—and the doctors, too, I wasn't sure what to think. I mean, you've never given me any encouragement, though I've been trying and trying to get your attention...."

Ruth looked at him, eyes wide.

"George, you are a patient. I can't."

"Well," he said, chin out. "I'm going to be discharged soon, and I was hoping, well, that we might see each other now and then when I am."

"Oh, I'd like that, George. I'd like to visit with all the boys after they get well. We get to spend so much time with you."

"No, that's not what I meant. I mean, see you. Like officially. Like a date or something."

Ruth smiled inside but held it back, put on her professional face. "Now, Mr. Smith, surely you are not making some sort of improper suggestion to your nurse...."

He looked at her quickly and sensed she was teasing him. He ducked his head. "Don't make fun of me, please."

Ruth immediately felt chagrined. "Oh George, no, I didn't mean to." She tilted her head down, caught his eye. "I'd love to go out for a date when you are discharged. We've had such fun together."

George beamed. "That's perfect. Now I can really work on getting well."

"But George, let's keep things as they are until then, can we? I'm already in trouble for 'fraternizing'. It will only get worse. I might lose my position here."

"Ah," said George, his voice lowered and crafty. "But if you weren't a nurse, we could date right now."

"Don't you dare, mister. If you make me lose my job—well, there wouldn't be any dating in the future. I'll leave and go. I'll go to be a nun and you'll never ever hear from me again!"

"Okay, I promise, for now. But the day I'm discharged, expect me."

Ruth wasn't sure if she felt happy or bullied as they walked back to the ward.

The rest of the winter passed slowly and coldly into a mucky, damp spring. Ruth was gradually included in following up the surgeries being done at the

San—assisting with care by the ever-changing rota of residents and doctors and 'her boys' as she had started to call them. She spent one day a week on the doom-laden Ward E, and despite the sadness and odours in the air there, found she was really enjoying the challenge of caring for the complicated patients. She and Jocelyn got along well, and often took meals together, planning their approaches on the ward.

Jerry was being put through the wringer—a pneumothorax first, then a rib resection that didn't help. He had a bout of pleurisy that left him weak and weepy. Ruth spent extra time with him, and because they were inseparable, with George. Ruth tried to keep a professional distance between them, but he was awfully persistent in trying to get near her, capture her attention.

Part of the TB treatment included lots of fresh air, including walks outside around the San if the patients were able to tolerate it. Ruth found that when she'd lead a group around, George would often come along, helping with the sicker men, joking with her and the other nurses. He seemed so kind, always there when one of the men needed a wrap adjusted.

"Thanks, George," she said to him one day. "You've been such a great help."

He gazed at her. "I'd do anything to help you. Anytime." The intensity of his look made Ruth blush, and she quickly bent to adjust the blanket around another patient's wheelchair.

"Come on, Ruth! Can't you see he's sweet on you? Give the guy a break, won't you?" The other men joined in and before she could stop it, George had picked up her hand and kissed it. Much cheering from the men.

Unfortunately, Mrs. Graham heard about this and the next morning there was a summons. Ruth dragged into her office. Surely they wouldn't send her home for this.

"You have an admirer," Mrs. Graham began.

"I didn't encourage him. He just keeps following me around."

"Hmmm. That's not what I've seen. You seem to spend a great deal of time in that corner of the ward."

"That's only because Mr. Bousquet is so sick," Ruth argued. "I can't help that they are friends."

Mrs. Graham paused. "Yes, I can see that. I'm just concerned. It's far too easy to be persuaded by these men, so lonely and far from home. Some of our best students have had to leave—either through marriage or...," she shuddered, "an unplanned pregnancy. It always seems a pity to lose good staff that way, to end up wives and mothers, their careers behind them."

"But that's what most women want, surely? A loving partnership? What was wrong with that?"

Mrs. Graham smiled sadly. "I was lucky in my marriage. Bob never wanted children and was happy to let me continue to work. Not that I would have stopped, mind you. My career is important to me. I sense yours is to you."

Ruth thought so, too, but the idea of being in charge of her own home, of raising little babies—well, that had started feeling exciting. Maybe the memory of her mother's long days of work was fading. She needed a reminder.

"Matron? Would it be possible for me to arrange a visit home? My mother could use my help. If you can spare me, of course. It would just be for a few days."

Mrs. Graham nodded. "You've earned a bit of a vacation. If that is what you'll get!" She coughed. "Likely it will cool George's affection to have you away for a bit, too. Good idea."

Ruth wasn't sure she wanted George to stop looking at her with those cow eyes, but she'd done it now. Time to pack her bags.

Her father was coming to town the next week and would pick her up. She was in a state of excitement while she waited, gathering presents for the kids from the stores in Kingston, knitting an almost normal-looking pair of booties for the new one. They were only a bit misshapen. All those days sitting with the sick men, knitting, were paying off. Some of the men had taken up knitting too and there was always a lot of laughter in the knitting groups.

Beth preferred cards, and in the quiet times she'd spend it with the guys at the card table. Ruth had noticed one or another of them holding her hand under the table. "Weren't you going for a doctor?" she teased Beth one day as they walked around the residence.

"Oh, you know, any port in a storm," she said vaguely waving a hand. "I'm getting tired of all this spit bottle cleaning. Aren't you? Perhaps one of these guys will be healthy enough to be discharged soon. Larry is testing negative. And they do have their military pensions."

She saw Ruth staring at her.

"Oh, come on, little Miss Purity. Tell me you haven't considered that with your handsome George? Or even Jerry, though I suspect that would be a brief marriage. Hey, then survivor's benefits!"

"You are horrible. Poor Jerry. And George is just looking for a port himself."

They realized suddenly what Ruth had said and started laughing so loudly they scandalized the patients lying out on the verandas as they raced back to the residence door.

Chapter Thirty-Four

Marriage?

Family life is nothing but internecine strife and mutual exploitation, (Florence) asserts. Parents rarely speak to each other, siblings have nothing in common, and the weak prey upon the strong. Sons are lucky since parents are eager to get them out of the home. Girls use marriage to escape the stifling atmosphere chez Papa but then reproduce it for lack of education and understanding. Unhappiest are the unmarried women, whose slavery ends only when both parents die. Nightingale insists that parents should in fairness allow each child to go his or her own way and that each child had a right to a share in the family resources...

Gill, pp. 270-271.

T he next week, Ruth was packing when she heard her father's voice from the parking lot. He was talking to Mrs. Graham. Hastily, Ruth shut her suitcase and carried it downstairs, doing up her cape with one hand.

"What I don't understand," her father was saying, "is how this could happen when you say you have control over the students in your charge."

Mrs. Graham was looking at the letter her father had handed her, open-mouthed. "Here, Ruth. What do you know about this?" She waved the sheet of paper at her. It was filled with cramped handwriting.

"I haven't seen that before," she said.

"But surely you must be aware of its contents?"

"No—what does it say?"

"Don't play ignorant with me, daughter. He'd not be writing this without discussing it with you."

"Who? What?" She was confused.

"Let's go into my office," the supervisor said, her voice soothing.

"Never mind that. I want to go talk to him, right now."

Ruth, baffled, watched her father go up the stairs to the ward. A sinking feeling was beginning in the pit of her stomach.

"Ruth, come here." Mrs. Graham held the door to her office open. "There's been quite enough public discussion already."

Ruth looked at the curious faces in the hallway and agreed. She followed her in and shut the door.

"Ruth, aren't you were serious about nursing? We talked about this not a week ago, and I was under the impression you might even be ready to join the regular class. And now this...."

"What?"

"You can't tell me you didn't know George was contacting your father!"

"Contacting my father? Why?" Suddenly the chill was there, colder than before. "He hasn't gone and...."

"Asked for your hand. Old-fashioned of him, but he is from the country."

"But I never! He never even mentioned it to me!"

Mrs. Graham looked at her, eyes stern. "So you didn't know at all about this?"

"Well, he did seem to be getting awfully fond of me, but we haven't ...we haven't even been on a date! I only see him around the hospital and on walks with the other patients. I don't understand." She sat down, legs trembling. "I'm not even sure how he got our address!"

"What do you feel about it all? Does the idea appeal to you? He's almost ready for discharge." She turned and looked out the window. "A wedding might be good for morale."

Ruth wasn't sure what to do. Scenarios passed by her mind—a white wedding, with her father doing the ceremony and all the nursing students in jealous attendance, a smallish house she'd fill with love and children, the chance to sleep in a bit in the morning...she blushed to the roots of her hair...sleeping in, with George....

"I see you have a lot to consider," said Mrs. Graham, gazing at her sadly. "Not least, what sort of man asks your father before he asks you about such a serious commitment."

"A traditional one? One who values the input from his future wife's father? I like him!" Reverend Maclean had come back into the office. His eyes were twinkling now, though with what emotion, Ruth wasn't sure. Anger? Joy? Sadness?

"Perhaps," said Mrs. Graham. "Or one who doesn't believe you have a right to refuse. In any case, why not take your weekend time as we discussed, get away from the situation, and get your head straight about things?"

Ruth nodded. "I should go talk to George, I suppose."

"I suppose!" Mrs. Graham cleared her throat. "Be sure to tell me your decision, will you? I'll have to find a replacement. Married women still aren't allowed to be nurses. Ridiculous rule, but there you go. I had to wait until my husband retired to get back into hospital practice, even though he let me continue to work through his office. Feeling back then was that if you were married, you didn't need paying employment. Unfortunately, those are still the beliefs."

Ruth stood. The idea of not having to drag around the wards cleaning up other people's mess sounded attractive in her exhaustion. "I'll let you know," she said, and left, carrying her suitcase to the car. She put it in the back, and straightening her hair, walked back upstairs.

When she opened the door to the ward, a great cheer greeted her. Everyone was smiling, George, Jerry, the other men, the other nurses, even her father.

"Congratulations!" The resident came over and clapped his hand on her shoulder. "Our first TB bride!"

"Couldn't happen to a nicer girl," said Jerry. His cough darkened his sentiment, but it sounded sincere.

"George, can we talk?"

"Ooooooh," the men howled. "She's already calling the shots! Watch out, George!"

George, grinning like the Cheshire cat, came up to Ruth and took her hand. "C'mon, sweetie. Let's talk." He guided her outside onto the verandah and away from the others sitting there.

"George, you never even mentioned this to me!"

"I guess I'm old-fashioned that way, wanted to check with your dad first, to be proper. But you are all for it, aren't you? I mean, you do like me and all?"

He looked so comically pathetic Ruth found herself laughing and saying, "Of course I like you, George."

"Well, that's all set, then! I like you, you like me, soon we'll make a famileee..."

"George. Listen." Ruth held his shoulders, made him stop his manic dancing about. Was he feverish? She thought maybe so. "First, you are getting all worked up. That's not good. It'll send your temperature up and the doctors don't like that."

George immediately stopped. "You're right, of course, nurse." He grinned. "But can't I be a wee bit happy?"

"But George, I haven't accepted you yet. For that matter, you haven't asked me yet."

"Whoops, I guess you're right. Got all excited. Shall I ask you now?"

She recoiled. "No, no. I need to get used to the idea, and you need to get back into bed."

"Will you tuck me in?" he chuckled and reached for her.

"George! Behave!" Ruth tried to sound cross, but inside it thrilled her that this man, this friendly, kind man, wanted her. She'd never been wanted by a grown-up man before. She leaned forward and kissed his cheek gently. "I'm very flattered, really, but let a girl think. I'm going home for the weekend, as you know—can I think about things until I get back?"

"I suppose," George said, sounding tired now. His colour was a bit high, too.

"Time for bed, or you won't be well enough to get married, or even date! I'll tell you my thoughts when I get back. In the meantime, get some rest. I'd feel terrible if I made you sick." Sicker, she thought, mutinously. Surely she shouldn't be expected to tie herself to a sick partner? She shook her head. We're all just a step from illness, she reminded herself. What would Dorothea Dix say? That she was being selfish, no doubt. Ruth rebelled in her head. Why couldn't she hold out for a romantic story like the ones in the Whig that they all read to each other over dinner? She mustn't think any more about that all now. "Let's go, George. Father and I need to get on the road."

"Give me a kiss," George insisted.

"Maybe when I get back. Let me go now." Ruth detangled herself and led George back to the ward, settled him on his bed, with catcalls and whoops surrounding them.

She turned to Jerry. "Look after him while I'm gone, will you?"

"Sure thing," said Jerry, trying to sit up from bed.

"No, stay put. I'll bring you some fresh air from the north." Ruth put her hand on Jerry's forehead, noticed its warmth. Poor Jerry. He just wasn't getting well.

She waved goodbye to the ward and followed her father out.

Once they were outside, her father embraced her. "Congratulations, my dear!"

"Oh no, you don't. He'd never even asked me. I have to think about it all."

"What's to think about? He seems like a decent fellow. He even says he'd be willing to move to Cloyne. And you could get away from this disgusting nursing you seem to want to do, looking after these godless men. The swearing I heard when I walked in! I need to wash out my ears." He stopped and smiled widely at Ruth. "I'm happy for you, my shining girl. May you be as happy as your mother and I have been."

A chill screamed up Ruth's spine. Was she going to end up like her mother, after all? What was she going to do?

Chapter Thirty-Five

Time in Cloyne

The most important practical lesson that can be given to nurses is to teach them what to observe—how to observe—what symptoms indicate improvement—what the reverse—which are of importance—which are of none—which are evidence of neglect—and of what kind of neglect.

All this is what ought to make part, and an essential part, of the training of every nurse.

Nightingale, Notes on Nursing, p. 111.

B y the time they arrived at Cloyne and pulled into the driveway, Ruth was wearier than she'd ever been. Her father had spent the entire trip talking about the joys of married life, about how she could contribute to the parish and help her mother out, how the younger children would dote on her, and she could play with them, "until she had a few of her own."

Ruth initially tried to stop the endless blather by inserting tales of work at the San, but everything she mentioned seemed to make her father talk louder about marriage. It didn't help that her father's old Ford was gasping up the hills. There was still some ice on the roads and her father slowed to a crawl every time he spotted any, likely because the tires needed replacing. By the time they'd dragged through Kaladar, she was done with talking. She looked out the window at the passing scenery (trees, trees, rocks, trees) and thought of the fun time she and the girls had had shopping on their last day off. It was always an enjoyable trek down to the waterfront via Princess Street, passing all the shops they couldn't afford and dipping into the few they could. They'd gone to buy more stockings—senior nurses bragging about their whites, while all the juniors were stuck with the sturdy blacks. Then it was time to stop for a sandwich and a milkshake at The Superior Restaurant, and a turnabout home. They made a loud, laughing mob, and yet everyone turned and bowed out of their way. It was like their nursing uniforms made them royalty. Smiling as she thought about it, she was caught by her father.

"See, you're coming around to it, aren't you? You've missed this place!"

Ruth shook her head. "Of course I love it up here, but I prefer..." she paused. Best not to indicate how much fun she was having. "...having my career to work towards. I feel I'm needed." She emphasized the last word, knowing it was the only argument her father would hear.

He sighed. "Well, I guess that's true. They do seem to need you there." He laughed. "Especially George."

"Father," Ruth began.

"I know. No more about that young man."

"Thank you. I need to think about how I feel."

"Your mother will likely quiz you, I should tell you. She read the letter, too."

Ruth moaned. If she turned George down, that letter would figure large in her reasons for refusal. She'd read it on the way in the car and it had done nothing to help his cause. He wrote badly, misspelled a bunch of words, but worst, he seemed so sure she'd be grateful to leave nursing and marry him as soon as possible. The cheek of the man!

They pulled into the driveway, and the children spilled out of the house to greet Ruth. Every single one of them had something spilled on their shirt. The noise was intense, and Ruth was enveloped in greetings. She felt savaged by puppies. Dirty puppies.

Her mother stood in the doorway, a smile on her face. She stretched out her arms and Ruth ran to give her a hug. Her mother's abdomen was tight. The pregnancy was moving right along, and she seemed exhausted.

She looked down. "Yes, I'm afraid so. I'm feeling like our barn cat, always full in the tummy. It seems all I have to do is bake a loaf of bread and another baby comes along."

"And we love every one of them," her father added, swinging one of the little ones into the air. They all entered the house, everyone talking at once. Only Meg was missing.

"She's out getting in the wash," her mother explained.

"I'll go help," said Ruth, fleeing the sticky embraces. The wash was a perpetual task with all the children. She found Meg pulling diapers off the line, trying to fold them into three despite the chilly weather. There were dozens on the lines.

"Here, let me help—my fingers are warm."

"Ruth!" Meg hugged her quickly. "Thanks! This laundry never ends. I want to get it in before the weather starts." She gestured to the lowering skies. "Radio says snow. Brr."

"I'll take this line," said Ruth. Their backyard was criss-crossed with clotheslines. There never seemed to be enough space for all the laundry. She stepped to one of them and started pulling shirts off, tossing the clothespins into the nearby bucket.

"Do you think Father will ever spring for an electric dryer?"

"Not on your life. Not when he has all the helping hands around here. He's even got wee Angela sorting laundry."

Ruth stood with her hands on her hips, imitating their father. "About time, too! 'Can't expect to lie about all day!'" she quoted. "I mean, she must be three already, right?"

Meg nodded. "I wouldn't mind so much if this were MY house," she said. "But they keep having more babies. It needs to stop."

"Yeah," said Ruth. "Honestly, aren't ministers supposed to be continent or something?"

They laughed, guiltily looking over their shoulders at the house.

"So, how's the San? Still having fun?"

"Oh yes. And learning so much. But Meg, one lad...."

"Wrote to father. Yes, I heard the shouts of delight all over the house. You don't look too excited, though."

"No. The fellow never asked me—just wrote to Father. Plus, he's a patient, so we've never dated even. Plus...he's a patient."

"Ugh. Permanent nursing. And I don't imagine going behind your back would appeal to you."

"You're right! I thought we were just having fun, chatting on the ward, but he seems to have told everyone else it's more. And his letter made it sound like I was raring to go!"

"Pushy sod, seems to me."

"Exactly."

"What are you going to do?" asked Meg. "Father seems so excited."

Ruth snorted. "I am just about done trying to please our father. He never listens to me. He won't be happy until I marry a minister and birth an entire choir."

"That simply doesn't seem like you."

"It isn't. I really want to be a nurse now that I've worked in it for a while. It's challenging. I get to do good things. I can learn new things every day."

"You were always much better at school things than I was. I'd be terrified."

"But you can do everything else!" Ruth gave her sister a hug. "I'm so useless at the usual 'womanly' things. Still can't knit worth a darn. You should see the booties I brought. I think I'm the only nurse at the San who hasn't sent socks to charity. It would have been a disservice to the men!" She laughed. "I pity whoever gets saddled with me. I'll likely poison him."

"Yes, you would."

Ruth threw a diaper at her sister, who caught it and folded it expertly. She asked, "What do you think Mother will say?"

"I'll have to talk to her if we get a moment this weekend. I don't want to disappoint her, but I am not thrilled at the thought of being married, especially to a guy who doesn't even speak to me." Ruth threw a shirt into the basket with force but it flolloped, losing the effect.

"Then don't do it," said their mother, coming up behind with another basket of laundry to hang. "You want to be a nurse, be one. Just be good at that."

"I'm trying to be."

"Keep on, then. I'll talk to your father. Now, let's just enjoy this weekend with no more foolish talk. Come on. Have a cup of tea. That will solve everything."

Chapter Thirty-Six

Ultimatums

When you see the natural and almost universal craving an English sick for their "tea," you cannot feel but that nature knows what she is about. But a little tea or coffee restores them quite as much as a great deal, and a great deal of tea and especially of coffee impairs the little power of digestion they have. Yet a nurse because she sees how one or two cups of tea or coffee restore her patient, thinks that three or four cups will do twice as much. This is not the case at all; it is however certain there is nothing yet discovered which is a substitute to the English patient for his cup of tea; he can take it when he is nothing else, and he often can't take anything else if he has it not.

Nightingale, Notes on Nursing, p. 83

Somehow, Ruth got through the rest of the weekend. She even avoided the sad looks from Chuck, who tried to sit with her at church on Sunday. She endured her father's sermon about the joys of being a father and the importance of families to God Himself. That was easier to ignore given the squirming (and slightly smelly) child on her lap. At the after church social, everyone came up to her and asked if she 'had anyone special', winking at her until she felt quite nauseous. No one asked about her nursing course.

Finally, the weekend was over, and a local farmer offered to drive her back to Kingston. Ruth was relieved that he was one of the quiet farmers, given to the occasional mutterings about the weather and not much else. It was a restful trip, and Ruth used it to prepare her response to George.

She unpacked her weekend case and sorted out her uniforms. The next morning would be awkward if she didn't settle things, so she straightened her shoulders and headed to the ward.

"She's here," called out the man nearest the door. George looked up and then dragged himself out of his bed to come and greet her. Ruth looked at him with fresh eyes. Good looking, yes, wasted by TB, yes, a bit arrogant, definitely. Marriageable? She still wasn't sure.

"Let's take a walk," she said.

"Oooh," called out the soldiers, stopping when Ruth turned to glare at them.

"Watch out, George! She's on the warpath," one called.

They walked out into the hallway and towards the balcony, but there were too many listening ears there, so Ruth took him down to the social room.

"This is nice," George said, looking around at the comfortable sofas. "Alone at last."

"We're not really supposed to be here, but I wanted to talk to you without everyone around." They sat, Ruth carefully propping the door open.

"Sure, sweetie. Have you decided?"

"George, I was furious that you wrote to my father without even discussing things with me. That is not the sort of man I would be happy with, or who would be happy with me."

"But I thought...."

"That's just it. You thought, without once talking about it with me. I'm not interested in getting married, not now, at any rate. I want to finish my training and work as a nurse. I had a lot of trouble getting here and I don't want to give it up."

"But I heard you failed the nursing course. I thought you'd be ready for a change." George reached for her hand. "And I know you like me."

He has an unattractive whiny voice, thought Ruth. Could I live with that? He is still handsome, though, and smarter than anyone I've met until now. And damn the hospital rumour mill that told everyone I'd failed. Or Patricia.

"I didn't fail," Ruth said, gritting her teeth. "I've just been delayed a bit. I expect to restart the program in September."

"And what if you fail then?" George asked, more gently.

"I won't," said Ruth, then lost confidence. "Well, I might, but I want a chance to try. You understand that, don't you?"

"Of course," he said, smoothly. "Of course you should try again."

Ruth didn't care for the patronizing tone in his voice, but she soldiered on. "Until I get that chance, well, I must be very careful. I can't be seen to fraternize. I have to be focused on my learning and nursing and do the best I possibly can. I can't afford a distraction."

"I'm distracting, then?" George grinned.

Ruth laughed. "A bit. So I'm telling you now, I don't want you to do anything romantic or even more distracting until I've at least tried nursing again. Can you wait for that long? That means no touching, no letters to my house, no special times alone together."

"You mean, like now?" George captured her hand again.

"Stop it. I'm serious."

"How long do you expect me to wait?"

"George, you're still a patient. I can't 'see' you anyway until you are discharged. Totally against the rules. And even then, I'll be busy. Can you give me until the end of the year? I'll know for sure by then."

George turned red. He sat for a while. "That's an awful long time." He coughed. "A man has needs, you know."

"Like, first, to get well." Ruth stood, wiped her hands on her uniform. They were surprisingly damp. "Please be patient with me and focus on getting yourself healthy. That's the priority."

"Can you give me any hope, at least?"

"Oh George. I am flattered by your offer. I do value your friendship. I don't want to lose that."

"Friendship." George grunted. "Back to bed for me, then. I'll just waste away, lonely and sad...."

"Oh, I doubt that," said Ruth. "I'm sure there will be lots of other girls interested in you."

"But I want you!"

"Well, if you do, you'll just have to wait. I'm sorry, George, but that's the way it has to be. My family gave up a lot to send me to school and I owe them a good try at least."

"Fine." George turned to go. "Just don't expect me to be happy about it. No, don't walk me back. I can do it. And I'm sure you have some work to do." He strode out of the door at a much stronger pace than when they had come in. Ruth couldn't help but wonder if he thought pity might persuade her. She shook her head. She was becoming a cynic. Time for some toast with the girls.

After a snack and many laughs over the children's antics at home, Ruth felt better. She hoped George would settle down, but the look in his eyes when he left was angry, and she still worried he'd be plotting something, some way to force her hand. Was that love? She wasn't sure.

Chapter Thirty-Seven

George and Jerry

Affectation, like whispering, or walking on tiptoe, is particularly painful to the sick. An affectedly quiet voice and an affectedly sympathising voice, like an undertaker's at a funeral, sets their nerves on edge. Advice, such as what I have been giving, does more harm than good, if it only makes people affect composure and quiet when with the sick. Better almost make your natural noise.

Nightingale, Notes on Nursing, p. 58

The next few weeks ran along as smoothly as they could, given a new group of soldiers in the San, all coughing and needing assessments and X-rays. Everyone ran hard to get everyone settled, and several of the men who had been so long on Ward B were discharged home. Ruth was filled with mixed emotions watching them go. Some of them hadn't fully recovered, but their families had created special rooms in their houses or on their verandahs for their men to stay in. Or families set up little tents in their yards beside their houses and the men lived there, isolated from their family and alone as they healed. Public health did in-community screenings now and agreed to check in on the discharged men. They'd make sure they were taking all the treatments prescribed, and evaluate the ongoing pneumothoraxes to be sure they didn't need topping up. Anyone running low would come back to the San for an injection of more nitrogen. Ruth sensed they would miss the coziness of the San, though at least the weather was improving with the spring.

George and Jerry and a few other long timers remained inpatients. George still had a recurrent fever and lived too far away for an easy transfer home. The doctors watched him closely. Jerry, unfortunately, was wasting away, down so many pounds since he arrived Ruth feared he wouldn't make it. She and the other nurses kept smuggling him food from the dining hall, but he was often too tired to eat it.

The new patients still poured in. Non-military patients were on the increase, too. With so many men gone, families often lived in poverty, crowding into smaller and smaller places with more and more people. TB spread well in that environment, and so sometimes entire families would come in, coughing and ill. Sadly, the families would be broken up and sent to different facilities. There was talk of sending Pauloosie's charges back to Montreal, but the nurses fought it. "Did you see how they came in? Half wild, they were. I don't think they should go back there."

Pauloosie said nothing, but Ruth privately believed he must be enjoying his comfy place in Kingston. The San provided him with a room, meals, and even a stipend for translating. She wasn't sure if the same would hold in Montreal. She couldn't ask him, of course, since every time she got near to him even at meals in the crowded dining hall, he would stand up and flee. Damn that Patricia! She wished she could do something to stop her from telling all those lies.

Despite Ruth's avoiding him, George just would not behave and kept telling everyone they planned to get married. In the end, Ruth had to tell him there was no way they would do so, and a few frosty days passed while they tiptoed around each other. Ruth got another nurse to provide care to that part of the ward and signed up for more shifts on Ward E. She assisted with many treatments and rib resections and dared to feel like she knew what she was doing, most of the time.

She and Patricia no longer spoke, though Ruth pretended to obey her orders if they crossed paths. She missed having Mary's regular updates about Patricia's manipulations. It was worrying not knowing what she was up to, and since Theresa viewed gossip as the work of the devil, she wouldn't provide any fresh information. It was getting tiresome sharing a room with her, and Ruth hoped she'd rotate out soon. She knew Theresa hated the San, and she'd overheard Mrs. Graham reprimanding her for continual complaining. She refused to work with the men, too. How was she expecting to work as a nurse? She asked her once and Theresa explained. "I plan to work maternity and paediatrics, no other focus. They told me it would be fine."

Ruth didn't understand her. From what Mary had told her about the patients on her wards and what she'd seen in her rotating wards, the men seemed much more fun and easier than the women patients.

One day, coming on to the ward from her lunch break, she spotted Patricia in the ward's corner, giggling over George. Ruth walked over. "What's so funny?" she asked.

"You are," Patricia laughed. "You are being so 'oh don't touch me' with poor George. Did you actually say you were going to become a nun?" She burst out laughing. George was blushing terribly, a rash of pink on his pale skin.

Patricia went on, "Why bother to become a nun? You're pretty close to one already, with that little blue book you carry everywhere and the way no one can get close to you. Unless you really did get cozy with that Indian guy...."

Ruth, overcome with rage, stepped forward and slapped Patricia across the face. There was a brief silence on the ward, and then scattered applause. Patricia stood, her hand over her face, where a red mark was rising. "I'm telling Mrs. Graham about this. She likes me. You'll be out of here so fast your head will spin!" She ran out of the ward.

Ruth sunk onto the chair beside George's bed. She gasped for breath. She looked at George—he had stopped blushing. There was a tiny smile on his face.

"That's it. We're through, do you hear me? Not that we ever were anything!" She turned to flounce away, but caught sight of Jerry out of the corner of her eye. Something didn't look right.

She stepped quickly over to his bed, leaned over to check his chest. Jerry spasmed and coughed, and a huge spray of blood arced out of his mouth and all over Ruth. It kept running, out of his mouth while he gasped for air. She grabbed her stethoscope and listened to his chest quickly. "It's from your left, I think," she told him. Ruth turned him to his left side and ran for the suction machine. Moving swiftly, she started suctioning the excess blood out of Jerry's mouth. "Get a doctor," she shouted to the other nurse, who stood frozen in astonishment after all the scenes. She ran off.

"Come on, Jerry, there you are. Breathe slowly. It's just a bit of blood. You'll be fine." Ruth wasn't sure if she was lying or not, but she said it over and over while she suctioned him, tilting Jerry to help with drainage, mopping up the blood as fast as possible. It seemed to be everywhere at once. His sheets soaked through in no time and even the bedside table was spattered.

The doctor arrived and immediately started barking orders. A graduate nurse followed him and started an IV. Another appeared with ice for Jerry to chew to slow the bleeding. The doctor ordered morphine and fibrinogen to help do the same. They swooped around Jerry in an intimate dance, trying not to trip each other up. Amid it all, Ruth stood, holding Jerry's hand and telling him to breathe slowly, to not cough if he could help it.

"I think he's stable now. Let's move him to intensive care," the doctor finally said. As they wheeled the bed away, the doctor turned back to Ruth. "Good work, nurse. You'd better get out of that uniform ASAP."

Ruth collapsed onto the chair, tears starting now that the pressure eased off. Poor Jerry. It was likely all over for him now, he'd lost so much blood. Feeling dampness, she wiped her hand across her face, suddenly realizing she had blood all over her. Springing up, she ran to the dirty utility room and started mopping off. Now she'd probably get TB! There went her plans for good. Another disaster. Don't think about that now, she told herself. Just clean herself off as well as she can. She tried not to cry, but was just choking up when she heard a noise.

Mrs. Graham stood in the doorway. "Oh Miss Maclean," she said, her voice low and sad. "How did this happen?"

"I just went to look at him—he didn't look right—and then he coughed all over me." Ruth wept, tears mingling with the blood.

"I'm so sorry," Mrs. Graham said. "I brought you your other uniform. This one will have to be washed in carbolic, I'm afraid." Ruth nodded, and amazingly,

Mrs. Graham closed the utility room door and helped Ruth wash off her face and arms and get out of her soiled dress without more contamination.

"Thank you," she said, in shock.

"Wait—there's something in your pocket. Here."

It was Ruth's little prayer book. She took it in her hand and clasped it to her heart. "Oh please, please, don't let me get TB!" she said, eyes welling up. "And please God, let Jerry get over this." She turned to Mrs. Graham. "I hate this disease! It's so unfair!"

Mrs. Graham allowed herself a little smile. "Much of life isn't fair, unfortunately. It looks like his blood didn't get in your mouth or nose, correct?"

"I don't think so."

"Still," she said, "we'd better put you in isolation for a few days until we're sure you are okay. Is there any chance to go home again for a few weeks? You aren't likely to be infectious as yet, and it would get you away from all the rest of the patients and staff here."

"Oh, no—there are so many babies at home."

"Can you stay away from them? Just for a while."

"I can write to my father."

"No," Mrs. Graham said. "We'll call him, this instant."

Ruth slumped. It seemed she would never get away from home. Once she went back there, her family would get their clutches into her. She exhaled, weary to her bones. Maybe that wouldn't be so bad. Marriage was looking better every moment. She probably wouldn't end up covered in tuberculosis-laden blood as a wife.

Chapter Thirty-Eight

Despair

Now a nurse ought to understand in the same way every change of her patients face, every changing his attitude, every change of his voice. And she ought to study them till she feels sure no one else understands them so well. She may make mistakes, but she is on the way to being a good nurse. Whereas the nurse who never observes her patients countenance at all, and never expects to see any variation, any more than if she had the charge of delicate china, is on the way to nothing at all. She never will be a nurse.

Nightingale, Notes on Nursing, p. 127

C hanged, and clean again, she put on a mask and went back onto the ward to say goodbye.

"I'm off for a few weeks," she told them all. "Have to go home to make sure I didn't catch anything from Jerry. You all get better before I get back," she added, pointing at all of them, one by one. She ended with George. He was gaping at her.

"You were glorious," he whispered. "You knew exactly what to do. If Jerry lives, it's because you saved him. Look," he grabbed her hand, "I've been stupid, I know. But I really want to see you. I...I care for you."

Ruth looked down at him and gave his hand a squeeze. "I'll talk to you when I get back. I promise. Look after Jerry for me, will you?"

George nodded. "I hope I will be able to tell him that."

Ruth nodded, then her eyes filled, and she couldn't see very well. She ran out of the room, colliding with Mrs. Graham in the hallway.

"Miss Maclean, I can't reach your father. They say the number has been disconnected."

Ruth coughed. They must not have paid the bill. Too many children, not enough money, as usual. "It must have been disconnected in a storm."

"I'll telegraph him this afternoon. You must go back to your room and rest up. Take a long bath, soak anything that might have been contaminated. Be sure to wash out the bath with carbolic once you are done. I'll have the kitchen bring up your meals for the next couple of days—it's important to keep your energy up. But plan to stay in your room, with the window open, for a few days. We'll do a test after that and check if you have been infected. We'll move Theresa down the hall for now."

Ruth crept back to her room and curled up into a ball. Theresa came in and gathered her things, not once looking her way. Well, that's one good thing to have happened, Ruth thought. She couldn't stop all the scenes playing by her mind—her slap of Patricia, the gasps of the other nurses when she hit her, the bloody scene with Jerry. Everything was falling apart. Ruth cried and cried until her head was sore, and then she worried that her headache was because she had been infected. She rolled over and shut her eyes, willing herself to sleep. In her dreams she heard coughing, saw nothing but red, and the worried, kind eyes of George, looking after her as she left.

She woke the next morning to the sound of a tentative knock. Opening the door, she stood back as a masked nurse stepped in with a breakfast tray. It was Beth. She was crying, her tears wetting her mask.

Ruth wanted to hug her but stood back. "Beth—you shouldn't be here."

"Ruth… oh, I'm so sorry! I can't help feeling this is my fault! I shouldn't have told you to ignore Patricia. I should have gone with you and taken her out."

"What do you mean? This," Ruth gestured around the room, "this was me being caught by a TB spray."

"Really? I was told you were under suspension and had to stay in your room because of that. We were supposed to wear masks so you wouldn't see who we were."

"Oh." Ruth slumped. "How did that get around?"

"Guess! I mean, it's all around the wards, but it mainly about how you punched Patricia right in the middle of the ward."

Ruth sighed. "I did slap her, it's true."

"Why? You'll be done for sure now."

"I hope not. She was ribbing me about Pauloosie, and he could get sent back if they thought he was being inappropriate—and you know I just read the children bedtime stories!" Ruth sobbed. "I hope I'll still be allowed to continue. Mrs. Graham helped me tidy up after Jerry... after Jerry...." She gulped back tears. "Is he all right? He hemorrhaged."

Beth shook her head. "I don't know. I haven't been to the ward yet. I can ask, though. What do you mean she helped?"

"I was covered with blood. She helped me get cleaned up. I'm here in isolation until they are sure I won't test positive."

"Had Patricia spoken to her before then? Because that little miss is blowing up the story all over the place."

"No idea. You'd better go. I don't want to put you at any risk. From Patricia or TB."

Beth fled but called back, "Open your window this afternoon. I'll bring you news from the ward."

"Thanks, Beth." Thank God she had her as a friend, Ruth thought. This place was so lonely when everyone was whispering about her. For the tenth time, she asked herself if going back to Cloyne and marrying a boring farmer would really be that bad. She flung open her window with a bang, only to be hit with a blast of wind and rain.

"So now the weather is angry at me? Why not? Everyone else is." She closed the window almost completely, just leaving it open a crack. The icy air chilled the room immediately. Sniffling, she wrapped herself in her quilt and sat down to sulk.

She picked up her blue book of prayers and scrolled through, looking for one that might fit her situation. There didn't seem to be a prayer for victims of gossip, but she found an echo in the prayer for humility:

"Oh, blessed Creator, who in love formedst me, and by thy humility savedst me: Preserve me from the sins of pride and self-will; that I may humble myself before all men, serving them in lowliness and meekness all the days of my life. Teach me to accept unjust blame and criticism, and fill my heart with forgiveness and love for those who seek to do me harm, for the sake of Jesus Christ our Lord. Amen."

Ruth read this twice to herself, tried to rid herself of the anger that surged when she thought of Patricia. It wasn't working yet. She still wanted to really, truly punch her, instead of the mild slap she'd administered. In the face. A few times.

She knew how to punch. Her older brother taught her that. Poor Bill. They still hadn't had any news from him since he'd enlisted, except for a quick, multiply censored letter from France somewhere. Since then, they'd scoured the lists of those injured, killed, or captured, but there'd been nothing. She'd almost given up hoping for his return. Almost.

She flipped the pages in her missal and found "A prayer for Loved Ones far Distant" and said that one, too. She felt slightly calmer.

Maybe, she thought, maybe I need to try to win Patricia over with sweetness. Maybe I can make her happy and then she'll leave me alone. But what would make her happy? Other than me leaving, that is. She sipped her now-cold breakfast tea and puzzled, then remembered how her mother always told her you could catch more flies with honey than with vinegar.

She had an idea. Picking up her pen, she started to write. When the lunch tray came, she passed a note to the nurse delivering it. "Can you get this to Dr. Anderson? And this one to Mrs. Graham?"

The nurse nodded and fled. Clearly she was afraid of getting infected, so at least part of the gossip story had been corrected.

Chapter Thirty-Nine

Sent away

"It was the fashion to suffer from the lungs; everybody was consumptive, poets especially," wrote Alexandre Dumas, author of *The Three Musketeers,* in his memoir. *"It was good form to spit blood after each emotion that was at all sensational, and to die before the age of 30."*

Morens, p. 154.

Later in the afternoon, she heard a firmer knock on the door and Mrs. Graham stepped into her room.

"Oh, don't worry," she said, as Ruth stepped back. "I was one of the ones to get immunized back in the early days. I'm not too worried about catching TB from you and besides, I'm old now. Wouldn't be as much of a tragedy as it is with the young lads here." She patted the bed beside her. "Sit down."

Ruth did, gingerly. At the far end of the bed.

"Miss Maclean, I was struggling to figure out what to do with you. On the one hand, you are insubordinate, and you even physically attacked your mentor." She put up her hand to stop Ruth from erupting.

"I know. She is far from blameless in this situation, and you must trust me. I am investigating all the claims being made. You have powerful allies. The fact remains, however, stories seem to keep swirling around you and that is not what I expect from my nurses. We aim to live blameless lives. It's far, far too easy to paint nurses with a tawdry brush." She folded her hands. "I've worked all my life to increase the respect for our profession. These rumours aren't helping. I've even been called to the college head to explain what is going on!"

Ruth gasped. "I'm so sorry! But...."

"I'm aware, you are going to say none of it is true, and it isn't your fault Miss Brannigan is spreading rumours. But the fact remains, part of our job as nurses is to get along even with the difficult or malign. We don't have the right to take people to task, especially when we are as junior as you are." She sighed. "I've been told to release you immediately, without recourse."

"Oh no," Ruth wailed, her arms flying up in despair.

"Calm yourself. I argued we could not in all conscience discharge you until we were certain you had not been infected while in our care. I've arranged for you to go to the Toronto Preventorium until we can get all of this cleared up. I telegrammed your father. He didn't want you home with all the children at risk—he says there isn't room for you to be apart from them."

"He's right. Everyone is on top of everyone else. But what's the Preventorium? I haven't heard about that before."

"Your home situation is unacceptable. The Preventorium is a place designed to hold people exposed to TB in a safe place until we are sure they aren't infected. There are a lot of children there, too. You might continue some of the work you were doing with the Inuit here. In any case, your father will allow you to go, provided we cover the cost."

Ruth flinched.

"Now, he's not your responsibility, either. Your parents are your parents. You owe them respect, but you aren't responsible for their behaviour. Or their irre-sponsibility." Mrs. Graham cleared her throat. "The school has agreed to cover the cost of your recovery time. I have to say, selfishly, and although I hope you don't become symptomatic, in a way I'm glad this happened."

"Glad?"

"A lot of students have been harmed while at work here. Injuries, infections, these things happen. The usual procedure is to discharge them while crying crocodile tears. Because of Miss Brannigan, you became so well-known here that they didn't dare just send you off into the darkness. It of course isn't the best for you, but you may have inadvertently provided help for your colleagues. There's even talk of paying for sick leave."

Ruth sighed. "Well, at least there may be some good."

"Exactly," Mrs. Graham said, briskly. "So, cheer up. You'll have a lovely restful stay at the Preventorium. It's somewhat monkish, but you are used to that from the nursing residence." She stood to go. "We'll be sending you in the next few days. We want to get an X-ray and a Mantoux test before you go just in case you show active disease. Were you taking your temperature?"

"Yes." Ruth pointed to the thermometer in its cup, the graph of readings. Mrs. Graham peered at it.

"Hmm. You seem to be measuring a lot. Are you feeling well?"

"Yes, it's just that...."

"You are feeling anxious. I don't blame you. Such an unfortunate incident."

"How is Jerry—Mr. Bousquet? Did he make it? He was so sick."

"Mr. Bousquet? Somehow, he is holding his own. There is even some hope that this latest rupture cleared out one of his most infected areas. They are giving him blood transfusions and hope to do a lung resection in the next couple of days. With God's help, this will be all he'll need for now. He is very fortunate it hasn't spread to his other organs or bones. Perhaps," she gestured to Ruth's missal, "You could use this time to try for some divine intervention for him."

"I will," she said, earnestly. She'd try, but she didn't think God was speaking to her these days. She hadn't been overly observant for months now, despite carrying around the prayer book like a talisman. And after all her misfortunes, she seriously doubted God was looking out for her. But she still thought it might be worth asking for help for someone else. God might listen to that.

"Very well. That's all. I'll let you know as plans progress." Mrs. Graham stood. She paused. "Miss Maclean, I'm afraid I misjudged you. You continue to surprise me. The letter you sent to Dr. Anderson, recommending Miss Brannigan to replace you as your assistant and asking for his help in getting her OR experience—that was an unexpected kindness to one who has hurt you. I rather suspect you are growing up at last. I sincerely hope all of this passes and you can come back to us." She cleared her throat. "I only wish my other students showed half your responsibility."

She closed the door gently, leaving Ruth open-mouthed with shock. Had she really won over the dragon? She daren't trust her thoughts. Mrs. Graham seemed so willing to believe the worst about her.

She wondered if she would hear from Patricia. Her recommendation wasn't as truly selfless as Mrs. Graham thought. If Patricia worked with the doctors, there were two possible outcomes that would work in Ruth's favour. First, Patricia might meet the doctor of her dreams and focus there. And second, she might be caught out for her sloppy practice by someone other than the nurses with whom she was competing. A word from the doctors regarding her might rid Ruth of her for good.

Ashamed of her thoughts, she pulled out the well-worn missal and tried to say the "Prayer for Patience," but it didn't help. She didn't want to "meet bravely and calmly all that thou sendest us." She had to admit she was tired of fighting endless battles simply to live her life, to study as a nurse, to provide solace to her patients. She was exhausted. Perhaps the Preventorium was a good idea after all.

Betty cried buckets at her from the doorway when she found out Ruth was being moved. After listening to her wail, Ruth couldn't help but wonder if her weepies might be because of another romantic misadventure. Betty admitted yes. It helped Ruth with her guilt to understand it wasn't because she'd be away for what Ruth hoped would only be a couple of weeks.

Chapter Forty

In the Preventorium

THE IODE Children's Hospital, known originally as the Preventorium, started in 1912 in a large home and property in north Toronto donated by the late Sir Albert Gooderham. For almost twenty years, it provided treatment in a homelike atmosphere for children who had been exposed to tuberculosis. In 1941 it was thought desirable to use it as a convalescent hospital and in 1948 its role was changed to that of a children's sanatorium of 115 beds.

Rees, IODE Ontario—A Proud History.

T ransferring to Toronto wasn't simple. Because of the risk of transmitting infection, they couldn't just send Ruth on a train, so she had to wait for a truck going from Kingston General to St. Michael's Hospital in Toronto and catch a ride with the driver. It was a bumpy ride, and the fellow kept looking all scared eyes at her, so Ruth sat in the far corner and kept her mask on. It was too noisy to talk. Ruth was just as glad. She didn't want to answer any awkward questions.

When Ruth finally arrived at the Preventorium, her jaw dropped. The building was an enormous place, all painted white, with awnings and balconies on every side. A group of children played outside, running about after a ball. They shouted to each other in a gaggle of languages, seeming to understand the game despite that. The inside was packed to the rafters with people of all ages, mostly children, though a few adults squeezed in here and there. The hospital was free here for people from Toronto, but because she came from out of the area, she had to pay for her stay. As she came through the doors, the staff immediately took her to the main office where they worked out the payment details. After that, she was sent to be screened and allocated to a room.

The harried nurse that took her temperature had her desk covered with index cards, all marked with different colours.

"What are you doing with all that?" Ruth asked. "Looks like a lot of administration."

The nurse, Susan, sighed and gave a rueful grin. "Oh. That's the latest innovation in TB care, of course." She looked at Ruth. "You're a nurse, right?"

"Just a nurses' aide. I was in nursing school. Hope to get back to it."

"I hope so, too! We need you! So, I can tell you the ministry of health has decided we need to track every patient with TB in a new system, entering all this data on these cards. When they are discharged to the community, their card goes with them to a community nurse, who then knows where to find them and how to follow up. If they have homes and give us the right information, that is. And all of this, in addition to the bills we must prepare for the Department of Health to get paid back for their treatment. It's a nightmare, but if we don't get the bills sent to the DOH, the municipality won't get refunded for the costs, and they aren't happy." She brightened. "You're only here because of an exposure, right? No symptoms?"

Ruth smiled inside. She knew she'd end up being put to work. Free help was too hard to find.

"So maybe you would help me fill these out? All the information is on their hospital charts, but it needs to be transferred over. It would be such a help if you could because you know all the terminology!"

"I'd love to help. I'm wondering though if I am working here...."

Susan looked at her sharply and smiled. "If we could reduce what you are paying. I'm sure we can work something out, not a salary or anything, but cover costs of food or something. The Imperial Order Daughters of the Empire, who are funding the Preventorium, don't have a lot of money. And as you can see, there's a lot of demand. The original plan was to look after children exposed to TB only, but their mothers would come along, so there are a few wards of women as well. And the immigrants coming over from Europe! So many every week!"

"I heard all the languages when I came in. It must make it hard to maintain order! I understand about the pay. Covering my costs, though, would make my sponsors happy," said Ruth. "I hate to think of them having to pay for me. The Kingston San doesn't have much money, either, but they arranged the fee for me."

"I wouldn't fret too much. After all, you got sick working for them, didn't you? Now, let's get you settled, and after that I can show you how this all works." She laughed, a short bark. "Which remains to be seen. If it works, I mean."

They stood and walked through several hallways to a long ward, where all the beds lined up, with a cupboard between each one.

"This doesn't seem like it would prevent transmission." Ruth said.

"This is for people not showing symptoms. Once you start—I hope you never do—you get placed in a smaller ward with others who are actually ill with the disease."

Ruth frowned. This wouldn't be much better than going home and bunking in with all her siblings.

"This is the women's ward. The children stay in another ward and their mothers spend most of the day there, just come back to sleep. It's quiet most of the day, if you need to rest." She looked closely at Ruth. "Do you need a lie down now, after your travels?"

"I think I'll be fine. Maybe I will just unpack and have a bit of a wash."

"After that, come join me to help with the paperwork. No time like the present. Can you find your way back?"

"I don't think so—such a confusing place—and so packed with people!"

"I'll draw you a little map on this notepad. If you get lost, ask for Susan Richie's office."

Ruth took the map and started unpacking the few things she'd brought with her. She didn't plan to stay long. She was glad she'd brought a little lock for the cupboard door. The size of this place meant everyone wandered anywhere. She washed her face and hands in the washroom at the end of the ward, and, pulling out the map, started her way back to Susan's office.

Amazed, she wended her way through the hallways crowded with people, staff and patients, both. The children swarming around were the most startling to Ruth. This didn't seem at all like a good place to prevent infection. She practically saw the germs floating about. After a few wrong turnings, she arrived at Susan's office.

"You found me! Fantastic. Let's get you oriented and set up, and then we'll head for dinner. Here's your desk. I cleared it off while you were getting settled. I hope it will be okay?"

The tiny desk was piled with paperwork but had a window beside it and a comfortable seat. Ruth sat, eager to get started.

"We'll start with the ones closest to discharge," Susan explained, handing Ruth a stack of cards and a pile of charts. "Those are due to go home next week. Honestly, I don't know when they think I'll have time to do all this. You're a godsend!"

She handed Ruth a fistful of pens and sat briefly beside her, showing her all the information that had to be transferred: name, address, contact person, dates of admission and discharge, medical orders. "You've got good handwriting, I hope?"

"I think so," said Ruth, but by the dinner hour her hand was cramped from so much writing. The pens kept clumping, and she had to stop several times to rinse them out. Her fingertips were blackened by ink, despite her careful filling of the pens. She kept being distracted by the noises of the children playing outside, too. It made her lonely for her family. She was watching them and wringing out her hand when Susan came up beside her.

"I know," said Susan, sympathetically. "Lots of writing. I keep trying to get some of those new ballpoint pens, but they don't seem to make them quickly enough. And they are so expensive!"

"Ballpoint? What are those?"

"From what I've seen, they are like a regular pen, but the point is this tiny ball that rolls out a bit of ink at a time. No blobbing, no need to blot anything. And they go on forever! I saw one at the store the other day and wanted it. We do so much writing it's hard to keep the pens filled and happy. As you have seen. Don't worry too much about your pens as you go on—we clean them all at the end of the day. Throw them in the cup if they give you grief." She stood, checked her watch. "It's almost dinner hour now. Let's get them cleaned up and we can grab dinner."

Ruth gathered the pens and stacked up her cards, after blotting the top one.

"Wow," said Susan. "You did a lot of them! That's fantastic!"

They took apart the pens and put them in a basin to soak clean. "We'll let them dry out and refill them after dinner. That way, we'll be ready to dive in tomorrow morning. That is, if you'll still be up for helping?"

"Yes! It's actually kind of interesting reading about all the histories of the patients. What varied lives they all lead!"

"And yet they are all getting TB. Or getting exposed to it. It's a sad state of affairs. I wish we'd get a handle on it."

"Me too. The surgeries I've seen at the Sanatorium are all pretty brutal."

"Have you been able to see the surgeries? I never got into the OR before they placed me here. I'd like to get back to real nursing."

Chatting and laughing about nursing school and their experiences, they wandered down to the dining hall, finding a corner table away from most of the crowds, where the other nursing staff from the Preventorium joined them. Susan introduced Ruth all around, which made her feel very welcome.

After dinner, Susan looked over at Ruth. "You've had a busy day. Why don't you head on up to bed? I'll ready the pens. Don't want you to get sick while you're here. Bad for business." She smiled, patted Ruth on the back. "I'm so grateful to have your help. See you tomorrow. Shall we say 9 AM? I'll do some ward work before I get started on administration."

Ruth smiled, relieved. She was tired. "Now the last challenge: finding my bed," she said.

"Oh, I'm heading up that way," said one of the other nurses. "Follow me and I'll set you right. You'll figure this place out soon enough."

Ruth followed her to the dorm, where most of her roommates already lay sleeping. She found a letter on top of her covers, from Kingston. It was from

George. He said he missed her and hoped she stayed well, and then gave her the news that Jerry was still in intensive care. Ruth fought back tears. She wished she could be there, see how he seemed for herself. And how sweet of George to write to her! She really must write back. Stretching, she told herself, yes, she'd write the next time she sat down to write to her family. Tucking the letter under her pillow, she headed to the bathroom. She gratefully managed a quick wash and threw herself into her bed. No one was talking, the silence blissful. In no time at all, she fell asleep.

Chapter Forty-One

Settling in

If children remained in the home, then (Nurse Dorothy) Deming was firm on her prohibitions against kissing, advising physicians that their patients "must understand that the family's love is shown in other ways while (they are) sick, and the family must take individual responsibility for keeping the rule: No Kissing." Dorothy Deming wrote "Home Care of Tuberculosis: A Guide for the Family" in 1949. She also advised that infants and young children should never be allowed to play in the sickroom, though older children could stand in the doorway...if possible, children should be sent away to live elsewhere until family physicians felt confident about their safe return.

Burke, p. 143.

The next morning arrived suddenly with a clanging of bells. The rest of the room seethed with women getting up and wandering to the bathroom. Ruth laid back for a moment after checking her watch. It was only 6 AM. How was this supposed to be restful?

One of her ward mates came by and sat on the bed beside hers. "You okay? Because we're supposed to report anyone who isn't."

"I'm fine," said Ruth, hurriedly. "Just waiting for the rush to pass."

"Okay, but I'm just warning you, you've gotta hurry if you want a decent breakfast." She leaned forward and stage-whispered, breathing unbrushed mouth smells into Ruth's face. "Some of these girls eat enough for seven." She sat back. "Better get moving."

Ruth pushed her covers back. She wasn't overly concerned. She was used to a slice of toast for breakfast, with marmalade, if she was lucky. Still, she didn't want to miss that.

She hurried through her morning ablutions and was quickly dressed, teeth brushed and all, ready to head down to the dining hall. She was astonished by what she saw there.

A huge banquet was laid out, eggs, sausage, ham, porridge, honey, breads of several kinds, even pastries. Ruth couldn't help herself. Her stomach urged her into the line, and she loaded up her plate, balancing it and a cup of hot coffee as she searched for a place to sit.

Her bad-toothed confidant waved to her and pointed to a spare seat. Somewhat unhappily, Ruth went over to join her.

"Good, you got some of the good stuff. Are you going to eat both sausages? Cos they watch me and I wasn't allowed to take all that I wanted."

Ruth handed over one of her sausages, but quickly dug into the other, just in case that, too would be demanded.

"Did you notice?" the other asked, waving her arm about. "No men. Only women." She burped. "On even days the children go first."

"Who watches all the children?"

"Oh, the nurses feed them. They have to get them to eat, and I've never been good at getting my brats to do what I tell 'em. Besides, they're probably infections, little runts." She laughed, showing her teeth with bits of the sausage embedded in them. "I know my little 'uns have something wrong with them all the time. I'm enjoying my break, let me tell you."

Ruth turned her head to avoid having to see her neighbour, pretending to look around the room. She gulped down her breakfast and slurped her coffee so fast she burned her lip.

"Well, I've got to run," she said, standing to go. "I'm working this morning."

"Work? Are they paying you? How much? Could they use my help?"

Ruth didn't answer, escaping with her tray to drop off the dishes. She fled so quickly she was sure her stomach was going to give her trouble later. The heavy breakfast wasn't something she'd ever gotten used to. From now on, she vowed, just a quick piece of toast and coffee. Far away from that woman.

But what to do now? It was still only early, and she wasn't due at work for an hour. She decided to explore her surroundings, wandering the halls of the Preventorium until she was hopelessly lost and had to ask for directions.

There were so many people here. Children ran everywhere, and the noise was incredible. They all had runny noses and food down their fronts and several of them needed a diaper change, badly. She shook her head. And her father wanted her to live like this, with little children all about? She could barely stand running the Sunday school at home, and that was only for an hour once a week.

When she got to the office and found Susan, she couldn't help asking how they all got placed there.

"Well, this is a spot for children who were exposed to TB but haven't shown symptoms as yet. It's designed to keep them away from both well people and those who are actively spreading the disease, hoping to get them healthy enough to fight off TB themselves. TB seems to be going wild of late, and we don't know for sure why. Some argue it's all about overcrowding in homes, or because of all the new immigrants. You are an outlier."

"I was pretty heavily exposed—one of my patients bled all over me. Since I was working in the San, I guess they thought the likelihood of me being positive was high. They were going to send me home, but my mother has all these tiny babies and there was no place for me to stay."

"Ah. And, probably, they also figured you could help out while here."

Ruth laughed. "Yes, I seem to be sent places to fill staffing holes. Still, could be worse."

"I called the Kingston San, and they are delighted you are working here, and they won't have to pay for you. My next question is, if all is well in the next week, would you like to move to the staff accommodation for the rest of your stay?"

"Oh, would I! Do I just need to stay negative?"

"Yes, we'll test you in a week and if all is good, we'll bring you up to our place. They still want you to stay here for at least a month, but if you are clear, there's no reason for you to stay in the dorms."

Ruth told Susan about her breakfast chum, and over some inappropriate laughter they started work.

Ruth's work at the Preventorium seemed to expand to fill any free time. Whenever she was finished with the charting and the discharge cards, she'd be sent to make beds or sort laundry. She didn't mind, really, as it passed the time, and the staff were all so glad to see her, but it was exhausting.

Once a week she tried to write to her parents, reassuring them she was still well and not laden with TB, but often she was too tired to make up cheery stories. They didn't write back, and she was left wondering until Meg finally sent her a big fat letter filled with news from all the family.

Ruth sat down in the staff room to share it all with Susan, and they laughed over the notes from the little ones. Funny crayon pictures of Ruth's mother, heavily pregnant, and of her father, bushy eyebrows and all, were pegged up on the bulletin board to share with everyone.

Ruth sobered up when she read Meg's letter, though.

"It's my mother," she said to Susan. "This pregnancy is really taking it out of her. Meg says she's resting most of the day, which must be driving her wild. She's used to working twenty-six hours a day."

"How is she managing? There are still six wee ones, right?"

"Yes. I don't understand why they don't do something to stop the babies from coming. It's not like we can afford them." Ruth shook her head. "Meg says she's taking over the Sunday baking—that's good. We always serve food after service," she explained. "Most of the families up around there are poorer even than we are, and so we share what we can, plus it brings them to church. My mother is a fantastic cook, but fortunately Meg can almost do as well."

"Do they need you there?"

"Oh heavens, no! I burn everything and I'm no good at sewing. Though," she paused, "I suppose I am getting quite good at cleaning and tidying."

"You know," said Susan, "when you finish your nursing course, you'll be earning good money. That will be more useful to your family than someone who can wield a mop."

"Oh thank you, Susan! I always feel so guilty here when I know how hard things must be at home. But I so want to graduate and start working as a full nurse. I love the figuring things out in nursing, and I know the money will help. My older brother Billy was sending money home, but he's ... he's...."

"Oh, no—is he a casualty?"

"We haven't heard. That's the hard thing. No news is good news, I guess, but keeping up hope is so difficult."

"I'll bet." Susan rose and turned on the kettle. "Only thing for it is another cuppa. You want one?"

"Lovely."

"Didn't you get some other letters today?"

"Oh, yes." Ruth frowned. "One from the dratted boy back home who still wants to marry me and birth children to fill up the church. If I'd ever considered that, this place has cured me of any desire."

"I hear you. Creepy little vectors of infection, all of them. Still, if you had your own..."

"Ugh. Not after watching my mother give birth all those times. I dread my maternity rotation in school. I'll have to keep myself from shouting at everyone, 'What were you thinking?'"

Susan laughed. She pulled out two cookies from the tin they hid behind the silverware. "Sweet?"

"Oh, don't say that, either. The other letter is from a patient who also says we're made for each other. He keeps calling me that." She reached out her hand. "I'll take one, though."

"Must be nice to be in such demand. No one is proposing to me, even people I don't want to."

"That's the company you keep. There's no male under fifty at this place. You need to get a transfer." Ruth bit into her cookie with gusto.

"Don't I know it. I'm hoping for a change soon. I want to get a position before the WRENS take all the good jobs."

"Well, there we go. Our task for next week. Find you a new job. One with handsome men about."

Following their chat, after they were done with the paperwork for the day, they pored over the newspapers and the newsletters from the local hospitals, searching for a position for Susan. They wrote application after application and finally, after another two weeks, an offer came through from The Hospital for Sick Children.

"More vectors," cautioned Ruth.

"Yes, but it's an exciting place to be! I hear they are going to open up a research institute. And they do so many interesting treatments and see such unusual things. I'm excited!"

"When do you start?"

"In two weeks, probably just after we get rid of you. Good timing. It wouldn't be the same here without you."

"I'm going to miss you, too. I hope you write."

"As long as you promise to write back."

Ruth blushed. Susan had told her she should write more to her family, but by the time they got done for the day, she felt she had nothing to say.

"I promise," she said, giving Susan a hug. "You've made my stay here positively tolerable."

"And then when you graduate, you can come and work with me in the big city. Get away from the small places for good. You haven't been able to see much of Toronto while you are here. Maybe before you go, we can take a day to explore."

"I'd love that!"

True to her word, before they went on their separate ways, Susan took Ruth around the downtown core of Toronto. The cars and noise and gigantic buildings and people were quite overwhelming, and though she had a fun day, on the train back to Kingston, Ruth thought she might prefer to stay where she was. Kingston was manageable, at least.

Chapter Forty-Two

Home again

Separate marked utensils

Spitting only into sputum cups

Sputum cups to be boiled every day for ten minutes and its contents burned

Patient's bedclothes to be kept separate and boiled at home

Dwellings to be fumigated at least once a month

Dust-gathering corners to be swept up every day

And, most importantly and therefore usually in bold or capital lettering:

NO FONDLING OR KISSING OF OTHER MEMBERS OF THE FAMILY, PARTICULARLY NOT OF CHILDREN

MARRIED PARTNERS TO SLEEP IN SEPARATE BEDS PREFERABLY SEPARATED BY A PARTITION

MOST IMPORTANT; THE SURVIVING HEAD OF THE HOUSEHOLD IMMEDIATELY TO NOTIFY THE DISPENSARY OF THE DEATH OF THE PATIENT

Dormandy, p. 312.

G etting released had taken over a month, what with all the requirements for checks for discharge. Amazingly, Ruth hadn't converted to positive on the skin test, and her lungs remained clear to X-ray. She didn't enjoy the gastric lavages to do the last check, but, she told herself, at least now she can understand what the patients were going through. The good food helped her, too, so by the time she was ready to return to Kingston, she felt healthier than she had since starting there. Her old room seemed blissfully quiet after all the racing and shouting children at the Preventorium, and someone had draped her bed with her mother's afghan. She wrapped it around her, sighing gratefully.

Mrs. Graham appeared delighted to welcome her back. "Now, my girl, back at it. The next nursing intake is in September. You should be ready for it. I plan to recommend you for acceptance. Your colleague, Miss Richie, has written a recommendation as well."

Ruth hugged the astonished matron, then jumped back, blushing. "Oh, I'm sorry, Matron—I'm just so happy! Thank you, thank you!"

Mrs. Graham tutted. "Don't thank me. Thank your colleagues. They'll be very glad you're here."

Ruth sang to herself as she unpacked. She hung up her uniforms and heard excited knocks on her door. Opening it, she saw Jocelyn and Beth, and a smattering of other nurses from the San.

They all talked at once. "Are you all better?"

"We missed you!"

"We're so glad you're back!"

"I'll bet some people are going to be extremely happy you are back," one nurse said, winking.

"None of that," Ruth said firmly. "I will not allow any new rumours. No romance for me!"

The nurses all gathered into the room and started updating Ruth on the patients, the doctors, news from the school. It overwhelmed her, and Ruth was glad when they left. It was so nice to be welcomed, but the babble exhausted her. She shut the door and laid down on her bed, closing her eyes. Suddenly, she sat bolt upright. No one had mentioned Patricia.

Ruth had her first shift the following afternoon. She poked her head into the children's ward and smiled at the sight of Pauloosie in the corner, reading to a young boy. The other children were running around the ward like well children. He waved to her. She waved back and, encouraged, entered the soldier's ward.

So many unfamiliar faces in the beds. For a moment, she stopped at the door, stunned. A new nurse Ruth hadn't met came up to her.

"Hi—I'm Anna Sellers. Lots of changes, eh?"

"Where are they all?"

"Oh, a bunch of them have been discharged home or somewhere. They seemed a bit better, and we had a fresh wave of men in."

Ruth strolled down the ward. She spotted a few recognizable heads. Over, playing cards, she thought it was ... "Jerry? Jerry?" She walked swiftly over.

He stood. He stood! "Miss Maclean! It's so good to have you back!"

She stopped herself from hugging him, but barely. "You look—you look so well!"

"I know. C'est incroyable. But they despaired with me and gave me the chance to try a new drug. It seems to be working. Now," he waved at the rest of the card table, "They all are on it."

Ruth looked at the other men, all smiling, with nary a cough between them.

"It's true," said Anna. "Right after you left the medication came here. The doctors started with the sickest..."

"That was me!" Jerry inserted.

Anna went on, "...to test it out and voila! They are really recovering. It is almost unbelievable!"

Ruth's heart soared. So many young lives—maybe this meant they would go on, get over this dread disease. She sent a mental thank you heavenward.

"Unfortunately," Anna gestured to the ward, "We still have a lot of work to do. Can I give you report? I'd like to get home."

"Of course," Ruth said, and soon they had their heads together, talking over the patients' needs and doctor's orders. Ruth sprung into her work, turning patients, checking temperatures, providing water and tidying.

She was so busy rubbing one man's back where a hot spot warned of an impending pressure ulcer that she jumped when she a hand tapped her shoulder. She spun around. It was Dr. Anderson.

"Glad you're back in the traces, Miss Maclean."

She laughed. "Not as glad as I am. How are you?"

"I'm missing my right-hand nurse." He smiled. "The good news is, we aren't having to cast as many people lately. Did you hear about the Streptomycin? It's a miracle drug!"

"It sounds like it. Such good news. All the men are talking about it."

"I only hope we can get enough of it for everyone. Meantime, we do still have some patients who are struggling with bone TB. I'd like to book you in to help me tomorrow, if that would work."

"I'll check with Matron. Isn't Miss Brannigan able to assist you?" Ruth couldn't resist asking. She was exploding with curiosity. She hadn't seen Patricia anywhere.

"Ah. That... didn't work out. Besides, I heard you are applying for nursing this fall. Good to update your experience."

Ruth shook her head. You couldn't scratch yourself here without someone knowing about it.

"I wanted to say thanks," Ruth said, tucking the covers around the patient with a final calming pat. "They told me you spoke up for me. I'm very grateful."

Dr. Anderson snorted. "I like competence. You are competent. It seemed ridiculous to oust you because of some sleazy rumours." He smiled again. "Talk to you tomorrow, then."

Ruth turned to the next patient, a song in her heart. He said she was competent! In all of her life, she'd heard that only a few times.

As she worked her way down the rooms and the ward, she missed a familiar face. Where did George go? When she reached Jerry, she had to ask.

"Where's your partner in crime, Jerry? Did he go home?"

"Last I heard he headed off to Toronto to check on some girl in the Preventorium there. They discharged him two weeks ago. Didn't he catch you?"

"No—I never saw him. Did he really go to Toronto?" Ruth blushed. It was flattering, she thought. Then a chill passed over her. She'd been so busy at the Preventorium she'd barely written to anyone, collapsing into bed right after her shift. She knew she'd sent a letter to George once, but she didn't remember if she'd done any more. Would he be angry at her? She knew her mother had sent a scolding note after she'd been there a few weeks and hadn't written.

Jerry looked puzzled. "That's odd. I was sure he'd have connected. He seemed intent."

Ruth felt worms tumbling about in her stomach. Happy worms or worried ones? She couldn't tell.

"Well, he missed me. I guess he wasn't as determined as all that."

Jerry grinned. "I imagine he will find you before long."

"Well, enough of him. Let's get you checked over."

Ruth examined Jerry, glad to observe his clearer breathing and lack of fever. It seemed his main problem now would be recovery from all his surgeries.

"You seem to be doing so well! What happened after I left?"

"After I cough all over you? I am so sorry about that."

"Don't be silly. You could hardly control that."

"I don't remember the first days. I think they gave me a bunch of blood, sent for the priest, the usual. Sacré bleu. Then they started this medication, eh? I think they figured they wouldn't hurt me any more than I was already." He coughed, a normal clearing the throat one. It did Ruth good to hear it. "They did another surgery to cut off the mauvaise bits. I'm still sore from that, but other than that, well, I am like a new man. What's left of me, that is."

"I'm so glad. Let me get the nurse to give you something for pain. Meantime, it is still rest period. Into bed you go."

She settled Jerry in and went to get the nurse.

After the rest period, she led the men in their post-op exercises. She was glad she'd remembered all the steps, the stretches to correct the slumping after lung removal, the abdominal tightening exercises. The social support staff had continued the painting classes in the main lounge, and she was enchanted to view the men's creations. In another corner, a group of men whittled toys over a collection box, bits of wood flying all about. She sensed a new feeling of hope, and it warmed her.

"We can't wait until they let us go outside with this." One man lifted his whittling project, a gnome. "I hear the weather next week will be dry, so we should be able to."

"I hope so!" The nurses still pushed the patients out into fresh air, but avoided having them out in the rain in case they got chilled. Spring in Kingston was a varied season, with sudden storms and winds. Outside time took careful planning.

At the end of her shift, everyone was tucked in bed, backs rubbed, beds tidied, all around them clean as a whistle. Ruth looked over her domain, well-pleased. She was glad to be back, but also so tired. After the different duties at the Preventorium, the work here seemed backbreaking. Never mind, she told herself. You'll adapt.

She handed over the ward to the night nurse and wearily headed outside for a breath of air.

"You never wrote," came a voice from the darkness.

Chapter Forty-Three

A threat

The use of cod liver oil and tomato juice is a MUST. This combination of food and medicine has been proved to be a preventative and possibly a cure for tuberculosis of the bowel.

Ongwanada, p. 15

R uth jumped. "What?"

George stepped into the light. "You never wrote to me," he said, his voice dripping acid. "You could have written."

Ruth hung her head. She should have written. She wasn't sure why she hadn't. "You only wrote to me once, George. I heard you'd gone home."

George snorted. "I did. Your home."

"What?" She froze.

"Yeah. Drove up to Cloyne. Met up with your dad. He likes me. Your mother likes me, too. I told them all about our plans."

"Our plans? What plans are these?" A hot wire of alarm and anger burned up Ruth's spine.

"Don't play the fool. We're going to be married. We talked before you left. And I already spoke to your father, remember? He's all for it."

"I never said...."

"Yeah, everyone told me you were a flirt. I said you weren't, that you loved me. The guys all thought we were a done deal." He frowned. "But then you didn't write." His voice grew louder. "Maybe you need to be reminded of our agreement."

"I never agreed," Ruth cried, as George stepped closer, wrapped his arms around her like a vise.

"Give me a kiss. You want to. Everyone believes we've already been to bed together. I've even told your dad."

She was surrounded by the reek of alcohol. Ruth pushed at George, trying to break away. "What? You said we'd been ... intimate?"

George laughed, a nasty guttural sound. "Yeah. He cried, but I said I was still willing to marry you. He was SO relieved. Especially when I told him about all the other men you'd been with, that doctor, even that Indian guy."

Ruth pushed him harder. "You!" She spat in his face. "How dare you? I never...you never even touched me!"

"Oh, yes, I did. We held hands in front of everyone, remember?"

"That's only because you grabbed my hand." She struggled, but George had a firm grip. The alcohol haze coming from him made her dizzy and her heart was racing. Her fear intensified as he pulled her toward the dark side of the building, the side with no open windows and more than a few looming bushes.

"Let me go!"

George put his hand over her mouth, pulled her head in against his shoulder so she couldn't escape. "Oh yeah, I'll let you go when I'm done. You owe me. I stood up for you back on the ward, remember. They'd have fired you if I hadn't." He swore. "It is not like other women would be seen with me after this disease. They all run away. Can't even buy them a goddamn drink." He breathed hard into her face, out of breath from her struggles. The mix of alcohol and tobacco almost made her retch.

Ruth struggled and kicked, pulling partway free. George grabbed at her. Ruth relaxed for a moment, then twisted, surprising George, and loosening his grip. Her older brother had taught Ruth a lot.

George lost his balance for a second and Ruth grabbed his arms and kneed him, hard, in his groin. She bet her father wasn't aware she knew that move. That she had time to form that idea surprised her, but the entire event seemed to float by in slow motion.

George gasped. "You'll pay for that," he said, reaching for her again. But she was free and ran, sobbing now, into the light. She raced along the path. Fortunately, George's tuberculosis damaged lungs slowed him up, and she was able to reach the building before him. She hoped the door in the back was unlocked. It was. She flung herself in through the door, slammed it shut and locked it.

Ruth shrunk below the window frame, peeking out at the sidewalk outside. She heard running feet above her—she must have alerted the other nurses. Good. She saw George storming around outside. While she watched, he pulled back his fist and punched a parked car. The car dented. He stood, holding his hand while he swore, then walked into the dark.

Ruth collapsed in relief, gasping for air and trying to sort out her feelings.

Nurses from the residence encircled her, demanding to know what happened. Ruth at first couldn't answer, her sobs blocking her ability to speak.

The relief supervisor arrived, clad in a housecoat. "What are you girls up to now? Didn't I tell you to just use the door, for God's sake? This isn't the 20s."

Ruth looked up, her tear-streaked face telling her story. The supervisor snapped into action.

"Girls—tea, with sugar. Miss Jones—get the whiskey from my room. Miss Forest—get a blanket from the linen closet."

The students leapt to obey and soon Ruth was wrapped in a cozy comforter, a hot toddy in her hand.

"Drink that," the supervisor commanded. "Got it down you?"

Ruth gulped the tea. It burned going down, but it felt righteous, like the damning of a vengeful God. Would she never be allowed to succeed?

"Was it the man we've been watching out for, girls?"

The other students shrugged. "I'm not sure," one said. "We saw a guy out in the street, but he looked different. Perhaps he changed his coat."

"He punched that car," offered another. "Looks like he's heading to emergency."

The supervisor lifted and spoke into the phone in a low voice. By the time she came back, Ruth was warmer, but she still shuddered.

She put her hand over Ruth's. "Now, they'll be on the lookout for him. Can you tell me what happened?"

Between sobs, Ruth related the story. The nurses looked on, mouths open.

"Okay," said the supervisor. "We're having trouble with a fellow attacking the nurses when they were walking home alone at night. You've been away, correct? You wouldn't have been aware. We told everyone to walk in a group."

"But that's hard," said one student. "Sometimes we get off duty late and there's no one around."

"I just stepped out for a breath of air! He must've been watching the door." Ruth gulped. "Has he been hanging around all this time?"

"We tried to get the police to walk more around here, but they stopped. They aren't too concerned, apparently. But you say you knew this fellow? Was he one of ours?"

"Yes," Ruth hiccupped, took another sip of her tea. "He was up on ward B. We were friends, I thought, but even though I said no, he told everyone we'd agreed to marry. He visited my family, he said. Told them we'd been...." She couldn't say any more, sobbing anew.

"What a crumb!" a student cried out.

"Oh, dear. There is a lot of talk about the nurses being too free with their favours. It would be easy to believe."

"But I wasn't!"

"Most of the accused nurses haven't either. It seems to be what the men are putting about to excuse their behaviour. I'm surprised it came to you—your Mrs. Graham rules her wards with an iron fist."

Ruth saw Patricia's face in her mind, leaning over George's bed. She was tiring of her family-acquired forgiveness rule. Time to take action. She shook herself, took a deep breath.

"Did you want us to call the police?"

"Oh yes," said Ruth, her voice still wavering but strong. "Can you call them, ma'am?"

"If you are sure? It can be rough reporting these things."

"I have nothing to be afraid of." Ruth squared her shoulders. "Would you call Mrs. Graham, also? She will need to know."

In minutes, an odd assembly stood around Ruth in the common room. Two senior nurses hastily dressed. Ruth, still looking a bit tumbled. Two policemen, pencils and notebooks in hand. And Betty, who had taken a cab over to provide support.

It was gruelling, reporting the incident. Ruth was questioned at length about her activities, and Betty being there wasn't helping. One policeman pointed at her, saying to his senior, "I've seen her around, sir. The Barriefield camp, sir. With all sorts."

Betty blushed but retorted, "Not with 'all sorts'. I only rode the bus a couple of times. Did you ever see her with me?"

"No."

"That's because she never was. She's been studying. She just now came back from Toronto, from the Preventorium. She got exposed to TB."

The police took two steps back.

"So, this isn't the same man you've been reporting, Ma'am?"

"I'm not certain. You said he went up to Cloyne, Miss Maclean?"

"Yes. He said he'd been staying with my parents, telling them lies."

"We should call them."

"No. My father already wants me to come home, but I don't want to go. I'm here to be a nurse. He'll demand I come back if he hears about this."

The policeman raised his eyebrows but shrugged. "Well, with his hand broken, this guy should be easier to track," he said.

The phone rang. It was the emergency room at the hospital. The junior policeman took the phone and talked for a few moments. He came back, notepad in hand, spoke into his senior's ear. He turned to Ruth. "How did you manage to get away, anyway? He seems strong. And you aren't that big."

"Older brother," said Ruth. "He taught me some tricks."

The senior policeman guffawed. "I'll bet. The emergency room reported he was there, broken hand and all—and walking with a limp. So we seem to have all the information to lay a charge."

"Oh no, please don't. That would make everything worse. I doubt he'll come after me again."

The policeman frowned. "Why did you call us, then? Throwing him in the drunk tank is all we can do."

"Please. I wanted to make a report in case he kept pestering me, and the others. Could you tell him I won't charge him if he stays away? Would that work? I really don't want this to be in the paper."

"I agree," said Mrs. Graham. "It's hard enough to recruit nursing students without this sort of thing being made public. Though I am tempted to push forward simply because this particular student has had more than the usual torment. It has got to stop. Someone has to be made accountable."

"Mrs. Graham." Ruth spoke quietly, but there was steel in her voice. "We both know who is responsible for this, and for all my other challenges. I agree someone should be held responsible, but I don't believe I should be sacrificed to do so."

Mrs. Graham had the decency to look embarrassed. "Yes," was all she said.

The meeting broke up and Mrs. Graham, Ruth, and Beth walked back upstairs together. "I am so sorry," Mrs. Graham said. "She pulled the wool over my eyes, too. I will deal with this," she added, more strongly. "Trust me."

Ruth said nothing.

Chapter Forty-Four

A bent ring

Sally left her room and although she was smiling she was unaccountably annoyed. The way Marcia Beach described her intention of devoting her life to nursing made her sound like a prig or an obnoxious misogamist. That wasn't true. She didn't object to love and marriage for others. It was only that her love was given to her work—to helping people—was that such a strong, unheard-of career?

Hancock, p. 9.

When Ruth returned to the ward the following evening, Jerry wouldn't meet her eye. Ruth worked through her routine, ignoring his quiet until she reached his bed at last.

"Jerry, what is going on? You've hardly looked at me all day."

Jerry sighed. "George came by this morning. With his hand in a cast. He wouldn't tell me what happened—do you know?"

Ruth said nothing, just looked down, straightened the already tidy blanket.

"He told me the police have it in for him. He was sad, acted hurt. Said someone reported him for a stupid stunt and now he isn't allowed to come here to visit anymore."

Ruth adjusted the bed table.

"Well," said Jerry, "he said there's nothing for him in Kingston, so he's heading back to New Brunswick. Told me to give you this." He leaned over to the bedside table, pulled open the drawer. He lifted out a small box.

"Oh, no," Ruth said.

"Oh, oui. He saved up from his disability pay for this for you."

She opened the box. Inside lay a ring, with a tiny diamond chip. It was bent and twisted.

"He said you said no."

"Not in so many words, no. But yes, I said no."

"He's usually a good guy, George. He just gets these ideas in his head without bothering to tell anyone else about them. He's been trying to get a job around here and they kept turning him down. It made him angry. He thought if you were with him, he'd do better. Anyway, he said you may as well keep the ring to remember what you'd turned down."

"A ring smashed into a knot? Yes. It will remind me exactly about George." She snapped the box shut. "Why don't you keep it? One day you'll meet a sweetheart who you can actually ask before assuming she's dying to marry you."

Jerry waved away the box. "Oh Ruth," Jerry said. "Come here."

Curious, she leaned down to hear his whisper.

"I don't feel that way about women."

She flipped up, eyes wide. A moment's pause, and then she smiled. "That's why we can be such good friends." She squeezed his hand. "Sleep well. I'm sorry about George going away."

"Are you?" Jerry asked.

"Well, really, no. He got me into all sorts of trouble. But I'm sorry you won't be able to visit with your friend."

"Wartime friends—some last, some don't. If we're meant to, we'll see each other again. He's a rotten card player, though. It'll be better with a different guy at the table."

"I'll say!" said the private on the next bed. "He cheated."

"Yeah," said another. "Good riddance."

Ruth stared wide-eyed at Jerry. How had she not known?

209

"You're too kind, miss," answered the private. "You think we're all nice people. Heck, you probably haven't even figured out Bruce over there—he's another bad 'un.'"

Bruce coughed out a laugh.

"Well, I guess I consider you all my brothers! Badly behaved, but good underneath."

The men laughed. Ruth turned back to Jerry, put her finger over her lips. No one would find out his secret from her. Jerry smiled at her, turned onto his side, and pulled up his covers.

Well. That explains a lot, thought Ruth. Jerry always hung around them, but never seemed interested in her or any other nurses. She'd assumed it was because he was so sick. Another idea crossed her mind. Maybe she could introduce him to her brother. They'd share a lot in common. Not that her father had any idea, of course. Getting them to meet would be a super-secret project. That is, assuming Billy ever came home.

She still hadn't spotted Patricia, and she didn't want to ask about that—time to let the waters settle. Dr. Anderson hadn't added anything to mentioning she hadn't worked out. Where did she go?

The week passed, and the mystery had not resolved. No one seemed to want to tell her. Ruth could stand it no longer and set up an appointment with Mrs. Graham. The matron already seemed to know what she wanted. She stood by her window, nervously twisting her fingers. Ruth had never seen her nervous. It was astonishing.

"Miss Maclean. I suspected I might be seeing you soon," she said. "I wasn't avoiding you. I've just been... awash in administration, you could say."

"I'm sorry to bother you," began Ruth. She wasn't.

"But you are wondering about Miss Brannigan. I would be if I were you. Such a malevolent girl. It's hard to even trace all the messes she started."

Ruth waited. A tiny bit of un-Christian joy started dancing in her chest. Would Patricia get her comeuppance at last?

"She attended the same nursing school as I did," Mrs. Graham explained. "I felt I should show some loyalty to a fellow alumnus. I admit I gave her a lot of latitude.

She told us she had a rotten childhood. Of course, she probably made that up, too. I wanted to give her every chance, and she was certainly smart enough. I tried pushing her to the San to teach her some humility, but it appears it had the opposite effect." She coughed. "It wasn't just your life she tried to ruin."

Ruth tilted her head, puzzled. What else happened?

"Come, sit down."

Ruth stepped forward and took a chair. Mrs. Graham sat opposite her. Her hands writhed in her lap. Ruth couldn't stop looking at them.

"Miss Brannigan has been busy. Your kind reference got her into contact with one of our more... adventurous residents. They became involved rather quickly."

They must have, thought Ruth. She'd only been gone for slightly over a month.

"Unfortunately, this resident is married. His wife created quite the scene. I didn't know about it at first. A new cohort of nurses' aides came in for the San and she'd moved back to the hospital rotation—she didn't have you to mentor, so there was no reason to keep her here."

Ruth's head spun.

"So... well... the dean found out about it. I was reprimanded at first, but he realized I hadn't been in charge of her at the time. The head nurse over there was relieved of her duties. There's a new nurse in place you'll be under when you go back to school."

"I heard. I assumed it was the usual rotation."

"No. She's new. A much more casual head nurse. I do hope it works out for the students. I prefer a tight ship myself."

Ruth said nothing. Loudly.

Mrs. Graham barked a laugh. "I see your point. Perhaps I didn't have as tight a ship as I thought. Has your friend Miss O'Donnell spoken to you? I'm afraid she's leaving, too."

"What? Why?"

"Those army boys. Always a bad bunch. Sowing their wild oats. I'm afraid she got rather caught up in the harvest."

"But she never said...."

"You were newly back and experienced that incident with Mr. Smith. I think she felt it might be inappropriate to mention."

"Oh. I've got to talk to her."

"Wait. Didn't you want to know about Miss Brannigan?"

"Is she still in Kingston?"

"No. She's seen to that. Again, unfortunately, she took the resident with her."

"Ah. She got her doctor, after all."

"Yes," Mrs. Graham said, grimly. "Honestly, this is like some sort of engagement school. Everyone keeps running off. I blame the war. And all the soldiers here all the time. The resident lost his position, as well. Last information I had about them said they fled off to the prairies to work there. His wife is still here, furious and threatening the school."

"You can't be held to account for Patricia—Miss Brannigan's behaviour. She is a special case. I don't believe I've met anyone like her."

"Oh, I have," Mrs. Graham said. "But that was when I worked in the prisons."

Chapter Forty-Five

Facing the family

Syringes

In some hospitals...it is necessary to boil the syringe and needle and even the solvent. ...When boiling hypodermic syringe and needle or when sterilizing them in a pressure cooker it is convenient to support them in a sieve, The point of the needle in the sieve swings free and so is protected from blunting. Attempts to sterilize a needle in a spoon over the flame of a lamp should be discouraged.

Suggested procedure:

Clean the neck of the ampoule with alcohol. Collect all the drug in the bottom of the ampoule by tapping the tip until the liquid leaves it. File the neck of the ampoule and break it, protecting the fingers with a sterile gauze or paper square; then withdraw the contents ... through the needle into the syringe...

Textbook of the Principles and Practice of Nursing, p. 724.

R uth swallowed her laugh and stood to go. "Thank you for your support, Mrs. Graham. I know it must have seemed I was more trouble than I'm worth."

Mrs. Graham smiled. "Well, yes. But then I remembered my time in nursing school, and I recognized how things can be twisted. Don't forget to get your application in for nursing school, remember. The deadline is next week."

"Mrs. Graham... can I take a few days to check in at home? I had a letter from my mother the other day before I came back, and she really wanted to see me. I didn't get a chance before the Preventorium."

"You may have this weekend, but only because I know you worked hard at the Preventorium. They were very grateful. Be back first thing on Monday."

"Thank you."

If she hurried, she might just be able to catch the milk bus. It left in an hour from downtown Kingston. She raced to the residence to pack and called a cab to get her to the station. She'd only get there mid-afternoon and have to leave early the next day, but that would have to do.

The ride up gave her time to wonder what to say. Had George really gone up and visited with her family? Did he tell them he wanted to marry her? What was she going to tell them?

Fortunately, they were surprised to see her, and everyone tumbled all over her at once, so no one had time to ask troublesome questions. Ruth had to admire the new baby, exclaim about how her siblings had grown, cheer on Meg's accomplishments as a seamstress, compliment her younger brother's ability to run and climb. She cuddled the little ones, played card games with the middle ones. It wasn't until later in the evening when the little ones had finally gone to bed that she could sit down with Meg and her parents. The new baby curled up in her mother's arms, napping until the next feed. For a moment, all seemed peaceful.

"So, how have things been going?" her father asked. "Are you feeling well?"

"Oh, yes. The rest did me good."

"We heard from an admirer of yours."

Ruth sunk into her chair, pulled the cat onto her lap for protection. Here we go, she thought.

"He spoke very highly of you. Said you were an asset to your profession."

"What?" She sat up. Surely George hadn't said that.

"It was a doctor you worked with—a surgeon, I believe. Was most upset when you had to go back to ward duty. He wrote to tell us he was going to recommend you for the next nursing intake. A Dr. Scofield, I believe."

Ruth shook her head. She only assisted him a few times. There's no way he would think that highly of her. Unless someone put him up to it.

"He mentioned working with a colleague who also spoke highly of you. It seems you have impressed the doctors, anyway. What do you think about trying again?"

"What?" Ruth was gawping, but the room seemed to spin.

"Ruth, dear, your father was asking if you wanted to try nursing school again. The six months we agreed to are almost finished. We'll understand if you want to stay home—it seems like you've had a terrible year, but...."

"Yes, yes, yes," Ruth cried. "I would love to try again. Thank you!" She leapt up to hug her father, startling the cat, who slunk off to the corner, insulted. "Oh, I'm sorry puss," she said, reaching out a finger to try to appease. Puss was having none of it and put herself out of touching reach and glared. There was a pause.

"So," Ruth hesitated to ask, "You didn't have any visitors from the school, did you?"

"No, dear, should we have?" Her mother put down the sock she was darning and looked at her closely.

Her father cleared his throat. "But what about your young man? George, was it? He seemed very keen."

"That didn't work out," said Ruth in a tone so flat they knew not to ask anything more.

Her father frowned at her mother but didn't say a word. Ruth could feel the tension draining from her like water out of a bucket. Finally, her father went to bed, and Meg left, too, to help soothe one of the little ones. Ruth and her mother were alone. They looked at each other for a moment, glad to be in each other's presence. Ruth's mother looked exhausted, dark circles under her eyes, her skin grey and grainy.

"Are you feeling well, Mother?" Ruth asked.

"Well, I am tired. This one still needs to feed all the time. The other children help, but there are so many of them! I wish I had a good way to prevent any more coming along. I don't think I can stand having another, though I love every one of them."

"Mother...."

"Never you mind. Your father wouldn't stand for anything your nursing knowledge might suggest."

"But Mother—"

"I know, I know. At least we're both too tired for any of that sort of activity to happen. God willing he'll lose interest." She chuckled, but there wasn't much heart in it. Ruth felt awful.

"Are you sure you don't want me to come home? Help out? I can," she said, though thinking her heart would break forever if she had to come back.

"Where would you sleep?" her mother asked. "Seriously, dear girl, you are the thing keeping me going. If you can get out of this... this... with a career, I'll feel as if I've done something right."

"Oh, Mother, you've done so much right. I couldn't do a half of what you do."

"Never you mind. Part of a parent's role is to raise children to live their own lives when the parents are gone. You're my success story. Go on back, write when you can. We'll be fine here."

Ruth hugged her mother tight. "Thank you, Mother," she said.

"And do watch out for the boys, will you? I didn't like the way that fellow seemed to take you for granted. You deserve to be wooed."

"Well, at least I'd like to have some input on the decision."

"Seems reasonable," said Ruth's mother. "Is he still around, that George fellow?"

"No, I think I've finally driven him off. He's gone back to New Brunswick, looking for work."

"Well, I do hope you meet nice man one day, though I've forgotten what it was like to be in a romance! Sometimes I think back to when it was just your father and me, how many adventures we had. Now it seems my adventures all deal with bleach and laundry. Speaking of which, would you mind bringing in the diapers? They should be dry by now."

Ruth stepped outside, tugged on the clothesline, pulling diaper after diaper off the line, listening to the squeak as it rolled. It was so quiet here. She could hear the hoot of an owl, rustling in the underbrush. She did miss the almost-silence. Kingston was always noisy, even on a Sunday morning when everyone should have been in church. Since the soldiers started moving into the area to take advantage of the upgrading classes, every moment seemed filled with rough male voices.

Pulling the last diaper off and putting the last clothespin into her mother's hand sewn bag, she sighed. She had two homes, it seemed, and both had a part of her heart.

Chapter Forty-Six

Proud parents

There were in 1946 still thousands of sanatoria and specialist hospitals crammed with young people seemingly condemned to an indefinite stay and probably to end their lives there. Three years later the sanatoria and hospitals were closing down.

White Death, p. 369

The rest of the weekend passed far too quickly, and her father agreed to drive her back so she could spend a little more time. She was quite teary-eyed when it came time to say goodbye to everyone. Almost the whole family, she thought. They still hadn't heard from Billy.

"Could you drop me at the nursing residence, Father? I'd like to catch up with Betty."

He grunted a reply. "Hope this is where you are the next time I come down here."

"Me too!"

When they got to the nursing residence, her father got out of the car and hugged Ruth long and hard. This occurred so rarely Ruth leaned back. "Are you well, Father?"

He harrumphed. "I was just so proud when that doctor wrote to us. I've seen you on the ward, so I know you have a gift, but it is wonderful that someone else recognized it as well. Your mother has the letter framed."

Ruth laughed. "No! She didn't show me."

"Well, she doesn't like to show favouritism. It's hanging inside of her closet."

So much like her mother. Her mother's closet was filled with drawings and report cards and prizes the children had won. All 'hidden' so no child would feel singled out. The children all knew the shrine was there, though. When their mother went to church, they'd gather and see what had been deemed suitable for it.

Ruth sobered. "Any word at all from Billy?"

"Nothing. I'm so afraid he... I wish they'd send us a telegram or something so we could at least have some idea...."

"I do, too," Ruth said, with passion. "But I'm sure he's still alive. I'm certain he'll be home one day soon."

Her father frowned. "I hope so. I pray he isn't a prisoner somewhere. Your mother worries so."

Ruth smiled to herself. Her father was worrying too, probably even more than her ever working mother. The whole time she'd been home, her mother kept knitting or cooking or cleaning. They'd only had those few minutes at the end of the day to talk. Even then, her mother was so tired she could barely keep her eyes open. Worrying took time. Her father had more of that.

Ruth waved goodbye and ran up the steps to the nursing residence and within minutes, Betty wrapped her in a huge hug.

"Oh, it's so good to see you! Are you well? Everything clear?" Betty waved her hand at Ruth's chest.

"Oh, I'm fine," Ruth responded. "Everything clear?" she added, waving her hand over Betty's abdomen. Betty slapped it away.

"Yes, thank heavens," she said, pulling Ruth around a corner to talk. "But I got caught out too many times for coming in late. Can you believe it? They are bumping me out until the fall intake. 'Give you time to reconsider your approach', the supervisor said."

"Ouch."

"Ouch is right. So, I got a job in one of the shops downtown and they're letting me live here until September. Hey—we'll be in the same class again!"

"If I get in," said Ruth.

"Hey, Patricia's gone. It's gotta get better, right?"

"I hope so. I am considering wearing a disguise." Ruth put her finger up like a moustache under her nose.

"No moustaches, please," said Betty. "We're done with men with moustaches."

Ruth nodded solemnly, and they burst out laughing, putting their hands over their mouths quickly to catch the sound.

"Walk on the weekend?"

"I'll see what schedule they have me on and give you a call."

"Before 9 pm, please, nurse. That's one rule they haven't changed." They hugged goodbye and Ruth set out in the late spring afternoon, a song in her heart to be back in Kingston.

When Ruth got back to the dorm, there was a note waiting for her. "Come to my office," it said, nothing more.

"What now?" Ruth groaned. "I just got in." At least she didn't have Theresa's judging looks to contend with. She'd been rotated back to the hospital when Ruth was away.

She pulled on her uniform, checked her hair, and dragged herself over to Mrs. Graham's office. When she entered, she saw her matron smiling from ear to ear.

"I have a surprise for you," she said.

Oh heavens, no, Ruth thought. She didn't want any more surprises. Ever again.

"Follow me," Mrs. Graham said. "We're heading over to the hospital," she added, still almost twinkling. It started to frighten Ruth.

"Is someone looking for me? Can I get unpacked first?"

"No. You are needed immediately."

Ruth slumped. It seemed she wouldn't get a break. She hadn't slept well at home, probably because she had to sleep on a blanket on the lumpy and over-squashed couch and the cat kept walking all over her face. Nothing for it. Immediate meant immediate. Pulling on her cape, she followed Mrs. Graham out the front door of the sanatorium and down the road. They hurried. The spring rain spread puddles over the sidewalks and walking took concentration if she didn't want to get splashes all over her legs and shoes. Mrs. Graham strode so quickly that conversation was impossible, and she didn't seem to want to speak, anyway. Soon they arrived at the General Hospital, and Ruth, breathless, followed Mrs. Graham, not breathless at all, up a set of stairs.

"Here we are." Mrs. Graham said, waving her arms in triumph.

"The orthopaedic ward? Am I going to work here or something?"

"Well, maybe. But that's not why we are here."

Ruth looked around. She looked around again. Mrs. Graham pushed her down the hall a bit. She froze. Did that voice sound like... Billy?

She screamed his name, running down the hallway like a mad thing. At the second wardroom, she spotted him. Yes, there was her brother, tied up in traction, but looking relatively healthy despite that and grinning so widely it seemed his head would break off.

She turned to Mrs. Graham, who had followed her at a more appropriate pace. "How did you hear?"

"Oh, it's this place. No one has any secrets. They just brought him here today. I knew you'd want to know right away."

"Thank you, thank you," cried Ruth, her eyes sparkling with tears.

"I'll leave you to visit. Remember, you're back on the ward in the morning, though, so don't stay too long."

Chapter Forty-Seven

Billy

"Apprehension, uncertainty, waiting, expectation, fear of surprise, do a patient more harm than any exertion. Remember he is face to face with his enemy all the time."

https://blog.nursing.com/florence-nightingale-quotes

Ruth flew over to Billy's side and squeezed his hand as if she was afraid he'd vanish again. "Where were you? We worried so!" She leaned in to give him a big hug. He hugged her back with one arm, so tight she could feel his heart beating. He seemed thin, almost like one of her patients.

Finally standing back, she took a good look at him. It truly was her brother, lying there with tears in his eyes and a scar down the side of his face, healed but still an ugly red. "I can't believe you're here! I just left Father—he drove me down. We were only now talking about you! I wish I could catch him before he got too far." Ruth caught her breath. "Are you okay? I mean, other than this?" She waved at the traction device. She so wanted to pull off the covers and check out his legs, but it seemed wrong unless he offered. What would be under there? She dreaded to imagine.

Billy smirked. His scar pulled when he did that, bringing the side of his lip down and tight. "It's been a bit of a ride. But I'm here now! What's all this about you becoming a nurse? Have to show me up yet again, don't you? Look at your uniform! You're all official and everything."

Ruth tried to keep from tearing up. He looked so much older, so weary. Broken. And scrawny. She shook her head, trying to focus on the positive. He was here, wasn't he? And alive! That was something. "Oh, silly, I'm still only a beginner. I'm hoping to get my bib and cap next year. But I want to hear about you! What happened? Where have you been? Are you okay? Tell me everything."

"One day," he answered. "Soon, I promise. For now, can you help me write to the parents? I'm not sure what to say."

"They'll be so, so happy to know you are okay! Mother has been worried sick."

"I feel awful. They didn't let me write from where I was. And," he waved his right hand, wrapped in bandages. "I seem to have ruined the bit that holds a pen."

"Oh, no—more injuries?" She peered at him, a question on her face.

"I'll explain it all later, I promise. For now, let's write a telegram for the family. They'll be getting the official one soon, and I don't want them to worry."

"The official one?"

"That I've been wounded in duty, former prisoner of war, you know, the lot. Let's write something happier?"

Ruth grabbed a pen and paper, and they wrote a brief note. "Home safe. In KGH but fine. Love Billy."

She ran the paper down to the switchboard and they called it in to the telegram office. Racing back, she found Billy asleep. She sat beside him, marvelling. How had he survived? His eyes fluttered open, his pupils dilated with fear. He looked around in a panic. She clasped his hand tightly in hers.

"Never mind, Billy, you're safe now. You're here, in Kingston. I'm right here with you." She said the words she'd said to so many men over the past months and fortunately they had the same soothing effect. Billy squeezed her hand, his eyes slowly closing again. It took at least an hour before he slept deeply enough to release her hand.

All that time, Ruth watched him ease into sleep, relearning his face. He'd grown up while away—no longer her big brother boy, he had turned into a man, with a set to his jaw that was new. She wondered what he'd seen. He had been captured, he said. What had they done to him? If he was like her father, he'd probably never speak of it. Her father had served in the trenches for a bit of the Great War, but he never mentioned it other than getting weepy whenever he led a prayer for the soldiers serving far away. And having those sudden bouts of anger, out of nowhere. They'd all tried to live with it, but her father could be scary sometimes. She hoped that sort of change hadn't happened to Billy as well. She wanted Billy to be able to speak of things, release the tension.

A telegram waited for her when she got to her residence. "Tomorrow."

Her poor father would have to baby the ancient car down from Cloyne again. Ruth wondered who would come to visit. Surely not the entire group! They wouldn't all fit in the car anymore, and Ruth was sure they wouldn't be allowed to visit Billy. She wished she'd added something to the telegram to warn them off, but it was too late now.

The next day, back on the ward, she worked her early morning rounds, feeling the revulsion that always came back after a few days away from emptying bedpans and sputum bottles. The smells always turned her stomach for the first few hours on. She looked forward to getting back to different tasks. Clattering away in the utility room testing urine before the morning insulin doses, she didn't notice her sister Meg creeping up behind her.

She jumped. "Meg! You're not supposed to be in here!"

"I pretended I was a relative. I am a relative, anyway. Just not one of theirs," she said, waving at the ward behind her. "Everyone is over at the hospital with Billy. I wanted to come and see where you worked!"

"Let me ask if I can get a few minutes off," Ruth said. "I don't want to get in trouble for unauthorized visiting." She spoke briefly to the other nurse who nodded approval. Ruth gestured for Meg to follow her outside onto the verandah.

"Are those patients lying down over there? Aren't they going to get a chill?"

"Part of the treatment," said Ruth. "Don't worry, they're all wrapped up nice and cozy. I should know. I had to wrap them!" She waved at a man who was watching them. He smiled and waved back. "Who came down here with you?" she asked.

"Just me and Mother and Father and the sprout. Sarah and one of the church ladies are looking after the other little ones. Mother couldn't leave the sprout behind."

Ruth nodded. The "sprout" was their nickname for the newest addition. They'd named her Donna, but she looked so much like a Brussel sprout they all called her that.

"Father grumped about having to drive down again after just bringing you, but he cheered up as soon as he saw Billy. They are so excited!" Meg stopped smiling. "They didn't ask him while I was there, but do you know what's wrong with him? Why does he have all those things tied to his leg?"

Ruth didn't know what to tell her. She'd peeked under the sheet after Billy fell asleep and she saw one leg only, the other had been amputated. And the other leg didn't look too good—it had a greyish cast to it that didn't seem healthy. It would be too discouraging to explain. "He's got a leg injury," she finally said. "All those poles and such are to keep his legs in traction until the bones heal together."

"Like a cast? Why can't they cast him?"

"I don't know for sure. We didn't have time to discuss it. He seemed too tired yesterday, and I had to work this morning. I'm hoping we can talk later today. Has he told Father anything about what happened?"

"No. He just tells them silly stories. I had to come away. It made me sad. He's obviously badly hurt, and he seems so lost. I hope they have someone work with him a bit. I don't want him to end up all silent and broody like Father."

Ruth agreed. "I'll find out what I can when I get off this afternoon. Are you staying overnight?"

"No, we have to get back. Father has a funeral service in the morning and mother—well, she's exhausted, as you've seen. We need to get her back for a good sleep. She was overjoyed to see Billy, but she doesn't have much energy after the sprout. Can you take some more time off? We can walk over to the hospital and catch them there."

"Can you bring them over to the San? I've just been off to visit you all. They won't want me to be away. We're always short-staffed here, and the patients keep coming. I've got to get the results back for the nurse to give insulins, and I've still got two new admissions to get settled before quiet time." She made a face. "Should I come home? Does Mother need my help?"

"Don't you even think it," Meg said. "We're fine. I've got things under control up there. Besides, you can keep an eye on Billy."

Ruth nodded, still fighting guilt.

"And don't tell anyone down here yet, but I have my own surprise to make everyone happy, pretty soon."

Ruth looked up. Her sister positively glowed. Meg nodded, smiling, "Yes, I think I'm engaged. You remember Wayne Madden, two houses over? With the big farm? Well...," she preened, "he has spoken to Father. After we'd talked. Not like your guy."

"Really," Ruth squealed. "He's so handsome!"

"He's also so kind," added Meg. "He's already offered to take us all over to his big house. Imagine! We'd have our own side, and Mother and Father and the babies and the sprout would have the other. He doesn't have any family left of his own. The boys would help him farm. And Billy could come back to recover, if he needs to. There's lots of room. And huge clotheslines!"

"Oh, that's all simply perfect," Ruth said, giving her sister a hug. "Are you thrilled, Meg?"

"Yes. Yes. I didn't mention it when you visited because all the little ones would overhear and they would go altogether too wild. They're going to love living on a farm, with all the animals. But Mother and Father talked about it with me on the ride down just now and if all goes well, we'll be married at Christmas."

Ruth squeezed Meg tight and skipped back to the ward, doing all her duties so happily the day sped by. Her parents popped by briefly, but they were emotionally wrought, and they had to leave the sprout with Meg in the car so they didn't stay for long. Relieved they didn't ask her to come home, Ruth hugged everyone and went back to the ward. More tidying to do. Today she could almost enjoy it.

Chapter Forty-Eight

Challenges

A very great deal as now written and spoken as to the effect of the mind upon the body. Much it is true. But I wish a little more was thought of the effect of the body on the mind. You who believe yourselves overwhelmed with cares, but are able every day to walk up the street, or out in the country, to take your meals with others in other rooms, etc., etc., you little know how much your anxieties are thereby lightened; you little know how intense they become to those who have no change; how the very walls of their sick rooms seem hung with their cares; how the ghosts of their troubles haunt their beds; how impossible it is for them to escape from a pursuing thought without some help from variety.

Nightingale, Notes on Nursing, p. 70-71.

The next few weeks flew by. Ruth was working her two wards and doing plastering assisting besides. When she was off, the spring weather in Kingston lured her out for walks by the lake and visits with her colleagues. And every moment she was off and it was visiting hours, she was over at the General Hospital, visiting Billy.

His progress was discouraging. She'd been right to be worried about his leg—they'd tried everything from massage to leeches, but the circulation wasn't coming back. The leg he'd had amputated was healing slowly, but even if it did, they couldn't fit him with a prosthesis while the other one was healing.

The third week he was back, Ruth was at his bedside when the surgeons came by to tell him it looked like he was going to lose his remaining leg. He listened to what they told him, his face whitening with shock. After they left, he turned his head to the wall for a long moment.

"Fine," he finally growled. "I'm going to be a bloody useless crip, anyway. May as well take them both. Won't make any difference."

"Billy...," began Ruth.

"No, don't you dare say anything. You're going to be a nurse, do something useful. Me, I'm just going to be a lump. You'll have to prop me in a shed somewhere, so I don't frighten the kids. Even my face...." He coughed out a bitter laugh. "I wish they'd killed me over there. That would have made sense. This is a bloody mess."

Ruth sat, shrunken into herself. The easy words she said to her patients didn't come as easily when it was her brother. What could he do? Would he ever be able to work? Have a purpose?

"Surely you are owed a bit of lump time," she began. "You've served, you've been a prisoner...."

"Yeah, and a fat lot of good I did over there. Months of training, we finally get sent over to fight, and the second attack I get sent on, the bloody Krauts get me. Spent most of my time in a goddamn POW camp, trying to keep the other guys alive. At least until I got the infection on my leg." He pounded his good fist on the bed. "And then, just as they were going to release me, one of them decided to knife one of the Brit POWs. For some reason I felt I had to get into it—you can thank father for that, him, and his responsibility code—and that's how I wrecked my hand."

"They say that will heal, though." Ruth sounded pathetically pleasing and hated herself for it. "At least there's that."

Billy glared at her. "Thank God. Imagine, me with two stumps for legs and one hand? What a treat I'd be to look after. Jesus, they'd have to wipe my ass forever."

Ruth shrugged. "Hey, I do that for patients every day. It's not so bad."

"You're not on the receiving end. Now, go away. I want to sleep."

She gazed at him, tears in her eyes. She didn't want to even think about the other things that might go wrong. He had a persistent infection in the stump he already had, and there was no guarantee he wouldn't get one in the new stump after his upcoming surgery. He was malnourished from his time in the POW camp, skinny and with patchy hair, and she wished they could wait longer to bring him back to health before they needed to cut him again.

She stopped to talk to the doctors on the ward as she left.

"He's awfully blue," she began.

"I'd be, too," one resident said. "Have they told you what our plans are for tomorrow?"

"Not fully."

"Well, first we're going to debride his existing stump, cut away the necrotic tissue, clean it up. We'll treat it with Streptomycin, hope that will slow any reinfection. We're also going to try applying a honey dressing."

"Honey?"

"Yes. We've seen some studies that recommend it as an antibacterial treatment. Given the infection is longstanding, the antibiotic may need some help. I'm tempted to try a new system of injecting the antibacterial into the leg directly, but I think we need better tissue integrity before I try that. Thus, the honey." The surgeon continued, "At the same time we'll be getting ready to amputate the other leg, below the knee to start. We want to leave him as much function as we can."

"Then what?"

The doctor looked at her sideways. "You're a nurse, right?"

"Just a nurses' aide."

"Well, after that, it's a long recovery, a lot of physiotherapy. After that, a fitting for prostheses. We might send him over to the Hopkins site for that."

"The Hopkins site? That's where I work!"

"Even better." The doctor actually smiled. "They have a lot more physiotherapists there at present because of the veterans and TB surgeries. And you'll keep a sharp eye on him, right?"

Ruth's heart lightened. "That would be absolutely perfect!"

The next day Ruth was in agonies of suspense waiting for news from the OR. Would Billy make it through? Finally at five o'clock, the phone rang in the hall and one of the other nurses answered it, calling out "Telephone call for Maclean."

Ruth raced to the phone.

"He came through the surgery okay," said the tired sounding doctor. "We cleaned out the wound, and the amputation went smoothly. He's going to be out for a while, though. We had to knock him out, of course, and the surgery was extensive. We'll want to keep him pretty quiet for the next couple of days."

"When can I see him?"

"I think if it's only you tomorrow afternoon should be fine. Can you inform his other family?"

"I will. Thank you, doctor, thank you so much for letting me know."

Ruth hung up and ran downstairs to the main desk, making up the telegram as she went. She was sure everyone would be holding their breath at home, too.

Chapter Forty-Nine

Healing

It seems a commonly received idea among men, and even among women themselves, that it requires nothing but a loving heart, the want of an object, a general disgust or incapacity for other things, to turn a woman into a good nurse. This reminds me one of the parish where a stupid old man was set to be schoolmaster, because he was past keeping the pigs. Apply the above receipt for making a good nurse to making a good servant. And the receipt will be found to fail...

The everyday management of a sickroom, let alone of a house—the knowing what are the laws of life and death for men, and what the laws of health for houses... Are not these matters of sufficient importance and difficulty to require learning by experience and careful inquiry, just as much as any other art? They do not come by inspiration to the loving heart, nor to the poor drudge hard up for a livelihood.

And terrible is the injury which is followed to the sick from such wild notions.

Nightingale, Notes on Nursing, p. 143.

B illy spent two weeks at the General before they arranged a transfer to the Veteran's Hospital. By the time it happened, Ruth was worn out from travelling back and forth, but she was determined to stay close as much as possible. She worried about Billy's mood—he'd gone so quiet since the surgery and not even her usual joking made him smile. She hoped being among the other soldiers would help.

At first it did. After the transfer, Billy was in a four-bed ward with three other soldiers, all wounded in action. Two of them also had amputations, the other one had facial and chest shrapnel injuries that caused severe scarring. The ward, designated rehabilitation, had physiotherapists in there most of the day, moving stiff limbs and encouraging exercises.

In the evenings, when Ruth visited, the men all joked around and acted like they were having a jolly holiday. They traded funny war stories, and Ruth hoped Billy would talk about what happened overseas. Maybe it would help him get over it. As the days passed, though, he grew quieter and quieter, and Ruth found herself tearing up as she left the ward.

One day, when the shrapnel soldier had gone out to the front for a smoke and fresh air, he caught Ruth as she walked by.

"Hey, Miss Maclean, your brother...." He stopped, looking uncertain.

"Hi, Corporal. What's up?"

"I don't want to say too much." He paused, scratched his head. "It's just, I think he's ...he's planning."

"Planning what?" Ruth's heart stopped. Surely not....

The corporal continued. "He goes awful quiet when you're not there. I got to thinking he's thinking about a way out."

She shivered, wrapped her arms around herself to steady her breathing. She'd seen something, too, a deadness in her brother's eyes, a shiftiness. She saw it in another soldier a few weeks back. That one now lay in the General, in intensive care. They were still investigating how he'd gotten all the pills he took.

Ruth couldn't stop herself from protesting, "No! He's healing!"

The corporal kicked a hapless dandelion to death before answering. "Yeah, his legs are getting better, they say, but... He doesn't seem to see his way on from here, Miss."

Ruth swallowed the sob that clutched at her throat. "Do you have any idea what's going on with him?"

"He's like a lot of the guys. I reckon they can't stop seeing the things they saw. We talked about that POW camp, though, and it seems like they knocked the light out of him there. Did he tell you he was over a year behind the wire? That's gotta do something to your mind."

"I didn't know—he won't talk to me." Ruth wiped her eyes, shook herself upright again. Forward, always forward, she told herself. She could hear her father's voice saying it. "Thank you for telling me, Corporal. He always seems cheerful when I'm there."

"Yeah, that. It might be good, ma'am, if you don't mind me saying so, if you didn't visit quite so often. It's hard for him to pretend to be okay." He crushed the cigarette he'd been smoking under his boot, really ending the dandelion's life for good.

Ruth realized, suddenly, how she'd been doing the very thing she'd counselled so many families not to do, exhausting the patient with cheery visiting. She blushed.

She'd do as he suggested, but she sure as heck would get someone else to check on Billy. She wondered. Time for the psychiatrist? She'd seen them work miracles with some of the men so wasted by TB that they couldn't see how they would live. She'd have to be careful, though. If they suspected Billy was planning to harm himself, he'd be off to Rockwood in a flash, and that wouldn't be good for anyone. She had heard from Mary what the treatments were like. Meantime, she'd ask around, find out if there was anything her brother could do, even if disabled. There had to be something.

The next casting day, she pulled Dr. Anderson into the treatment room before she brought in their patient and told him Billy's situation.

"That sounds terrible, Miss Maclean. I've seen your brother, and he does seem depressed. Not that I wouldn't be, in his position. What will he be able to do from here, as a double amputee? I'd be lost."

"Me, too. I'm trying to find something for him. But in the meantime, I don't want him to go down so low he can't get back."

He peered at her. "You don't suppose he's planning to take drastic steps, do you?"

"Oh no," she said quickly, fingers crossed behind her back. "And even if that was the case, it's not like he'd be able to do anything, right?"

"It would be difficult, but not impossible. I had a burn patient once that managed to throw his bedside table and then himself out of a third-floor window. He had burns over seventy percent of his body, too. Determined." He realized what he'd said and turned to Ruth. "Oh, I'm sorry. I didn't mean to imply that would happen with your brother. I'm sure he's not that badly off." He put his hand on Ruth's shoulder, awkwardly.

Ruth pulled a tissue out of her pocket and wiped her eyes. It seemed like she leaked a lot lately, tears all the time. She felt like Betty after one of her beaus dropped her. Too emotional.

"I hoped you would write a referral for psychiatry, Dr. Anderson. Could you?"

He nodded. "I'll do it the minute we are finished here."

Ruth smiled through wavery lips. "I'll go get our patient then." She left, leaving Dr. Anderson gazing after her solemnly.

At least Jerry was getting better day by day. His temperature remained stable, and he didn't show any further TB progression on X-ray. He still needed physiotherapy and exercises to help him straighten his cut and chopped ribs and chest muscles, but they started talking about discharging him soon.

Enough men needed more exercise that the nurses decided it made sense to take them outside into the summer weather and do them together. Ruth and the others delighted in getting the patients out into the fresh air, and the patients liked the chance to talk with people not on their ward. The exercise classes soon became like mini socials, with Mrs. Graham desperately trying to maintain order.

Ruth didn't worry so much about order. She liked the idea of fun. There was little enough fun on the wards and most of the patients were young and had spent months lying about with little to entertain them. So she and the other nurses created ball games that would get the men moving their arms and legs, and brought out balloons and other silly things to play with.

Billy remained quiet and his ward mates lost patience with him and didn't try to draw him out anymore. Often when Ruth visited him, he'd be in his wheelchair, staring out a window, unwilling to talk or smile. Ruth performed wild antics, trying to get a rise out of him, bringing him treats that he'd end up giving to the rest of the ward. She had asked her mother to send down one of her quilts, but Billy just left it folded at the end of his bed. Ruth feared that as soon as his wounds healed he'd be sent to Rockwood.

One day, Billy had progressed enough to come outside in a wheelchair. Ruth took her break to visit with him, stopped at the doorway, uncertain of how to approach him. Still flat in affect, his face frozen in his depression, he sat still, wrapped in one of the gruesome scratchy crocheted afghans made of Mertex that the Women's Auxiliary gave to the hospital. The nurses put him by the edge of the field, forced to watch the others. The other men ran awkwardly about, their bodies in unusual positions as they dealt with missing bits in their chests. Ruth gazed at him, fretting. Even the sunny day hadn't reached him. He hadn't seemed to respond to the visits by the psychiatrist, or even the injections of adrenaline they'd tried to treat his depression.

She snuck up behind him, put her hands over his eyes. "Guess who?" she said in a low voice.

Billy startled so much she immediately regretted it. He thrashed in his chair, batting her away. "What the hell are you doing?" He pushed at her hands. "What is wrong with you?"

"I'm sorry, I'm sorry," Ruth fought back tears.

"Just go the hell away. Look after some other crip. Do something important. God knows I'll never be able to again."

Ruth, downcast, stood back. She noticed the blanket covering Billy had slipped, and she almost reached to pull it back up around him, but realized that was probably the wrong thing to do. Sad, she turned to go back to the ward.

Just then, one of the soccer balls the other patients were throwing around flew over towards Billy, and Ruth, alarmed, ran to gather it, but Billy caught it in his now healed hands and flung it back into the field, directly to one of the men.

"Good catch!" shouted Jerry, giving a wave. They played on, but Ruth noticed her brother now watched the play.

In a few moments, Jerry threw the ball over to Billy, who caught it again, tossing it back. In no time, Billy somehow ended up part of the game, as the men sent him the ball again and again. Ruth smiled as Billy's old competitive spirit kicked in. He was trying to throw better than the others. The first sign of hope she'd seen in weeks.

After exercise period finished, Billy's nurse came to take him back to the ward. He visibly slumped, but Ruth hoped it meant fatigue from the unaccustomed exercise. She caught up to Jerry as they walked back to the ward.

"Thanks for bringing Billy into the game," Ruth said.

"He looked a bit lost," said Jerry. "I trust he had fun, no?"

"He sure did." Ruth squeezed Jerry's arm. "It was so good of you."

"Hey, we all pull together, eh? And of course, I want to help the brother of my so capable nurse!"

Later in the day, Ruth went to Billy's ward to check on him. The nurse shook her head. "He's exhausted," she said. "He said he didn't want to go outside ever again. I'm really concerned. Perhaps the men being able to play when he couldn't really bothered him."

Ruth started to go to him, but the nurse put a hand out to stop her. "He said no visitors."

"But surely I...."

"Especially you, he said. I'm sorry." She shrugged. "I've put a call in to the psychiatrist, but you're aware of how busy they are. It might take a while."

Ruth nodded, then brightened. "Can you let me know when he gets here? I'd like to talk to him."

The other nurse said, "Sure. I hope we can find a solution for him. He seems so nice. When he's not angry, that is."

Ruth blushed. Did her brother cause problems for the nurses? She couldn't let that continue.

Chapter Fifty

August

The fact is, that the patient is not "cheered" at all by these well-meaning, most tiresome friends. On the contrary, he is depressed and wearied. If, on the one hand, he exerts himself to tell everybody, one after the other, while he does not think as they do—in what respect he is worse—what symptoms exist that they know nothing of—he is fatigued instead of "cheered," and his attention is fixed upon himself. In general patients who are really ill do not want to talk about themselves. Would-be invalids do; but again I say we are not on the subject of would-be invalids.

Nightingale, Notes on Nursing, p. 104.

The summer flew by, with Ruth working as hard as possible and trying to think of a way to cheer up Billy as she did. His wounds were finally healing, thanks to the good food provided at the hospital. It was a long stay, and Ruth was grateful his veteran's payments covered the expense of his care. She still spent much of her salary on fresh fruit and treats for him. She always bought enough for the entire ward, as Billy would just share anything he got.

His mood wasn't improving, however. Ruth finally got a few moments with his psychiatrist and came up with an unusual plan. It was up to Ruth to get the other doctors onside, and she worked hard at that, too, winning over Mrs. Graham, Dr. Anderson, and Beth for her fresh approach.

The next exercise period, Billy was rolled out to the yard, protesting all the way. Mrs. Graham insisted, though, and even took the role of pushing the wheelchair onto the field.

"Just give it a try," she told him firmly. "The men need you."

"What am I supposed to do here?" He batted at his wheels in frustration. "I'm useless! Let me go back in. I'm tired. I want to lie down."

No one listened. Instead, the men gathered for a brief consultation and made Billy a goalie. They jollied him into position and put one of the other amputees at the other end of the field, and in no time they had created an impromptu soccer game. It was exciting, if somewhat alarming, to watch as men who still hadn't adjusted to their damaged bodies ran here, there, and everywhere after the ball. Ruth held her breath as a kick soared towards Billy, but he caught it easily and threw it back into play.

Ruth smiled as she saw her brother sit a little taller in his chair. The next two balls slipped past him into the goal, but he tried for them at least, and his team members came by to encourage him.

The game progressed slowly because after almost every few minutes everyone had to stop and catch their breath. But it was almost a proper game, even if short. The final goal shot headed to Billy, and he stopped that one, too, before the physiotherapists called a halt. Billy's team cheered and circled him, patting him on the back. He was almost smiling, and as the team talked on, Ruth was heartened at the sound of Billy's voice, loud and clear, giving ideas for the next game's strategy.

Mrs. Graham stopped Ruth as she was climbing the stairs to the ward. "Aren't you abandoning your patients, Miss Maclean?"

"Oh, but I just stepped out for a minute...."

Mrs. Graham patted Ruth's shoulder. "I don't blame you. That was rewarding, seeing your brother come to life a bit. You know, I think you may be onto something here. Good for you to insist they be allowed to play." She paused. "I have some discretionary money. I wonder if I could find some trophies...nothing like a little friendly competition to get the blood flowing, eh?"

Ruth floated up to the ward. The game seemed to have helped, and Mrs. Graham even thought it was a good idea. Things were looking up.

She'd been terrified when she'd offered the idea to the doctors at their rounds meeting. Who ever heard of TB patients doing vigorous exercise? They were meant to rest and rest until they were almost mad. But even Florence Nightingale recommended exercise, didn't she?

"Ridiculous," Dr. Rosen had snorted in derision. "These patients need rest. If they run around, they risk reactivating their TB. Unsupportable."

Ruth quailed but stood firm. "But, Dr. Rosen," she almost curtseyed, "exercise is as important as rest, is it not? The patients need to keep their blood circulating, or they can get bedsores or pneumonia."

"Who...are...you?" the doctor growled. "You're not even a nurse. Should you even be addressing me? Surely there are some bedpans to empty somewhere?"

But, surprisingly, Mrs. Graham and Dr. Anderson spoke up in support.

"The patients are becoming so deconditioned on bedrest they are losing all muscle strength," said Dr. Anderson. "I'm worried that may lead to further problems. Their breathing and cardiac health are being affected."

"We try to keep them doing their exercises, but we don't have enough staff to get to everyone individually," Mrs. Graham added. "It's much more practical to exercise them in groups. And we do have the field beside us."

"And they don't like the regular exercises," added Ruth. "They say they are boring, especially the patients who are almost well."

Mrs. Graham frowned at her, and Ruth realized she should be quiet. Dr. Rosen looked ready to explode, his face scarlet and sweat popping out of his pores. Mentally, Ruth reviewed what to do in case of a heart attack.

The physiotherapist, Captain Martin, spoke up. "Besides, Doctor, many of our patients don't have TB. They are recovering from war injuries. Those patients need more vigorous exercise than chest expansion and stretches."

"Well. I suppose, if—you—recommend it, Captain Martin, we might give it a try. We'll allow a brief—brief, mind you—attempt at playing team games. If anyone shows signs of worsening, however, I am pulling the plug."

Over the next weeks, exercise time became instead a soccer tournament. They started a play roster and picked members of each team. Billy's team members found out he had played soccer all through school and pushed him to be captain. One of the other amputees acted as captain on the other side. They made up names for each team: The Half-lungs, the Gimps, the Navvies and the Warriors, and the hallways were filled with laughter and shouts as they teased each other. Mrs. Graham had to threaten cutting the games if they didn't follow quiet hours. So instead, there were whispers and giggles. Ruth loved going to work. Everyone seemed so light.

She knew she was making progress when she spotted Billy practising with Jerry on their own one afternoon. Billy didn't have the same rest requirements as the TB patients, and Jerry was doing so well they were allowed some time to practise in the late afternoon. It warmed Ruth's heart to hear Billy laugh again.

He still had dark times, and Ruth reduced her visit time so he could have them without having to put on a smiling face. If only she could find something for him to do, some work to look forward to. She changed the time she visited Billy to time spent hunting for a job for him. It was discouraging. There were so many veterans in the city, attending the local high school or the colleges to upgrade their skills, most of the starter jobs or ones that would hire an amputee were already taken. Ruth began to share Billy's despair. She knew if Billy had to go back to Cloyne, he'd end up trapped at home, unable to go anywhere on his own. It would kill him.

Chapter Fifty-One

The game

It is the result of all experience with the sick, that second only to their need of fresh air is their need of light; that, after a close room, what hurts them the most is a dark room, and that it is not only light but direct sunlight they want. You had better carry your patient about after the sun, according to the aspect of the rooms, if circumstances permit, than let him linger in a room when the sun is off. People think the effect is upon the spirits only. This is by no means the case.

Nightingale, Notes on Nursing, p. 90.

As the summer went on, Billie's progress was encouraging. The soccer competition seemed to strengthen him. Between that and his wounds healing, he seemed to recover some of his normal cheer, and his arm and body strength were returning. Ruth remembered him from pre-war times, always making the best of unpleasant situations. He used to make their father laugh even when stormy, danced with their mother around the kitchen. She really wanted to see that Billy return.

No more dancing for Billy, realized Ruth, sadly. She still didn't have any idea what his future held. When he sank into his sad periods, she worried he'd descend into alcoholism. It horrified her to think of him ending up like so many of the injured vets she saw downtown, sitting on street corners, begging for change. She batted the vision away, leaning even more into her work.

It was a good thing for everyone that they had the games as a distraction. The news caused gloom—Russia and Turkey were fighting, and there was talk of a 'rematch' of the last war, this time fighting against the Communists. Everyone listened to the news, hands clenched. Several of the soldiers had either been to Turkey or knew others who had. They didn't relish a return. And the horror of the atom bombs still resonated.

The soccer practice created a hopeful structure to the days. Every day, the nurses rushed to get the patients dressed and out on the field. The fitter ones would play, and the ones still on restricted activities would demand to be set up in the yard so they could watch. Those confined to barracks watched from the windows, and every time Ruth looked up, she saw every window filled with pale ovals of patient faces.

Some patients wanted to start a baseball team, too, inspired by the start-up of the Kingston Ponies baseball club in March. Baseball required upper arm and chest strength, though, and the recovering TB patients didn't have that. So, for now, they focused on soccer, arguing more of the patients could take part. Instead, the men followed the Ponies on the radio. They certainly exercised their lungs, as they cheered their own teams and the Ponies. The hospital hallways rang.

"Good lung expansion," said Mrs. Graham once again. Everyone else just loved the enthusiasm.

By now, the four hospital soccer teams had played each other a few times, working towards the "championship" game. On the game day, two games were planned, one between the lowest ranking teams, the other between the top. The administration set it up for the end of summer, the second week of August.

Ruth woke that Saturday with a song in her heart. Today was the big game! Billy's team ranked in the top two. Ruth, on day duty, fretted through the first game while she got patients washed, dressed, and fed. It seemed to take forever, and of course the ones who should rest refused to do so. At long last, everyone was tidied or propped somehow to see the game, and Ruth escaped. She had one of the other nurses cover for her that afternoon, and she raced down to the field just as the players came on.

Billy and Jerry played on the same team now, so Ruth didn't have to split her support. Jerry, despite his lung and rib damage, still could run a bit, probably because he weighed almost nothing. Billy had his place in the goal, which they shrunk so that the amputees on each side could reach out with their arms to better stop the ball.

The opposing team, the Gimps, had cheated a bit, Ruth muttered. Their goalie still had his right leg, and stood, making it easier for him to stop high balls. She hoped Billy and the Half-lungs would hold their own.

Everyone who could, stood and sang, "God Save the King" and then it was time to start. Ruth crossed her fingers and added a prayer that all would be well.

The Gimps won the coin toss and before the Halves team even got organized, they'd scored on Billy. Cheering and slapping hands, they set up for the next play. Billy looked thunderous, and his face didn't improve when the Gimps scored a second time. A nasty kick to the high left side of the goal bumped off Billy's fingertips and slipped past into the net. Their fans groaned. Billy picked up the ball and threw it hard enough it almost hit the windows of the hospital.

Jerry called a timeout and walked over to Billy and spoke to him. When he ran back onto the field, Billy still seemed angry, but calmer. Ruth shouted to him, "Go Halves!" but only got a scowl in return. Her stomach twisted. Would this end up hurting Billy instead of helping him?

The Halves took the next play, everyone galloping in their own uneven manner to the other end of the field and kicking madly towards the goal. The goalie stood to block, but the ball bounced off him and rolled in low past his absent leg. Ruth cheered, and 'her' ward yelled in victory through the windows.

The shortened period finished, and everyone gathered to catch their breath. They were all overexcited, rubbing sore limbs, playing harder than they ever had in practice, gasping with exertion. The Halves gathered at their goal, surrounding Billy, who drew something on a piece of paper. Ruth smiled. Billy had been a successful coach for the high school team before he left for the war, and he had some excellent tricks up his sleeve. If he could get the team to do them, they might win.

The Gimps looked prepared, too. It would be an exciting second half. Mrs. Graham appeared at the edge of the field, holding up the trophies she'd found somewhere. The players cheered. The hospital administrators planned to set them up at the hospital and then take them to the Legion for ongoing display. Several Legion members from the Great War stood on the sidelines to applaud the teams, waiting to present the awards.

Jerry came over to Ruth before everything started. "We have the perfect plan!" he said, his voice raised in excitement. "Billy is brilliant."

"I know! Isn't he the best?" said Ruth. "Bonne chance!" Jerry waved and ran onto the field, stopping halfway to catch his breath.

Everyone was really pushing themselves, she fretted. Would they be all right at the end of this? The men had to continue—all of them were too excited to stop. She squirmed with guilt. Had she endangered everyone just for Billy?

Dr. Rosen had appeared on the field and watched the game with his brows furrowed. He stomped over to Ruth. "If anyone dies because of this foolishness, it's on you, Miss Maclean. Look at them! They can barely stand!" He walked off, heading for Mrs. Graham. Ruth saw him yelling at her, too, his arms flying about in rage.

Ruth turned away, seeing her nursing career evaporating. But it was worth it to see Billy so animated. Please, God, she begged under her breath. Let everyone be safe.

It didn't look good. The second half started, and it was immediately visible that the men had overdone it in the first half. Some men had to walk, kicking the ball while holding their sides to brace their ribs. Others moved forward and then stopped, bending over with their hands on their knees, catching their breath. Both teams suffered the same problems, so though the game slowed down, it remained evenly matched.

The Halves scored once, and then the game degenerated to each team kicking the ball back from their goal and then not quite scoring. The refs, two residents from the hospital, stopped calling out offsides and just let everyone run wild. Not that anyone ran. It looked more like stumbling.

Ruth was overwhelmed by the tension building up behind her. The spectators were shouting angrily at the players now.

"Come on, pick up the pace!"

"Score!"

"Man up!"

Some men even swore. When she glared at them, they dipped their heads in shame, but one seaman muttered, "I've got my pay packet on this. They'd better win."

Billy tried to do some fancy patterns with his team, but in reality they were barely standing now, everyone moving slower and slower. The referees, seeing the patients' exhaustion, blew their whistles. "That's it, boys! Time to call it."

The field filled with moans and protests from everyone.

"There's no winner," complained the captain of the Gimps. "We need a winner. Sudden death penalty kicks!"

The doctors looked skeptical, but soon everyone was yelling for a sudden death ending. Ruth frowned. It seemed like the wrong thing for them to be demanding, exhausted and broken as they were. After what seemed like an eternity, the doctors nodded, and each team set up to do their kicks.

"Hardly seems fair, miss, given that their goalie has an extra limb," said one man behind Ruth.

She didn't want to answer. She could only think of the pressure this put on Billy, how disheartened he would be if they lost. And what of the rest of the men? Would they end up sicker at the end of all this?

Chapter Fifty-Two

Sudden death

Exercise is medicine. Too much exercise (medicine) is harmful. Too little exercise is of no value. Too much exercise causes fatigue. Fatigue is POISON. Never become fatigued. No matter what form of exercise you may be taking, always stop short of the tired point.

Ongwanada, p. 13.

D r. Rosen tried to protest continuing the game, but the residents argued with him until he left the field. It had been decided that the first team who got the lead would win. No one wanted to draw it out to the full five kicks each if they didn't need to. The teams lined up, the goalies readied themselves. The whistle blew.

The first goal flew in, one for the Gimps. The Halves got their first goal in, too, their goalie spitting on the ground in frustration. Second round, the Gimps missed, as did the Halves. The tension was so high Ruth heard the birds in the trees—no one else was making a sound. She crossed her fingers, said prayers to whatever was listening, hoped against hope.

The Gimps set up to kick, and their ball sailed toward Billy. He tried to move his wheelchair to get over further, but it caught on the grass and he was stuck. Somehow, he propelled himself up out of the chair and caught the ball, pounding it back onto the field with a triumphant shout. The crowd exploded, cheering and whistling, but there was still the return goal to score to win the game. The physiotherapists helped him get back in his chair and straightened out in case he'd need to defend again.

Jerry was lined up to kick, but bent over, gasping, a stitch in his side. He tried to wave it off, but a doctor came up to him and spoke to him briefly, then directed him off the field. He collapsed onto the grass, lay back. Ruth wanted to run over, but knew she'd create an unwanted fuss. One resident sat down beside him, checking his pulse.

"Cheating! You can't sub now," screamed the other side.

The referees frowned, called the two captains in for a discussion. Ruth heard the tone of their argument but not the words, while the crowd waited, breaths held. Ruth felt a hand on her back and jumped, she was so tense. She whirled around.

"Betty! Oh, it's so good you're here!"

The men behind them whistled at the well-dressed Betty until Ruth glared at them.

Betty winked back at the men. "I came as soon as I could! Wouldn't miss the game."

"It's almost the end. They are doing penalty kicks, but since everyone is so tired, they are only playing until someone has the lead. It's one up for us now."

"Aren't they okay to play? I thought they were better?"

Ruth flushed. "Not quite. They're all so tired. I just wish it was over." She squeezed Betty's hand. "I'm afraid...."

They turned to watch the conversation in the middle of the field. The ref came over to address the crowd. "They've agreed the Halves can substitute a player, but it will be the Gimp's choice of player."

"Oh no," said Ruth. "They're going to pick the worst one."

Betty nodded. "I would if I were them."

The captain of the Gimps walked along the Halves lineup, examining each one. Finally, he plucked one player out, to the universal moans from the fans on the Halves' side. The selected player was Eric Rattie, a benchwarmer, used only as a substitute in previous games. He had thick glasses strapped to his head with elastic and a cast on his arm and had recently come through a rib resection. It seemed hopeless.

He shrugged and stepped forward to get into position. Billy called to him from the goal, and Eric ran over, listened hard, nodded his head. Coming back, he was a little straighter, walked with more confidence. He stood behind the ball, stretched, adjusted his glasses. Finally, he stepped back, readied, and ran forward.

The ball sailed forward, to the right of the goal, and the goalie moved over to meet it, only to watch the ball curve and head to the left. It slid in the upper left corner while the goalie tried to reach over, nearly falling out of his chair. He missed, and the entire hospital vibrated with noise. Cheers, applause, and groans, all in equal measure.

Ruth ran to Billy, grabbing him in a hug. He hugged her back, but detached and rolled over to the rest of the team. They all pounded him on his shoulders and jumped around until everyone was gasping and sitting on the ground. Jerry somehow got up and walked over to the group, but it was obvious he was hurting.

Mrs. Graham walked onto the field with two representatives from the Legion. The crowd quieted down for a moment while they presented the cups, the big one to the Halves, the smaller one to the grumpy-looking Gimps. Everyone shook hands, and then it was over.

Billy and Jerry came over to Ruth and Betty and were roundly cheered by the soldiers behind them.

"Are you all right, Jerry?" asked Ruth, touching his arm.

"Oh, you know me. I'm always fine. As long as I don't laugh." He gestured at his chest, where, Ruth knew, there was a network of old incisions.

Ruth wanted to say something nurse-y, but held back. This wasn't a time to remind them of their illness. Instead, she smiled and hugged him quickly. She couldn't express how grateful she was that Jerry had helped take Billy out of his shell. Billy was sweaty but smiling ear to ear. He looked ecstatic.

"I thought for sure you were goners when you had to use Rattie," said the seaman with the bet.

Billy grinned. "He was our secret weapon. Jerry here has been working with him, haven't you, Jerry?"

"Really?" Ruth said. "Good job!"

"Ah, he had the skills. Just looked like a drowned rat-tie...." he laughed. "Un peu de practique on his kick and we were tout préparer for this exact situation."

"Parfait, eh, Jerry?" Billy and Jerry smiled at each other, and Ruth sensed things falling into place.

The men from the Legion came over to congratulate Billy and Jerry. "Captain Maclean, I have a proposal for you, if you have a minute," said one. He and Billy headed off to a corner of the field. As Ruth was watching, Billy shifted from solemn to become animated and laughing. He shook the man's hand. When Billy rolled back to them, she had to ask.

"What was that about?"

Billy stretched his arms over his head and grinned. "The lads at the Legion have a team. They asked if I would come and coach them—for pay! And they have housing for me."

"Oh, that's fabulous! Congratulations!"

"Now I have something I can work towards. Thank God. I couldn't see any reason to...."

"I know," said Ruth, rubbing his shoulder. "Now you can focus on rehab. But wait, did you argue? It seemed as if you did."

"Oh, yes. I told them I needed Jerry to help me, and that I wouldn't come unless they took him as well."

"Good for you! And did they agree?"

"Yes, I had to make a pitch. They are afraid of TB, like everyone. But I persuaded them. I've gotta go tell him. He needs something to look forward to, too." He rolled off.

Betty squeezed Ruth's arm. "Isn't that fantastic? Now you can concentrate on nursing school, and you won't have to worry about him as much. The Legion takes good care of people."

Ruth smiled. She suspected Billy and Jerry would take good care of each other. "Let's get dinner," she said to Betty. "With luck, I won't be here much longer. I've got to enjoy the goods while I can."

"You're on!" Arm in arm, they walked in to the dining hall.

Chapter Fifty-Three

Progress

"I use the word nursing for want of a better. It has been limited to signify little more than the administration of medicines and the application of poultices. It ought to signify the proper use of fresh air, light, warmth, cleanliness, quiet, and the proper selection and administration of diet-all at the least expense of vital power to the patient."

https://blog.nursing.com/florence-nightingale-quotes

Meanwhile, Ruth hoped to enjoy some celebrating of her own. She'd reapplied to nursing school, and they were due to tell her if she'd been accepted any day soon. She could barely concentrate on her work until the mail for each day arrived. Every time it didn't include that fateful envelope, she had to fight to act happy as she worked on the wards.

The week after the big game, after a long tiring shift with two complicated pneumothorax procedures in it, Ruth dragged herself upstairs wanting only a bath and bed. Perched on her desk was a letter. THE letter. She grabbed it, sat heavily down on her bed, wondering how she was going to gather the strength to open it. What would she do if they had refused her? They'd make her go back to Cloyne, tail between her legs. Or will they, she wondered. Surely, the San will still need her as an aide. But that wasn't enough for her now—she wanted more.

She tucked the letter under her pillow and headed downstairs for supper. The news would land better on a full stomach. And maybe someone would come and sit with her while she opened it. Reading it alone terrified her. Wild swirls of despair were forming, like the ones that enveloped her when she'd slapped Patricia, and she'd worried everything was over. Ruth didn't want to become as glum as her father could be. But if they didn't accept her....

Dinner was a rather uninspired meatloaf and peas. The chefs had been out celebrating the games, too, and it showed. She shoved it down her dry throat and kept an eye out for Beth or Jocelyn. Both of them had been so supportive. She was sure they'd find something positive to say no matter the outcome.

She was half-heartedly spooning through a chocolate pudding when she felt a tap on her shoulder.

"That's not like you," said Beth. "You love that pudding. You usually gulp it down! Are you okay?" She sat beside Ruth with her plate of meatloaf. "Of course, this might have put you off your appetite...."

Ruth laughed. "It's...tolerable. The kitchen staff might be somewhat over-celebrated."

"Aren't we all? Such fun with the games! The whole hospital was in on them somehow. Even the women were excited and shouting. As Mrs. Graham would say, 'Good for their lungs'."

She dug into the meatloaf, took a bite, blinked, pushed it away with her fork. "But you seem down in the mouth. What's up? Is Billy worse?"

"No," said Ruth. "He was all smiles today! I'm so glad he's got a place to live when he finally gets out of here. He's got a long rehab ahead, but that makes all the difference. No. It's just I got the letter."

"The letter." Beth chewed her peas with a grimace. "What letter? Oh.... THAT letter? What did they say? Are you in? They didn't say no, did they?"

"Shhhh," Ruth said, looking around. "I haven't opened it yet!"

"What? How could you resist?"

"I was hoping someone would come and open it with me. I don't want to be alone when I see what it says. I'm afraid they'll say no, and I'll have to go back to Cloyne and wash diapers forever."

"You'd still have to do that in school, remember. The maternity rotation? Diapers galore."

"Yeah, but the laundry does them!"

"Only after we rinse them." Beth pushed her dish away. "That's enough of that dreck. I can always grab a peanut butter sandwich later." She picked up her pudding. "Let's go find out, right now."

Ruth stood, the butterflies in her stomach making her almost fall back onto her chair. "Okay. If you're sure."

A snort was the reply. Beth took Ruth's hand, pulling her to the stairs and up to her room.

"It's under my pillow," said Ruth.

"Well, get it," said Beth. "It's not going to bite you."

"No, but my father might!"

Beth laughed. "I'll bite him back if he does. C'mon. Open it."

Ruth ran her fingertip under the seal, flipped it open. The thick envelope filled her hand. That meant good news, she hoped. Finally, impatient with herself, she pulled out the letter and other papers and unfolded them.

There was a pause. Beth looked at her friend, reached out a hand when she saw tears sliding down Ruth's cheeks. "What does it say?" she asked softly.

Ruth looked up, a wide smile on her face. "I'm in! And they're funding me, too!"

"Really? Let me see that." Beth took the letter from her and read it over twice before letting out a loud whoop and waving it above her head as she danced.

Ruth joined her, and soon the entire floor was at the door, wondering what was happening. Even their supervisor joined in the excitement, for once not demanding quiet.

"You've got to tell your dad!" Beth pulled at Ruth's arm, dragging her downstairs to the phone.

Ruth blushed. The last time she'd tried to call home the line was down. She doubted her father had managed to afford to link it up again. She took a deep breath. Soon, soon, she'd be able to send money home, contribute. All of Billy's veteran payments were going for his hospital care. Turning to Beth, she said,

"Oh, they are probably in the middle of dinner or bedtime. I can send a telegram tomorrow."

"On no, you won't. This is big news. Let's go send it tonight."

"No, they'll think that something has gone wrong with Billy. I'll write them a letter tonight—that will tell them soon enough." She felt deflated, not able to share her news with her family. They'd be so excited!

Beth looked at her closely. "Well, you could tell Billy, anyway."

"Yes! What a fantastic idea! Thanks Beth, you're the best!" Ruth sped off down the stairs to Billy's ward and when she arrived and told him her news, he rose to the occasion and ordered the rest of the ward members to cheer her three times.

"Hooray for Ruth Maclean, future Super-nurse!" Everyone applauded.

"You'll need a red S for your uniform," teased Billy. Superman Comics were all the rage on the ward at present, all the patients excited about the Canadian creator, Joe Shuster.

Ruth laughed. "I'll be happy to wear a cap." She paused. "I could always hide a red S there? My secret identity?"

Everyone burst out cheering again, and Ruth's heart filled. She sped to tell "her boys", but there the reaction was mixed. "Does that mean you'll be leaving us?" one asked, a break in his voice.

Ruth went over and squeezed his hand. "Not for a little while. School doesn't start until September. And you'll be better by then, right? Heading home yourself!"

The patient, a young corporal with healing TB, smiled through his tears. "I'll try my best."

"That's the attitude," Ruth said, trying to sound cheerful. She'd miss the ward, and all of her patients. She knew she'd be discouraged from visiting because of the risk of bringing TB back. After her time at the Preventorium she wouldn't want to risk infection again.

"I must write to Susan!" Ruth spun around, and waving a hand, headed off to write her letters. Susan would be excited for her, and, besides, she wanted to hear how it was going at the new pediatric hospital. Smiling, she pulled up her chair to her desk and started writing, first to her parents, then to Meg, and then to Susan. It all became more real each time she told the story.

She was just finishing up Susan's letter when there was a knock on the door. She looked at her clock. It was almost nine PM. Who would be knocking at this time of night? Usually, her friends scratched at the door if they wanted to talk—less chance of waking others. But this was a firm knock. She straightened herself and opened the door. It was Mrs. Graham.

"I heard your news and wanted to come and offer you my congratulations." Mrs. Graham seemed stiff, awkward. It surprised Ruth.

"Oh, thank you so much, Mrs. Graham. I've so appreciated your support."

Mrs. Graham actually blushed. Ruth almost gaped in astonishment. "I...ah... I'm aware I haven't always seemed to be in your corner. I realize I may have contributed to your difficulties, and I am sorry. I'm certain you will succeed this time."

After a long, awkward silence, Ruth managed to ask, "Will you be coming back to instruct us?"

Mrs. Graham shook her head. "No. They've asked me to stay on here. Dr. Hopkins hopes to shift this hospital to an entirely TB sanatorium and wanted me to help with the transition. They'll be moving the veterans back to the main hospital over the next few months and admitting more TB patients. I think they'll be keeping the rehab floor here, however."

Ruth breathed a sigh of relief. It would be disruptive for the patients, especially Billy, to have to move. "There certainly seems to be a need for more TB support."

"Well, I'm hoping with the new medications it will be a short-term one. But I enjoy a new challenge." She smiled at Ruth. "I'd best be off. I just wanted to wish you success in your nursing studies."

"I so appreciate you coming over. Thanks, for everything."

The older nurse nodded and left, Ruth closing her door softly after her. She shook her head in amazement. She grabbed up her pen and added a postscript to Susan's letter—she'd never believe Mrs. Graham had actually come to her room to offer congratulations.

The rest of August flew by, and soon it was time for Ruth to return to school. She was awash with joy as she moved her things back into the nurse's residence. Classes were due to start the next week, and she was so excited. She already knew much of the first information they would be taught and could make a bed firm enough to satisfy the most exacting head nurse. Ruth hoped this meant she'd be able to focus on the harder things, as Mrs. Graham had suggested. Already, the new nursing students were coming to her for advice. It felt great.

There was more talk before she left about closing the Veteran's Hospital wings and turning it into a full sanatorium, changing its name to Ongwanada, which meant 'our home' in Ojibwa. Ruth liked that idea, remembering the native patients that she'd met. Ruth was glad Mrs. Graham would take the helm. Tuberculosis remained on the rise and despite the new medication, long bed rest and surgeries would still be required.

Ruth would miss the specialty practice she'd learned, but was eager to explore different things. Besides, she'd likely go there on rotation as part of her training, so she could reconnect then with all her friends on the staff. Perhaps she'd see Dr. Anderson in KGH, too. She knew she'd miss his support. It broke her heart a bit, too, to leave her cozy room and move back to the nurses' residence at KGH, with its myriad rules and chilly interiors, but new excitements awaited.

At least this time, she hoped she had a chance. Patricia was still AWOL, as was her doctor friend. Ruth prayed they were not causing any more damage where they were. In her more evil moments, though, she envisioned Patricia in handcuffs facing some terrifying judge. She'd deserve it, Ruth thought.

She had tucked away her last bit of clothing and was in the kitchen watching a classmate trying to work pleats into a senior's cap when she heard a noise in the hallway. It was Betty.

The friends embraced.

"You're back!" Ruth cried. "Didn't you tell me you couldn't afford it in the end?"

"Oh, my mother begged, and they decided to take me back for free. I'm going to start at the beginning again, like you. And I'm on probation. No fun adventures for me this year."

"I'm quite fine with no more adventures," Ruth said, scowling.

Betty snorted. "I'll bet." She peered at the cap on the table. "I still can't do that properly. My caps always seem chewed."

"Well, at least we have a few months before we need to do them perfectly." She pulled Betty into her room and whispered, "No unsavoury reminders of last year?"

Betty waved a hand at Ruth. "No. And not likely to be any. I've given up boys for Lent. And it's always going to be Lent."

"I'll believe that when I see it! You will be more careful, won't you? I don't want you to be sent away."

"Says the girl who had the most adventures last year of anyone in the school. I should probably avoid you—you're cursed."

"Not any longer. I've drawn a salt circle around my room...and see, I still carry my prayer book. I'm covered."

Betty looked doubtful. "That book had a lot of adventures, itself. Might you need a new one?"

"No, I'm counting on this little good luck charm. If it survived being sprayed with TB and came out clean, I figure it must emit magic powers." She waved it around her head, just to be sure.

They smoothed their uniforms and, after checking themselves in the mirror and adjusting their cuffs, headed down to supper. "I'm so glad we are here together," said Betty.

"Me, too," Ruth said. "Let's keep it that way!"

Tuberculosis

The prevailing thought that tuberculosis is on the way out is a handicap in its prevention. Any disease that is the first cause of death, excepting accidents, between the ages of 5-30 years, and which kills one out of every four persons dying in the age group 16-39 years in Canada, is not under control. From September, 1939, to June 30, 1944, tuberculosis killed more Canadians, in Canada, than did our enemies in all theatres of war. Krause, in 1918, stated that during the war of 1914-18, tuberculosis accounted for more deaths than shot and shell in the warring countries. The fact that tuberculosis caused more deaths in Canada than the infectious diseases during the five-year period 1938-42 bears repeating.

Tuberculosis Control, 1946, p. 1.

Bibliography

Angus, Margaret. *Kingston General Hospital: A Social and Institutional History*. Montreal: McGill-Queen's University Press, Montreal, 1973.

Barton, E. *Driven By a Dream: The Story of Ongwanada 1948-1998*. Kingston: Quarry Press, 1998.

Bond, Carolyn. "Ongwanada." Kingston Whig Standard, Jan 30, 1999. ·

Burke, Stacey. *Building Resistance: Children, Tuberculosis, and the Toronto Sanatorium*. Montreal and Kingston: McGill-Queen's University Press, 2018.

Crothers, Katherine Connell. *With Tender Loving Care*. Kingston: KGH Nurses Alumnae, 1973.

Dormandy, Thomas. *The White Death: A History of Tuberculosis*. London: Hambledon and London, 2001.

Eyre, Jessie G. *Tuberculosis Nursing*. London: HK Lewis and Co, Ltd, 1949.

Gill, Gillian. *Nightingales: The Extraordinary Upbringing and Curious Life of Miss Florence Nightingale*. New York: Ballantine, 2004.

Hurt R. "Tuberculosis sanatorium regimen in the 1940s: a patient's personal diary." *J R Soc. Med* 97(7) (2004): 350-3.

Hancock, Lucy Agnes (1946). "General Duty Nurse." *Kingston Whig Standard* June 25, 1946, p. 9.

Harmer and Henderson. *Textbook of the Principles and Practice of Nursing*. New York: Macmillan, 1955.

Hurt, Raymond (2004). "Tuberculosis sanatorium regimen in the 1940s: a patient's personal diary." *JRSoc Med* 97(7): 350-353.

Jones, Kingsley (2000). "Insulin coma therapy in schizophrenia." *JRSoc Med* 93:147-149.

Nightingale, Florence. *Notes on Nursing*. London: Gerald Duckworth & Co. Ltd, 1952.

Ongwanada Sanatorium. *Information and Rules for Patients*. Undated. Museum of Health Care, Kingston, ON 004.028.031.

Pearce, Doreen. *A Little Book of Devotion for Nurses*. London: A.R. Mowbray & Company, 1948.

Rees, Bonnie. "IODE Ontario—A Proud History." Retrieved from https://www.iodeontario.ca/ Accessed August 3, 2023.

Rogers, Jude. "Life as an NHS Nurse in the 1940's." *The Guardian*, June 24, 2018. Retrieved from https://www.theguardian.com/society/2018/jun/24/life-as-an-nhs-nurse-in-the-1940s

Wherrett, G. J. "Progress in Tuberculosis Control in Canada." *Canadian Public Health Journal* 32 (6), (1941): 287-292

https://blog.nursing.com/florence-nightingale-quotes

Acknowledgements

M any, many thanks are due to the various members of the Kingston General Hospital School of Nursing who provided background and interviews to add colour to this book. Special thanks to Diane Peacock, who steered me to classmates and other sources of information. I remain envious of the camaraderie between KGH grads even in retirement. Any errors or misunderstandings are of course, mine.

Thanks also to Rowena McGowan and the staff at the Museum of Health Care in Kingston, ON. (museumofhealthcare.ca). They were very helpful in pulling out resources and provided the photo for the cover from their collection. The Kingston Library provided assistance with research as well—I am extremely grateful.

I had the pleasure of workshopping this book through the Writers Rendezvous group at Kingston Seniors Association (https://seniorskingston.ca/). This group is an incredibly friendly environment, for which I am deeply grateful.

Biggest thanks go to my publisher and long term friend Tim Covell, who is unfailingly supportive and fun to work with. I recommend Somewhat Grumpy Press (https://somewhatgrumpypress.com/) as a small publisher, and that's not just because I started it—it is now in much better hands with Tim.

And of course, much love and gratitude to my sons, my dear friend Les Howie (who didn't die of TB), and my long-suffering other friends who have been always available for a chat or a laugh as I struggle on. I am able to do what I do because of you.

About the Author

Dorothyanne Brown (DA Brown), BNSc, MSc, is a retired registered nurse, writer, freelance editor, and sometime artist. She enjoys learning about past medical practices, and used this curiosity, her nursing experience, and her degree in epidemiology to help create this book. She plans to follow Ruth through her nursing education in subsequent novels.

She lives in beautiful Kingston, Ontario, and shares her home with visiting foster cats and a variety of needle-felted sculptures. Her three children are scattered far and wide but always provide balance and wisdom. Dorothyanne lives with multiple sclerosis, and spends her non-creating time volunteering, facilitating classes in managing chronic disease, and occasionally playing the ukulele.

Recycled Virgin

also by Dorothyanne Brown

T he former Blessed Virgin Mary has had enough. She's spent the past 2000 years looking after others, only to find that her true story has been erased. No one knows the real Miryam, the flesh and blood mother, the woman who taught the foundations of a world-wide religion to her often disobedient son. As she lives through her latest reincarnation, she struggles to understand why she keeps returning. Will her study at a Theological College finally allow her to free herself? Will she be able to retell her story, make herself real?

"A real page turner and thought-provoking read." (Amazon Review)

Recycled Virgin was published by Somewhat Grumpy Press in 2020 and is available from most booksellers.

ISBN: 978-1-9992884-2-6 (paperback), 978-1-999-2884-1-9 (ebook)

Help support independent authors and small presses. If you enjoyed this book, please leave a rating and review at your favourite retailer or review site.